SUCCUBUS SOUL

VERAS ACADEMY

LINA JUBILEE

Crimson Fox
PUBLISHING

Succubus Soul by Lina Jubilee

© 2019 by Lina Jubilee. All rights reserved.

Published by Crimson Fox Publishing and Lina Jubilee.

Crimson Fox Publishing, Turner, OR

www.crimsonfoxpublishing.com

Cover by Ali Lawson Book Design.

ISBN: 978-1948661546

CHAPTER ONE

"So remember: Visualize. Create. Control."

The dashing Nelian guard struck a pose in front of the makeshift outdoor classroom for each of those three keywords. He'd repeated himself at least a dozen times over the past forty-five minutes. But I wasn't complaining. Each of those poses was tailor-made to show off his lean, sculpted biceps.

"Visualize. Create. Control." His dark green brows pulled together, his fingers poised in a circle in front of him. Then he waved his arms with a flourish, a thick growth of vines growing from his palms, creaking as if someone were step-ping on squeaky wood. The vines were curling into a cone in an imitation of soft-serve ice cream, but I wasn't focused on that. The more he was in *control*, the tighter his ass got, that brown-and-green leather clinging to him in all the right places. I pressed my thighs together under my calf-length plaid skirt, pushing down the building buzz between my legs, trying to *focus*. *Focus.*

The lecturer's long, green hair tousled a bit in the light breeze, catching on the pointed tip of his tawny ear. My hand subconsciously moved to the bright red hair covering my own pointed ear. The thick, straight strands were dyed—carefully styled. Anything to hide the fact that I was one of them.

A Nelian. Half-Nelian.

Mom and Dads didn't want to do a blood test to determine which of them, exactly, had contributed DNA to my twin brother, Sage, and me. But frankly, there was no way my biological father wasn't Alarik, king of the Nelians, the elf-like race of aliens who'd come here from their flora-overrun planet over twenty years ago in an initially misguided attempt to save Earth.

None of my other dads had pointed ears.

Rajani stopped chewing on her pen just long enough to lean over and whisper, "I bet he could show off a lot of *control* in the bedroom." Her red lips curled up into a smile as she arched her back, tossing her wavy, black hair over her shoulder and showing off her hourglass curves in her bright pink sari. The move worked. The lecturer paused in his pattern, his eyes dancing pointedly in her direction as he topped off another soft-serve vine sculpture. Only the plant life sputtered off wildly as his gaze lingered in our direction, and the "control" part of his demonstration seemed like a joke as the vines spread out and wrapped around the nearby oak tree offering us shade.

Rajani and I both giggled like schoolgirls half our age, earning us an austere look from Professor Chastity, our primary combat instructor. She was a knockout even at around age fifty, and she stood to the side of the guest lecturer with her hands clasped tightly behind her back.

"Ah, that is," sputtered the Nelian man—Connak, son of one of my father's most trusted guards. Sure, Nelians didn't really age like humans did, but it was nice to know my friend and I were taking turns fantasizing about a man in his early twenties. "Visuals. Crontrol. Create. I mean…" His arms trembled.

Professor Chastity stepped in from where she'd been leaning against the giant, blooming oak tree in the back yard

2

of the Academy. "Thank you, Connak. I believe the class gets it." Her gray-and-black eyebrow arched, her silver bob especially severe as her gaze narrowed on Rajani and me once more. "Unless Bryony and Rajani apparently have questions for our guest lecturer?"

"What time is the *guest lecturer* off the clock?" asked Rajani under her breath, but he heard her. Everyone heard her.

We burst into laughter once more. The rest of the class glowered, and Derek actually *shushed* us, a familiar, inviting scent of old books and fresh grass hitting my nostrils as he leaned closer, his finger to his shapely lips.

My best friend since I could remember, and just a few months younger than my brother and me, Derek was like if a model for a college campus gear catalogue had walked off the page and onto the real thing. Smooth, flawless, umber skin peeked out from his form-fitting, sleek workout shirt that clung to every bit of the muscles he'd earned through sweat and tears over the twenty-one years he'd been on Earth. His close-cropped textured black hair framed a perfectly-oval face with high cheekbones that made his hazel brown eyes pop beneath his thick-rimmed black glasses. He had his notebook open in front of him as well as his tablet, and he'd written down Connak's three keywords at least four times in each. Derek didn't mess around when it came to studying.

The cheeky bastard had this idea that he could beat me to being valedictorian when we finally graduated in a few months.

The shushing just caused Rajani to giggle more, but I made a zipper motion over my lips, complete with "turning the key," and winked at Derek, trying to stop myself from smiling. He rolled his eyes and faced forward.

"Okay, then," said Professor Chastity, all business. "Let's please give a round of applause for Connak's, uh, *enlightening* demonstration."

No sooner had the halfhearted claps begun—though to be fair, Rajani was sitting straight on up on her calves, clapping *too* hard, as if she'd just watched the most riveting performance of Shakespeare—than the period bell rang from the main building a few dozen yards away. The other members of the class gathered their things—foldable tablets for most students, though some preferred paper and pen like Derek—and broke off into groups as they headed back toward the old sports center that had been converted decades ago. First into the headquarters for the small Natch team called Veras, then into Veras Academy, the number one institution in the Midwest that instructed Natches on how to use their powers safely and responsibly, from first grade through college, accredited and recognized and everything.

Daddy Alarik had used *a lot* of influence to make that dream come true, with no small help from Papa Zander.

I guess I should back up. Beginning about half a century ago, about one in three people started being born with superpowers. All kinds of powers. Rarely alike. No one knew exactly why, but these naturally occurring phenomena led to superpowered-gifted individuals being called "Natches"—short for "Naturals"—compared with "Typicals," the remainder of non-powered humanity. As the years have gone by, the percentage of Natches had grown. It was probably almost one in two births these days. Good thing Papa Zander had a foothold in government. He was the leader of the Renegades, a small group of Natches who didn't used to see eye-to-eye with Veras on how best to protect Natch rights. They got along pretty well these days, though.

Shortly before my brother and I had been born, our mom —Aurora Haddix, member of Veras—and our other two dads —Pop Nash and Dad Jayden—had gone up against the Nelian invaders who'd thought that to save Earth, they'd had to rip down everything unnatural. It had taken some *convincing* for them to change their approach to saving Earth from environmental destruction.

But change it they had—and it had worked so well. When I'd been little, the Earth had been on the brink of climate-change-related destruction. Now? There was still damage the planet needed to heal from, but Earth had a bright future. We all had a bright future ahead of us.

Thanks to the work of my family. Nearly every single important figure in this historical marvel was part of my family.

That came with having so many fathers and uncles.

They took care of things for you.

Yup, nothing but peace and prosperity ahead for my generation. Made practicing how to use our powers awfully pointless, if you asked me.

Rajani was telling me something about this show she'd watched the night before and Derek was flipping through his notebook and scrolling through his tablet screen at the same time as we walked back to the Academy. *Focus,* I reminded myself. *Live in the moment. Only a couple of months until graduation, and then everything will change. Cherish the now.*

"Your Highness!" called Connak as he jogged up beside us. He put one fist to his opposite shoulder and bowed.

Subconsciously, I tugged on my hair to make sure my ears were covered, but there was no missing the giggles from Hazel and her gaggle of friends as they pushed past us and headed toward the main building.

"*Your Highness,*" mocked Hazel with a flourish of her hands. Her long, black-and-blonde-striped hair shifted over the ruffled shoulder of her blouse as she bent in my direction, her little perfect nose remaining upturned and snooty, her blue eyes offset by her peachy pale complexion. She acted all prim and proper, but her ability was rather vulgar: her hazardous breath turned things to stone, just like her icy heart.

Her companions curtsied and snickered some more.

There was Pepper, gorgeous and lanky, her black hair in braids that complemented her medium-brown skin. She shot light out of her fingers that could temporarily blind someone if she focused hard enough.

Sheila, short with fair red hair and freckled white skin, was beautiful when not smiling condescendingly at those around her. She could create a doppelgänger of herself who could fight alongside her.

And Jerry, the only man in the gaggle, as stuck-up as his girlfriends. Wavy, brown hair, a chiseled tanned complexion, and the tallest one of the group. He looked like a supermodel, the kind that never smiled except when enjoying watching someone else make a fool of themselves. He had an ability to "fix" physical objects that were broken, though he clearly didn't relish the idea of becoming something like a mechanic. He was a glamor hound through and through.

I watched them out of the corner of my eye until they slipped inside.

"Connak," I said, straightening my back. "Don't call me that here, okay? Or anywhere, really. Seriously." As the son of Normak, one of Daddy Alarik's most trusted guards, Connak had been a fixture practically my whole life. We might have had a little fling at one point—he *was* freaking stunning. But it hadn't lasted, nor had it ever gotten far. He'd told me he hadn't felt the Nelian *sense* toward me, and that had been that.

Rajani, on the other hand, hadn't transferred to Veras until her high school years, and she was far less familiar with Nelian courting rituals. Flings were fine, but if Connak didn't feel those pheromones unique to his kind, she had no chance of making more than a little dent in his heart.

I may have been half-Nelian, but I honestly had no idea what this "sense" was all about. I'd never felt it.

But that wasn't going to stop my other best friend. She twirled one of her luxurious curls around her finger as she clutched her tablet to her chest, sizing Connak up and down and up again.

Derek, oblivious as usual to anything but his studies, only just now looked up from his book and tablet, only just now noticing we'd stopped, turning around and shuffling back toward us.

Connak flinched somewhat under the power of Rajani's gaze, but he remained as stiff as a board. "I cannot call you anything but, Your Highness. You are heir to the Nelian throne—"

"Bup, bup, bup." I placed two lace-covered fingers on Connak's lips, causing his head to tilt in surprise. Rajani's smile grew wider. "None of that talk here, please."

"But, Your Highness, everyone *knows* who you are—" he started.

"Yeah, and I don't need the constant reminders, thanks." I flicked my bright red hair over my bare shoulder, wondering if my green roots were showing yet.

Connak was undeterred. "But your father requested that when I make this trip to your prestigious academy that I remind you that you need to be starting to make arrangements now for your move to the heart of Nelia."

I held up a hand in the air. "I know. But that's months away."

"You're almost finished with your education," he continued. "Which means that you can soon assume the throne. You can start visiting on the weekends, getting to better know the populace."

"The weekends?" What was he talking about? I had two months yet. I was overcome with the sudden *need* to run and hide behind a bush.

A shriek pierced the air from the nearby playground as the elementary-aged kids were up to their fun and games. The sound was like a slap straight to my senses.

I turned on my heel, my plaid tie soaring outward in the wind, whapping against the black bustier I'd paired up with my plaid skirt decked in red and black, the colors of the school's optional uniform. I was in university, after all, and most of the older students liked to exhibit their own style. But I could make "preppy" my own when the mood struck.

"The people of Nelia eagerly await your rule," continued Connak, unabated.

Rajani seemed to be eyeing our escape routes, knowing I'd want to weasel my way out of this conversation as soon as possible. I opened my mouth to say anything—the right thing —whatever would get him to move on—when Derek stepped between us, all of his studies forgotten, his books and tablet clutched tightly to his brawny chest with one arm.

"She was promised she could have the full Veras Academy education on Earth before she moved to Nelia."

Connak bristled. "Of course, but her father thought—"

"She has four fathers, and I don't recall them agreeing with her mother to make any adjustment to that promise."

"Well, no, not a formal agreement, but His Majesty simply thought—"

I stepped forward, slipping my lace glove into Derek's free hand. The thought of him standing up for me warmed my heart—and I'd gladly do the same for him.

"I want to wait until I graduate," I said, straightening my back. "And not a moment sooner."

Derek's gaze met mine, his smile lighting up his eyes. If he weren't my best friend, I'd—

"Look out!" screamed Rajani, in time with a sudden chorus of shrieks from the playground, no longer punctuated by giggles, just screaming, *shrieking*.

"The kids!" said Derek, growing tense, dropping my hand and his books all at once, striding toward the danger without taking a single moment to analyze what was going on.

Children streamed toward him, away from the play-ground—away from the steaming hot playground equipment that glowed red, ready to explode.

"The temperature kid," said Rajani, nodding at me. "Must have gotten out of control." As college-level students, it was our duty to be at least somewhat informed about all the kids wandering the campus grounds. She sent a sly, suggestive gaze toward Connak. "Visualize, create, control, honey."

Crossing her arms in front of her, she started running through the crowd of kids, her skin morphing into metal scales that would protect her from almost any attack...

Except concentrated heat, as the metal on the playground equipment could already attest.

Growling, I snapped to it. "Jani!"

Derek was already pelting a sizzling swing set with his ice bombs, small snowball-sized concentrated projections of ice. It wasn't his bombs that would prove most useful just now, but his father's steadier stream of ice blasts. Only I didn't think the man was on campus just now.

Sure enough, the first ice bomb to impact exploded on the ground, sending ice shards willy-nilly in every direction—including toward the lone child remaining amidst the playground equipment.

The child was crying as steam poured from his hands.

It grew hotter then, his rosy skin turning tomato-red, his wails growing louder as the air wavered and morphed around him.

I bolted forward, not even sensing if Connak joined me, focusing on nothing but that child, nothing but protecting him—from himself, from the blast. Protecting my friends from danger.

CHAPTER TWO

RAJANI SLOWED AS SHE NEARED, NO DOUBT FEELING THE HEAT ON her metal scales, the metal casing having turned even her long, wavy hair into stiff alloy. She stopped moving, the heat likely expanding her metal skin, making it difficult for her to move. She collapsed. Derek readied another blast, only to pull his arm back as he seemed to realize—his theories catching up to his practicums—that his ice bombs would just melt in the steam, that his shrapnel was too difficult to predict and wouldn't do an adequate job of cooling the area. Connak's swift, silent feet brought him to my side and then in front of me, a giant vine growing outward from his palms, but to what end, I couldn't be sure.

We had a panicked child here. And there was no reaching a panicked child with force and chaos.

Just as the plume of steam exploded outward from the boy to meet the intruding vine, threatening to engulf the entire playground, I got close enough.

Protect him, I spoke inside my head. *Protect them all.*

"Pumpkin, what's going on?" asked Papa Zander in my head. I didn't know where he was—I didn't have time to wonder. He was a telepath with an innate connection only to those he cared about most. He must have picked up on my

stress, but I had no time to explain. What could he possibly do to help in the next two seconds anyway?

Protect! I answered back—to him, to myself, to anything listening.

And I did. Visualizing the bubble of protection. Creating it, projecting it with my mind. Controlling it, shaping it in the air with my hands. Around the boy. *That's it. Soft, warm, inviting.*

With a shrill hiss, the steam exploded outward, hitting the faintly visible pinkish walls of my protection, straining against it—pushing. Fighting. Demanding chaos.

Protect, I thought. "Protect!" I said out loud.

The bubble fought back, soothing, comforting, conforming to the child's needs, trapping him and the steam inside. The air outside the bubble growing blissfully cooler, Rajani was able to move and breathe again, Derek shuffling to her side, helping her up. Her metal scales faded away, revealing skin, and Connak slid in beside them, taking her other side.

"It's all right!" I shouted, knowing my voice alone would travel along the bubble of protection like a speaker inside it. "It's okay! We all make mistakes."

The quiet sniffles of the boy penetrated into my mind first, his form still shadowy behind the mists inside my bubble. "Zora pushed me." He hiccupped.

A playground fight turned dangerous.

"It's okay," I said again, as soothingly as I could.

There were others headed our way now, people attending to the children, Veras members and instructors here to offer their help.

Mom was the only one of the new arrivals I allowed to penetrate my concentration, the hand she offered on my shoulder not just a message of support, but a gauge of the situation. Was I handling it? Did I need the boost in my ability she could offer?

I shook my head.

"It was my turn on the slide," said the boy between hiccup

sobs. "And Zora said she didn't care, and she pushed me, and when I tried to get up and tell Miss Lacey, she pushed me harder and—"

"It's all right," I said again, quieter this time. "We all lose control sometimes. But it's time. It's time to breathe deeply and focus. Get the temperature back to normal. Let it go. Let go of the anger, the frustration…"

As I spoke, the steam inside the bubble retreated, dissipating, the child inside revealed. His blond hair was scruffy, and there was a patch of dirt on his cheek, along with three small scratches on his neck.

"That's it," I said, my muscles beginning to ache at the strain of holding the bubble up. "It's okay."

With that, the temperature grew stable again, the steam gone, and the protection bubble collapsed, my aching legs stumbling. Mom grabbed hold of me on one side and a couple of pairs of strong arms swept in on the other side. I turned to see Pop Nash and Dad Jayden.

"All right!" called Dad Jayden, taking charge, as ever. He patted my back and pushed his glasses up his nose, his all-white full head of hair the perfect complement to his pale cream skin, marred only by the slight indentation of wrinkles around his eyes and mouth. Somehow, any sign of aging on him only gave him a more distinguished appearance, like one of those former movie stars you knew were hot in their youth and had somehow just become more handsome in their sixth decade. "Are you all right, Bryony?" he said softer to me.

I nodded and he set about with the other instructors, who were helping the temperature-controlling boy dry his tears, directing him inside to the infirmary, no doubt.

"Our baby's getting so strong." Pop Nash noogied my hair as if he were a big brother. I might have laughed at it when I'd been five or six, but it was getting a bit old.

Straightening, I patted my messed-up hair. "Thanks. I think." I stared at him. The silver threading through his close-cropped golden hair was at odds with his still rugged and youthful appearance. Even well past forty, he filled out a workout suit like a man several decades younger who had to try much harder to build muscles. It came more natural to him, bulky as he was, though he certainly had a love for the workout.

"*Nash*. She's too old for roughhousing." Mom stepped forward to push a strand of my hair I'd missed away from my cheek. She smiled, her deep red lips tugging upward at one corner, the slight grooves forming around her mouth only making the smile seem more beautiful, earned after a lifetime of similar ones. "I can't believe you and your brother are almost graduates." Tears pooled at the edges of her eyes and Nash slipped in to put his hand on her shoulder. Those deepening grooves around her lips and her salt-and-pepper hair were the only clues that she was older than she looked. It was no surprise she'd caused four men to fall in love with her—the fact that she could boost their powers in very, uh, *interesting* ways aside. They loved her. All four of them.

Which I appreciated sometimes—having four doting daddies could do that to a little girl—but not so much at others.

At some point, Hazel and her entourage had made their way back outside. Instead of tending to the children like some of the other students, they were simply glaring our way, Pepper and Sheila pretending to be examining their nails, and Jerry mimicking Hazel's catty pose, a single hand on his hip.

They all looked gorgeous—coiffed and not a thread out of place—and it was clear they thought the idea of lending a hand here could lead to disheveled clothes or an immediate need to touch up their manicures.

The thought made me want to hurl.

"*Bryony has four daddies and her mummy's a whore,*" said a ten-year-old Hazel the first year she transferred to Veras Academy. *She was on a swing, monopolizing the entire set with her friends, and singing this as a song.*

I stiffened as the song hit my ears by the big oak tree. Derek looked up from the book he was reading to put his hand—tentatively, waiting for my reaction—atop mine.

"Runs in the family because her aunt's a slag, too," continued Hazel in her song.

I jumped to my feet, my fists clenched, and Pepper burst into laughter at something—at the sight of my face. My short, green hair. My pointed ears.

The only known half-Nelian, half-Earthling in the world.

"Someone's touchy," said Hazel in her snobbish English accent before she descended into giggles along with Sheila and Jerry, the four of them forming a bizarre pack the moment Hazel had transferred. "You don't see me going around acting all special. My family actually worked for their money—and until someone's stupid family got involved, we used to have so much more!"

Sheila let out a little gasp and her doppelgänger popped out of thin air beside her in an identical pose, their hands over their mouths, her clone seeming to be sitting on nothing, as there were no spare swings. Then it seemed to realize its predicament and stood, crossing its arms, acting almost as if a separate entity from its host —one equally in thrall to exchange student Hazel Thorne.

Hazel had introduced herself the first day as heir to the Thorne Biodegradable-Mushroom-Root-Formerly-Plastics fortune, making sure to express her displeasure that mushroom root packaging apparently cost far more to make and produced far less profit than old-fashioned plastic.

Her grandfather and father had campaigned hard against the Nelians' reach extending to the United Kingdom. And had failed. Their heir turning out to be a Natch had been the perfect opportunity to send her abroad and get in good with the Nelian king behind all the changes, Pop Nash had guessed out loud once in front of me shortly after her transfer.

Though Daddy Alarik had little to do with the running of the school. Everyone knew his lover and children were here, though.

My parents had all asked me to be kind to her. If the Thornes learned to embrace their reduced fortune for the betterment of the world, even more of their class were likely to follow.

Unfortunately, Hazel had never given me the chance.

"Four daddies, four uncles, one mummy, one aunt," sang Hazel. "Whore's a Haddix family trait, what you think about that?"

Her friends giggled, the extra Sheila laughing so hard that with a little pop, *her clone vanished into nothingness again.*

"You take that back!" I shrieked, but then there was an explosion on the ground in front of her, ice shards soaring this way and that. The girls and Jerry screamed, covering their faces, running for the hills.

Derek smirked at me, his arm out in front of him. "What?" he said. "She can't carry a tune."

"You all right, sis?" Sage jogged over from where he'd no doubt been comforting Lacey, a Veras member who focused mostly on instruction of the little ones. I checked behind him to make sure Lacey was in one piece at the moment, considering the stress of the situation might have brought on a relapse.

Her natural state was a literal pile of goo. Stretchy and convenient, depending on the task at hand. But limp and gooey.

She had to focus to stay all together like a human being, and it caused her great pain, but she rarely showed it. She was as beautiful as Uncle Bo, her older brother. Blonde and willowy, peachy like a summer's day.

She was also almost nine years older than my brother and me and the dope was totally besotted.

"Yeah," I said, brushing him off. He sent me a knowing look across those blue eyes, as if we had some sort of telepathic twin connection that would tell him otherwise, but he didn't say anything more. Fit and bulky, he resembled some kind of mix between Nash, Jayden, and Zander—though he had Zander's dark, wavy hair. It was impossible to tell who'd fathered him, but all of our parents were convinced I'd saved him in utero, protecting him against Mom's powers and bringing us both into existence against all odds.

Not that I could remember any of that, of course. I absentmindedly ran a gloved hand over the patch of skin on my upper arm and Sage exchanged some words with Mom and Pop Nash. There was no missing the pointed stare Hazel directed his way. *In your dreams, asshole*, I thought at her, hoping my curling lip was enough to convey the message. It seemed to work. She turned on her heel, her clique following a moment later, returning back to the college wing of the Academy.

I snapped back into the moment. *Rajani!*

I met up with Rajani, Derek, and Connak, the latter two supporting the limping Rajani between them, and Rajani chuckled dryly as she saw me. "Good job, Bry. Smarter than me."

"I'm glad your instinct was to help," I said, looking pointedly at Derek for a second as well. I gave them both a slow smile. "I just wonder if we need more practice in coordination." Thank Mother Nelia that there was really no need for fighting anyone anymore. Practically no need, anyway.

The Renegades took care of the few Typicals who acted out in prejudice. The Nelians and Earthlings were at peace now.

There was almost no reason to be devoting all of our childhoods to learning how to make the best of our powers at all.

"Um, Derek, I don't really need *two* people supporting me on my way to the infirmary, but I do appreciate the offer," said Rajani, clearing her throat. Her eyes went wide and she tilted her head twice toward the Nelian on her other side.

Rajani was the type of friend who thought it was *awesome* that both my mom and my aunt had four lovers—husbands, in my aunt's case—each. The type whose next words after finding out were, "Sign me up for some of that, please."

Clamping my lips together, I slid an arm through Derek's and tugged him away. "See you later, then, Jani. Thank you for taking care of her," I added to Connak.

"Your Highness," he said once more, bowing ever-so-slightly. I flinched but tried not to cringe outwardly.

The crowd dissipated, another bell going off in three short rings, which meant an "incident" had caused the cancellation of the class—it really wasn't *that* abnormal, with so many kids just coming into their own with their powers.

Derek and I hadn't moved an inch toward the college building, and it wasn't until Derek massaged the back of my hand with his thumb that I realized I was spacing out.

So oblivious, I'd even tuned out Papa Zander's voice in my head.

"Your mother tells me it was just some kid freaking out," he said. *"And that you saved the day. Pumpkin?"*

Yeah. Um, yes. It's all fine, I answered back.

"Zander?" asked Derek out loud.

I nodded, though to tell the truth, I'd been thinking about a whole lot of nothing before I'd had my telepathic conversation.

I searched the dwindling crowd for Hazel and her groupies, but they were gone, Sage and Lacey and all the little kids, too. Mom, Dad Jayden, and Pop Nash spoke with Professor Chastity a few yards from the entrance to the main recreational area, the one with the kitchen and the dining hall as sleek and utilitarian as any gym-converted-to-mess-hall could be.

"Bryony!" said Dad Jayden, waving toward us.

"Way to go, pumpkin," said Papa Zander over the telepathic bond. *"Excuse me, though, as I've got a delegation to greet."*

I couldn't keep track of what the Renegades were up to these days.

"Bry?" asked Derek. "You okay?"

"Yeah," I said quickly—perhaps too quickly. Derek gave me a slight *hmm* and studied me with those warm hazel eyes.

"You're worried about inheriting the crown," said Derek, speaking aloud the anxiety I'd tried to squash and suffocate and keep from putting into words.

"Your books!" I said, searching around us. "You dropped your tablet and notebook—"

"Bry!" Derek cupped my chin gently to get me to turn back to him. The fluttering in my stomach was at odds with the way I felt secure at his side. "If it's bothering you, you need to tell your parents. I'll go with you."

A sharp whistle caught my attention. "Bryony!" called Pop Nash from near the door. Even from here, I could see the slight dance of flames in his palm as he straightened his back and did his best not to show that he'd caught his daughter in a somewhat uncompromising position.

But that was ridiculous. Derek was my best friend. My rival for valedictorian. I'd grown up with him.

I mean, I *did* want to find love. Just *one* love. I wasn't my mom or my aunt. But Derek... Derek was safe. I couldn't imagine jeopardizing that.

Besides, he had plans after graduation and I... I'd had plans forced on me.

"My dads are calling me," I said, my voice wavering. I gave his hand a squeeze and pointed to the haphazardly strewn pile of his notebook and tablet nearby. "Don't want to forget those. We've got exams coming up." I tapped the side of my head. "And I think *you're* the one trailing behind me by .4 points?"

".3." Derek cracked a small smile. Of course he'd know the precise difference in our GPAs. "But, Bry, you don't have to keep brushing this topic off."

"See you at dinner!" I shouted, already fleeing toward my escape.

And right into another situation I wanted to escape from.

I could tell by the glimmer in Dad Jayden's eyes. They only lit up like that when he was with Mom or Papa Zander —and when he had some really "exciting" news to share about Veras Academy.

No one could ever say he didn't deserve to be headmaster of this place. He'd put *everything* into it.

Maybe a little *too much* of himself into it.

"There she is," he said, as if he hadn't spoken to me just

moments before. "Our hero." Professor Chastity, her arms crossed tightly over her chest, gave me an approving nod. "Our princess," Dad Jayden added.

He wasn't one for pet names with his kids like my other dads were.

No. He meant it literally.

"Why do I have a feeling I'm not going to like the next few words out of your mouth?" I said, trying to inject some nervous chuckles into my voice. They came across more terrified than jovial.

"Bryony," said Mom softly—though still admonishingly.

"The Renegades are bringing back the Natch delegations from New Zealand, Great Britain, and Japan," said Dad Jayden, nonplussed. "Their royal families have decided to send their princes to be guests at our Academy for a brief cultural exchange."

I nodded dumbly, my mind racing. Exchange students? Or guest lecturers? That was a first. Interesting. *What does this have to do with me again?*

Mom slid her fingers through mine, her mouth parting slightly. "The thing is, darling, your fathers and I thought—"

Pop Nash wrapped an arm around one of my shoulders and squeezed me to his side. "You're going to get hitched!"

CHAPTER THREE

THREE NATCH PRINCES WERE ON THEIR WAY HERE, TO THE Academy. Their countries put more stock into their royalty these days than they had before the Nelian invasion, New Zealand even naming a royal lineage in the past couple decades to reward a Māori Natch who'd prevented a tsunami from devastating the island nation. For a second there, I thought with a chilling sense of shock, that they intended me to marry all three of them.

Then I realized that mattered far less than the fact that they wanted me to marry *any* of them.

"What are you talking about?" I snapped, jerking out of Mom and Pop Nash's grip. My voice grew thick as my posture stiffened. "You're joking. You're *arranging* my marriage? Do you hear yourselves?"

Mom swallowed visibly as she exchanged a look with the others gathered around. "Now, that may have been a crude way of putting it"—Pop Nash shirked under her harsh look— "but we've been discussing the matter with Alarik, and it might do the Nelian-Earth alliance a lot of good to have it strengthened with a marriage between the heir to Nelia and the heir to one of Earth's nations."

"You. *You* of all people think it's a good idea to arrange a marriage," I sputtered. "You never got married because you couldn't decide between four people!" I didn't bother to weigh the fact that according to Nelia tradition, a Nelian can marry any number of people they feel drawn to—as my aunt, Alanna, had married four—because I was too angry to be reasonable.

"Bryony Haddix," said Dad Jayden sharply. "Don't speak to your mother—"

Mom laid a gentle hand on his chest, stopping him. "No, I understand. Honey, it's not what you think. You don't *have to* marry any of them." She bit her lip and her eyes darted over my head. I turned to see what she was looking at and found Derek several yards behind us, ducking slowly into the college wing door. "If you've felt the Nelian sense with some-one, I'd be the first to wish you joy and happiness," continued Mom, "but you haven't—"

"I don't know!" I threw my hands up in the air. "I don't know if I've felt it. I don't know what it's like. Maybe since I'm half-Nelian, I'm defective—not like we can compare me to any single other living creature on Earth or Nelia combined." My aunt had chosen not to have children—appar-ently, Nelian women could turn that on and off with a thought. Did it work the same for me? Who knew? Between schoolwork and responsibilities and hanging with friends and having the Nelian heir stuff hanging over my head, I hadn't gotten beyond second base with anyone.

I was a late bloomer. So sue me. Rajani could tease me all she wanted, but I had other things to think about.

And now my inexperience was going to bite me in the ass because my parents were picking up the slack and arranging my life for me in every way conceivably possible.

"Baby girl, please, calm down." Pop Nash stepped closer to me and I realized I was pacing, my hands threading through my hair and clutching two clumps of it by the roots. "I spoke too hastily, okay? You don't have to get married to one of these princes. You don't have to marry anyone."

My eyes bubbled up with tears as I stared up at him.

"Of course you don't have to marry any of them," said Mom, scrambling to embrace me. "We just thought... We thought you might *consider* it," she said as she pulled away.

"It would be a pivotal moment in history." Dad Jayden's lips were a thin line. "The joining of Earth and Nelia—"

"I'm already proof of that!" I stepped back and tossed up my hands. "And Princess Alanna married four Earthlings."

"But this would be a formal alliance between two *royal houses*," continued Jayden, pushing his glasses up his nose with one hand. "It would be symbolic—"

"Jayden," whispered Mom harshly under her breath.

He went silent.

Everyone was quiet enough for my brain to clear so I could hear Papa Zander's telepathic voice over our bond. *"So they told you."*

You knew? Of course, I snapped back at him. *My whole family is against me.*

"I'm picking up the delegations right now. The boys are headed straight to Veras Academy."

I sent Papa Zander an image of me sticking my tongue out and hoped he got the message.

"What about Sage?" I asked, looking this way and that for my brother. But that was right. He must have gone in already. Lacey was nowhere to be found, either.

"What about him?" asked Dad Jayden.

I whirled on him. "You're not arranging a marriage between him and some princess?"

"Sage isn't a Nelian heir," said Pop Nash.

I ground my teeth. "And why not? Because he doesn't have these?" I flicked aside a chunk of my hair and jabbed a finger at my pointed ear. "You always told us you were *all* our fathers."

"We are," said Jayden.

"Then why am I the only Nelian heir? He has the 'prince' title when it's convenient."

"Bry, you *know* why," said Nash bluntly.

My blood boiled. "You don't know that Daddy Alarik isn't Sage's biological father! Maybe he just didn't inherit the markers. I mean, wouldn't it make more sense for us to share the same dad?"

Professor Wade, the resident Veras Academy scientist, had explained that it certainly wasn't impossible for another one of Mom's lovers to be Sage's father—I didn't want to think about what that meant, exactly—but I wasn't completely wrong, either.

They were the ones who'd never done a DNA test. Squeezing my ear in frustration, I let out a low growl.

"Bryony, stop that," snapped Mom, tugging my hand away from my head. I let her, but I still clenched my fists.

"Before this gets any more heated," said Professor Chastity, interrupting, "why don't we agree to a cease fire?"

I side-eyed her, listening, but not letting my traitorous parents out of my sight.

"Bryony, you and the princes both have been informed about the possibility of a marriage," she continued.

"And how much advanced warning did *they* get?" I muttered under my breath. Pop Nash turned away and Mom averted her gaze.

"But you've all been informed that there's no harm done if none of you agree to it," added Professor Chastity, unabated. "So you just have to treat them cordially through a few inter-actions and then it'll all be over."

"I can do that," I said through clenched teeth.

"Alarik and the princes' parents do expect *some* effort," said Dad Jayden. I whipped my head in his direction and his chin dipped, his posture slumping somewhat. But he contin-ued. "A date or two with each."

"Should we invite a camera crew along?" I suggested harshly. "Broadcast the charade to the world?"

"That wouldn't be too bad an idea—" said Pop Nash, but Mom elbowed him and he let out an *oof*.

"No cameras," said Mom. "And if there's no spark, then that's the end of it. We promise." She sent a sharp glare toward Dad Jayden.

"Fine," I said. "But you better mean that."

Though if they didn't, I wouldn't feel one ounce of guilt for shirking all responsibilities and abdicating my throne to spend the rest of my life traveling with Derek, taking in the splendors of the world.

***

THE SPLENDORS OF THE WORLD JUST SHOWED UP ON MY doorstep. Not the verdant fields and bounteous mountain variety. The what-business-do-you-have-being-so-hot-*and*-born-into-riches variety.

It didn't matter. I would not be moved.

"Class," said Professor Wade, threading his hands behind his back and trying to appear serious. He was shaking somewhat from potentially messing up his duties as our biology teacher in front of royalty or because even he turned to gelatin in the presence of such blinding beauty. They were probably at least twenty years younger than the married professor, whose husband was a Typical, but the nervous researcher was clearly more used to having his face shoved up against his dozen computer screens than being in the presence of such exquisiteness. "May I introduce—that is, well, these are our guests who are going to be observing for a bit."

"Please," said the prince standing in the middle. His proper British accent lent an air of regalness to his words. "Don't go to any trouble on our account. We're merely here to observe a few days or perhaps weeks." His eyes scanned the classroom and landed pointedly on me. "Think of us as exchange students."

Without thinking, I fluffed my bright red hair over the front of my shoulder, as if to hide my ear better.

But *someone* would have shown or told them what I

looked like. I didn't think the dyed hair and unexposed ears alone would do the trick.

Professor Wade scrambled to snatch his tablet, his shaggy black-and-gray hair whipping over his glasses. "Perhaps before we begin, Your Highnesses can share something about yourselves. About your bodies of power—I mean, your countries and abilities and…" He said something then, in what I guessed was Japanese to the prince of that nation. Though Professor Wade was Filipino-American himself, his Natch abilities also made him a genius—he'd probably learned to speak all the languages in the world on a lark.

"Please," he said when the Japanese prince nodded at him. He gestured to the middle of the projection board.

"Now *that* is what I call a guest lecturer," mumbled Hazel under her breath a few seats over. Pepper and Sheila giggled. Jerry was too frozen in his seat to react, the only movement the slight brushing of his fingertips across his loose collar.

"Not another one of those *nature-loving freaks*," said Sheila for emphasis, as if what Hazel had been implying needed to be said out loud.

All four of them sent a scathing look my way. Perhaps they did think it needed emphasis.

I sank down into my chair. Of course these princes would come to interrupt the only class I had with neither Derek nor Rajani this semester. They would have had my back. As it was, I was in no mood to disturb the class, however already off-course it may have been, to draw more attention to myself.

But the three princes had already zeroed in on me.

"I'm Prince Trey," said the only prince who'd spoken thus far. He was dreadfully pale, his skin as white as snow, which somehow beautifully complemented the white-gold of wavy, short but coiffed hair and the round, bright blue of his eyes. Tall and neither too thin nor too broad, there was the hint of defined muscles popping out even under his ornamental garb, a white suit decorated with all sorts of colorful military-style ribbons, complete with golden ropes encircling his shoulders and a little ceremonial cape hitting his mid-back behind him. His posture conveyed not a hint of sagginess, his overall air that of one of superiority, though his dazzling white smile softened that somewhat, whether intentionally or not. "I'm the third in line to the British throne—currently seating my grandfather—after my mother and older brother. No one expects me to ever sit on that chair." He winked, and Sheila let out a low groan. She was too easy. They all were.

He continued. "My family inherited the throne after an alliance with the European Natch Coalition decreed that ceremonial positions in our quarter of the world should be reserved for Natch families only. It doesn't hurt that we have a claim through the original line on my great-grandfather's side, all the way back to John of Gaunt."

He leaned forward aggressively, as if he expected some kind of challenge. "Right," he said, standing taller. "My abilities are…" His proper London-style accent gave even the word "are" a distinguished flair. "Instructor, may I demonstrate them on you?"

Professor Wade, who'd been hanging back in the corner, jumped to attention, his expression slack, as if totally unexpecting to be noticed. He cleared his throat and tried to seem more in control. "Of course, Your Highness."

Prince Trey nodded. "Right. Well, do a little jig."

Without a moment's hesitation, Professor Wade began to dance, pumping his arms up and down in a line in front of his fast-flying feet.

The class broke out into laughter, but my blood went cold. Unless they had prearranged this demonstration, he was *controlling* him. It wasn't funny.

"All right, that's enough, professor. Thank you. You're in control," said Trey. Professor Wade stopped dancing at once and stood there, blinking. Trey turned back to the class as if he hadn't just overridden our instructor's free will. "I get others to do as I command." His smirk grew broader, and I could practically hear the gleam shining off those perfect teeth. "And I don't mean just because I'm a prince."

"He can *command me* any day," mumbled Jerry, and his gaggle of gal friends tittered in response.

I sat up straighter, refusing to crack the slightest smile, looking anywhere but at Prince Trey.

"Okay, well, then, thank you," said Professor Wade, gesturing for the class to settle down. "And you, Your Highness?"

The prince from Japan stepped forward next. He hadn't reacted to any of Prince Trey's smarmy sense of humor—neither of the other princes had. His black hair hung more loosely over his dark, dark brown eyes, his amber skin smooth, the perfect complement to a sharp, angular face that seemed sculpted by a master's hands. His dark blue pants—*hakama*, I thought they were called—popped against his white kimono folded across his chest. He was thin but tall, and though difficult to tell through his puffy sleeves, there was a sense that he carried himself in the manner of a man confident in his lean physique.

"I am Prince Rio," he said, the slightest touch of an accent to his words, to the way he spoke each consonant carefully, almost too precisely. "I am second in line to the imperial throne of Nihon. My grandfather married my grandmother, who was a Natch unbeknownst to him, and their heirs have all manifested abilities over time." He paused a second, then with a rush of noise that could only be described like a zipper across the air around us, the curtains opened up behind me, letting in a stream of light. Everyone turned and began to murmur. Prince Rio seemed motionless, but the more I stared at him, the surer I was that his lips curled up in the smallest of smiles. "My ability is simply speed," he said after the class quieted down.

I turned around again and stared at the window. So he'd physically gone there and opened them himself, not with telekinesis like Uncle Rhett? And no one had seen him move.

Impressive.

Dangerous.

I tapped a finger atop my desk and tried not to let him know he'd rattled me.

"And you, Your Highness?" Professor Wade asked the third prince after a spell.

The last prince sat on top of Professor Wade's desk and made no move to get up, letting out a throaty growl halfway between irritation and the need to clear his passageways. "Prince Zeke," he said succinctly, running a hand through his shoulder-length red hair. He was broad-shouldered and shorter than the other two, though just barely, and certainly a head taller than me at least. His tanned complexion spoke of many hours spent in the sun, his gray eyes penetrating even from here. He barely seemed to have made an effort to dress ceremonially: a simple navy business suit and a navy tie, loosened at the collar of his crisp white shirt.

"New Zealand named my father king about ten years back," he said, his Kiwi accent combined with his laid-back attitude somehow making it seem as if it were no big deal at all. He rubbed his stubble-covered chin as if to hammer that point home. "Ceremonial position, though, eh?"

He waved his hand in the air, and the classroom disappeared—replaced seamlessly with an endless, gorgeous field at the base of a majestic set of mountains, even though we were all still in our desks. The class collectively gasped and Sheila outright shrieked, Hazel nudging her to be quiet. A bright, yellow flower grew up around the leg of my desk, and I reached out for it. But my hand closed in on itself, grabbing nothing, seeming to pass through the bloom without disturbing it in the least.

Prince Zeke waved again and the scenic view vanished, replaced now with empty blue sky, fluffy clouds and—

Pepper, Sheila, and Hazel all let out a collective scream, followed shortly by virtually everyone else in class. My stomach leaped up into my throat as I realized we were falling, the clouds soaring higher, barren ground appearing below us, moving closer—closer.

"*Enough*," snapped Prince Trey as he stepped in front— through the sky—of the falling desk housing Prince Zeke.

It was then I realized that Zeke's longer hair wasn't fluttering at all, that none of us were actually moving. "Stop this illusion at once," said Prince Trey.

Prince Zeke waved his hand quickly and then we were all back in the classroom, the deep breathing, the murmuring ringing throughout the room the only sign anything had happened at all.

"Thank you," said Prince Trey, dusting off the sleeve of his jacket as if we'd all actually fallen out of the sky. "Zeke, you're in control."

Prince Zeke tossed his head back and looked away, but he caught my eyes as he did and smirked as Professor Wade tried to calm the class into silence.

Hazel shot to her feet, her legs still trembling from her fright, and offered the princes a resounding round of applause, quickly followed by her clique, then the rest of class, more reluctantly, stumbling to their feet.

I didn't move, yet it was clear all three princes' attention was zeroed in on me.

Command. Stealth. Deception.

These princes were not to be taken lightly.

I had a perturbing, if irrational, feeling—these were the princes of several of Earth's most prosperous nations, after all —that it wasn't just these so-called dates I had ahead of me that warranted my growing sense of impending doom.

CHAPTER FOUR

"Wait, wait, wait, wait," said Rajani, holding both hands out in front of her, as if I were pushing my force field of protection against her. I wasn't. "You have to marry a prince and you're just *now* telling me…?"

I groaned and punched my pillow, burying my face into its fluffy cushion. "I don't have to—" I started.

"Bry, I can't hear a word you're saying."

Sighing, I sat back up on my twin XL bed, socked the pillow once again for good measure. "I don't *have to* marry one of them," I said, trying to force a flittering smile on lips. "So my parents claim. But they also *didn't happen to mention* any of this until just this morning, so…"

Rajani chewed her bottom lip, cradling her own pillow to her chest on her bed across the room from mine. Both our comforters were thick, black, our academy-issued sheets red beneath. I'd been to Rajani's parents' place, though, and she'd decked her room out there to the nines, with floral patterns and pastel colors that popped much more than the plain white walls of our converted bedroom. I wondered briefly what it might have been like to have a place all *you* like that. A place anywhere but here. A place *on Earth* anywhere but here, that was. I'd lived here all my life—half my parents were founding members of Veras. First, I'd shared a room with Sage, and then I'd gotten a roommate in middle school. She'd moved after a few years and in high school I'd been assigned Rajani, who went home every summer. Not that having an academy-decked dorm room to myself all summer was better.

There were kids in the warmer months, then, too—kids without parents, and Derek, since his parents were in Veras, too—so it was always a school. Never just a home.

My aunt and her four husbands had a place of their own —Lacey's home-away-from-home since her brother lived there. I'd been envious more than once that my own parents had never settled on living arrangements that would bring us all together as a family.

Then again, since our family was so unconventional, maybe that wasn't such a bad thing.

"Okay," said Rajani, having clearly thought things over. That made one of us. "So these princes are handsome?"

Why was that the first question she asked? Never mind. This was Rajani I was speaking to. "Does it matter?" I growled.

"Uh, yeah, it doesn't hurt, that's for sure." She rolled her eyes. "Never mind. Grapevine answered that for me anyway. *Everyone*'s talking about their display in your biology class."

"Yeah, we didn't really *learn* any biology."

"Oh, Pepper says there was *quite a lot* of rough biology on display."

"What does that even mean?" I clutched the pillow hard. Pepper was an idiot.

My phone buzzed from the nightstand housing the small, utilitarian lamp beside my bed. Derek was messaging me. Probably to ask why I was so late to dinner.

I curled my knees up to my chest. The princes were likely in the dining hall getting dinner, too. I'd wait until midnight to go eat if I had to.

Rajani's stomach grumbled, but she didn't comment on it.

"All your parents want you to do, at minimum, is go on a date with each of them. One date each."

"You make it sound so *reasonable*."

Rajani shook her head. "If it were me, I wouldn't even blink. Yes, wine me and dine me, charming storybook princes." She lay back on the bed, a dreamy look clouding her eyes.

"And what happened to a certain Nelian guard?"

She giggled. "He said he'd give me a *personal tour* of Nelia sometime. Maybe over spring break."

"We're supposed to go to the beach over spring break. Just you and me," I said. True, we'd just planned on kind of winging it—no reservations were made or anything, but Pop Nash had said we could borrow his car. A girls' road trip. To the *real* beach at the ocean, not the lake.

"Yes, well, by then *you* might find yourself occupied with one or more princes."

"Or *more*?" I groaned and lay back in my bed, rolling toward the wall so I could avoid looking at her wriggling eyebrows.

After a moment of silence, Rajani spoke more quietly. "I'm sorry all this pressure is on you. I know it hasn't been easy."

"I haven't taken this Nelian throne business seriously at all, though," I admitted softly. "I just... always begged my parents to stop putting it all on me right now. To let me focus on just being a student like everyone else."

"And now we've almost graduated." She let that hang in the air for a while. "Have you told them? That you want to travel?"

"I can't," I whispered. "After all these years of asking them to wait until I graduate, I can't just be like, 'Um, yeah, so can we wait yet again? I still want a normal life, thanks.'"

Rajani laughed softly. "I think your idea of a normal life is pretty skewed, Bry. Growing up here, having five parents, being a princess..."

Moaning, I put the pillow on top of my ear, blocking out the sound, the light—everything.

Not *everything*, though, apparently, because the muffled sound of a knock on the door came through.

"Coming," said Rajani, her bare feet padding to the door.

I pushed the pillow harder, her conversation with whoever had arrived too muffled to understand clearly.

I let the pillow slip slightly.

"I'll leave you two to it, then," said Rajani softly.

There was some shuffling, then the door closed, and the cheesy aroma of mac and almond milk cheese coupled with the citrus scent of lemon marinade reminded me that today was chicken and mac, two of my favorite dishes.

"Did someone bring us—" I started, shooting up, for some reason not expecting to find Derek there holding a tray, Rajani nowhere in sight.

The corner of my lip twitched. "You know, sneaking into a girl's room is frowned upon at Veras Academy."

"Yeah, if you're thirteen years old," said Derek, placing the tray on my nightstand and moving my phone out of the way. He frowned when he looked at the screen, probably noticing the unread messages from himself. "You never miss a meal."

Letting out a rough, choking breath, I shifted to sit nearer the stand, picking up my fork. "I've never had reason to." I poked at a noodle, not finding the desire to move the creamy goodness to my lips.

Derek sat beside me on the bed. "Not even to skip seeing Hazel and her cohorts' faces?" he asked, nudging me.

"Not even then." I brought the empty fork to my mouth, tapping the tines against my lips. "Though seeing Hazel drool over my brother has almost made me lose my appetite a few times."

My brother, the traitor, had had nothing to say about this predicament in which I found myself. He fretted constantly over Lacey since she was almost always in pain—except when she was around my aunt, Alanna, whose Nelian ability drained the powers of those around her for a time.

It worked on every Natch and Nelian but me, the mix of both.

Who knew if it'd work on Sage. He was a Typical. The only one allowed to live here, to get an education from some of the top Natch instructors around the globe. He could have gone to a Typical university, but his only career plan had always been to teach at Veras alongside half our parents. Having a Natch girlfriend likely played into that now, too.

He was family. And family had each other's backs—so I thought.

"So," said Derek. "I take it you met the princes."

I didn't ask how he knew what was eating at me. He was observant, and the rumor mill worked fast at Veras Academy. He'd also know there'd be no way I would have kept this information from him for long.

We trusted each other like that. In some ways, Derek was more my brother than my own flesh and blood—but as soon as I had that thought, I felt a prickling of my scalp and a quiver in my stomach. I didn't want to think of Derek as *that* kind of family. Even if he was safe and *home* and everything I was going to miss as soon as we graduated.

Dropping the fork to the tray, I dabbed at my eye with the napkin beside the tray.

Derek wrapped me in his arms, pulling me toward him so that my cheek rested on his shoulder. That inviting scent of ink and paper and musk calmed me, drying most of my tears before they'd even fallen. "You could tell them," he said. "Tell them you don't want to marry any of them."

"They want me to go on one official date with each," I said, my voice catching in my throat. "Just for appearances at the very least."

Derek swallowed beside me but didn't comment on it. "You should tell them you don't want to be queen," he said after a moment, his fingers rubbing massaging circles on my elbow.

"I can't."

"Can't?" Derek's fingers stopped moving. "Or won't?"

I pulled away from him. "Is there a difference?"

Derek removed his glasses for a moment and massaged his temples. He looked hot with or without them—he could have had a dozen girlfriends by now if he'd ever gotten his head out of a book—but there was something about his bare face that would have made it so much easier...

To kiss him.

I squeezed my eyes shut tightly. He was my best friend, and we had such different plans after graduation. I wasn't going to risk what we had or ask him to change his plans for me.

"Do you *want* to go on these dates?" he asked, slipping the glasses back over his nose.

My adrenaline was spiking slightly, some kind of unperceived threat telling me to be wary. "Excuse me?"

His shoulders sagged, his voice growing flat. "I *saw* them, Bryony. In the dining hall. They look like fairytale princes or fucking movie stars or something."

"And?" I asked, biting back my tongue to tell him the same applied to him. He didn't deserve to hear it just now. "When you think of me, you think of a drooling, doe-eyed lovesick slut?"

His eyes bulged. "I said no such thing!"

He knew how I felt about the Hazel fan club talking about my family that way. I knew I was putting words into his mouth, but what else could he have been implying?

I stood quickly, practically tripping over his defined thighs to tower over him. "Well, I don't know what else you mean."

The color drained somewhat from his face. "I don't know. All I know is people are talking, saying you have to marry one or all of them—"

"One or *all*?" I scoffed, looking at the ceiling as I tried to bite down the fire boiling inside me. "Why does everyone assume I'm going to have a freaking harem?"

"Because your mom and aunt do, obviously," snapped Derek. He stood now, too, gaining the upper hand, a head and a half taller than me.

I crossed my arms tightly and didn't let him make me step back. "And that's what you think of me. Just a harem collector waiting to happen."

"You've made out with"—he counted off on his hand for show—"at least four Nelians, and Harry Turner in eleventh grade and—"

"Oh my god!" I shrieked. "Do you hear yourself? I've barely dated anyone and you—"

"You date guys just to make out with them!" He swallowed. "You're never *serious*. That's not normal!"

He may as well have slapped me.

"And I suppose the time I found you plastered all over Hazel Thorne in a dark hallway after Homecoming sophomore year, that was just *normal* dating and not an utter goddamn betrayal of your best friend!"

Derek's lips went thin. "That was a mistake. I've told you that a dozen times. I've apologized a hundred times!"

"How would I know, really?" I shrugged, biting back the sob threatening to choke out. "If you don't know *me* by now, maybe I never knew you at all."

Derek opened his mouth and then closed it.

I turned away so he wouldn't see me trying not to cry.

"Bryony, I'm sorry—"

"The door's over there," I snapped.

I could feel him stiffen behind me.

"If I walk out now," he said, "things are just going to be awkward between us." He put a gentle hand on my bare shoulder, and my stomach fluttered with heat at the touch.

"Maybe they should be," I said quietly. "Can't have the princes think I'm not taking their dates seriously. Or maybe I can. Since I apparently just collect boyfriends like souvenir spoons."

"That's not what I meant. I'm just concerned you're afraid of commitment—"

"Go," I said, pinching my upper arms until it started to hurt. "Just go. I have a whole life to prepare for. That won't involve you." That came out harsher than I'd intended. Of course it would involve him, even if we just checked in with each other every so often.

"I see," he said quietly. The door opened and still, I didn't turn around. "Then I hope you're happy."

The way he said it, I wasn't entirely sure he believed in those words.

I turned around to apologize, to get him back, but the door shut in my face.

I clenched my fist, hesitating, warring with myself to take those few steps forward.

No. Set him free.

But I'd show him. I'd remain a queen without a man, a queen without an heir.

I'd go on those dates and send those princes packing.

I didn't care how incredibly gorgeous they were. A sudden flush of heat spread out throughout my entire body, erupting from my groin. Startled, I stumbled to the bed, the tingling coming out of nowhere.

My breaths grew shallow, the images of the princes in front of the classroom dancing through my head.

But which one? All of them? Was this the Nelian *sense* my parents had told me about, those pheromones that denoted whom you were meant to spend your life with?

But which?

I grew hot, eager to touch myself, to think of each prince, my best friend in turn—now, in the middle of this situation, after that conversation!

Sobbing, I sat on the edge of my bed, ashamed at myself

for being the promiscuously-minded woman Derek had accused me of being.

Me, a virgin—technically.

And then I pleasured myself anyway until the tears dried up.

CHAPTER FIVE

I'D SUCCESSFULLY AVOIDED THE PRINCES, DEREK—ANYONE, really, even Rajani when she came back into the room because I'd pretended to be asleep—for the rest of the night.

But it was Friday morning now and there was a day of classes to get to, so I couldn't stay holed up forever.

"Bry, we're going to be late." Rajani poked my thigh through my comforter with her tablet's stylus. "And now you definitely won't have time for breakfast."

My traitorous stomach gurgled then, reminding me of the cold, untouched food on my nightstand that still had to be returned to the dining room, and the fact that I hadn't eaten since lunch.

"I *know* you're awake," hissed Rajani. "I've just been letting you think you're pulling the wool over my eyes to give you some space." With a flourish, my comforter flew to the bottom of my bed, the sunlight trickling in around the blinds an affront to my senses.

I grumbled and sat up, clutching my stomach as it growled and growled.

Rajani, all dressed and ready for the day, sat beside me. "I was going to say you can't report yourself to the infirmary over this, but you look like shit."

"Thanks," I muttered, rubbing a hand atop my frizzy, wild, red hair, taking note of everything. It *did* feel like a bullet train might have hit me in the night. On top of which, I was hungry and achy. No food plus using my powers plus the stress of the day before had done a number on me.

A soft bell chimed out over the hallway speakers, the warning that we only had five minutes to get to first period. The college division was a little laxer with tardies and absences in general—but not for the daughter of the founders.

My eyes blinked blearily toward my phone on the nightstand, but as I swiped it to get a look, I found no additional messages from Derek awaiting me. Instead, there was just a clunkily written text from Daddy Alarik, who insisted on using Earth technology but always managed to make an adorable fool of himself doing so.

No. Not adorable. I was too mad at him over this whole prince debacle for it to be adorable.

Sweet supernova, he wrote, his ridiculous nickname for me. He wrote it so often, autocorrect always got it right for him. *Cat PLEASE meet 2day 2 discus your marry.* Beside the word "marry," there was an emoji of a bride.

Muttering under my breath, I crumpled the thin, sheetlike phone into rest mode in my palm and tossed it on my bed, burying my hands in my face.

"Bry," said Rajani, her voice growing serious. "Do you need me to go with you to the infirmary?"

"I'm fine," I snapped, harsher than I'd meant to. I sent her a flittering smile. "I'm sorry. I don't want to talk about it just now. But get to class."

"Should I say you're sick?"

"Sure," I said.

She stood warily, watching me with her bottom lip pinched between her teeth, her tablet clutched to her chest. "I'll skip, too, if you need me."

"I'm fine." Smiling kind of hurt just then, but I did my

best impression of it anyway. "Go. The Renegades try to guest lecture here on Fridays. You might get Torynt as a teacher."

She rolled her eyes. "You say that like it's a good thing." She smoothed down the wrinkles in her blouse even so, her dark irises glowing. "He's such a flirt."

But in a committed relationship with a Natch rights lawyer. A polyamorous relationship in which he shared his girlfriend with more than one man—

Okay. I really needed to get *away* from this place. The harem gene was just too damn infectious.

Once Rajani left and the second bell rang, I was left alone with my thoughts. Those thoughts were soon enough interrupted by Papa Zander.

"Pumpkin," he said in my head. *"Why aren't you headed to class?"*

Without formalizing the words, I just sent a bevy of images at him: the princes, my other dads telling me about the marriage, Daddy Alarik's almost indecipherable text— everything. Well, almost everything. I sent a brief flash of me arguing with Derek, but some things were just too personal to share with a dad.

I could feel Papa Zander probing my brain in the silence.

"You're hungry," he said. *"Meet me in the dining hall for breakfast."*

I sighed.

"Come on now. It's nice and empty. Well, almost empty. Alarik's here. We can talk to him together."

He said that as if he'd be on my side.

DRAGGING MY FEET, FRESHLY SHOWERED AND DRESSED, I DIDN'T think I could find an excuse to take any longer in getting to see my two dads who were only here part of the time. The dining hall was pointedly empty, the only sounds along the way the thumping bass of students without classes in their dorm rooms listening to music, then the echoing lecture of instructors seeping out from classrooms.

Papa Zander walked with a tray from the kitchen, and I noticed Professor Kouta, a former Renegade turned full-time Veras instructor and a pretty good chef, hanging up an apron and nodding at me before walking away. He wasn't normally a cook here, but...

"Supernova!" cried Daddy Alarik, distracting me. He waved from a table in the middle of the empty room, a lock of his long, green hair falling just slightly out of place.

Doing my best to smile, I shuffled over, comparing my form-fitting jeans and dark purple T-shirt to the native Nelian attire he wore. Earthy, leather, and cotton, it complemented his flawless pale-brown complexion well, his angular features popping against the frame of his green hair. As Papa Zander sat down, I compared the two. They couldn't have looked more different. Zander was bulky, Alarik lean. Zander was shorter, dark hair flecked with white, his face lined with the beginnings of wrinkles but somehow more warm and handsome for it. Papa Zander looked as if he'd *lived* here on this Earth, had struggled for a long time. Daddy Alarik looked as clean and pristine as the Nelian world that had spawned him.

But I knew both had seen and done as much on this world as anyone could.

Their semi-frequent absence during my childhood could often be attributed to the work they'd done saving this planet and all the Natches on it.

"You're making me blush," said Papa Zander out loud, his voice deep.

"Stop reading my mind," I snapped, but my mood softened as Papa Zander pushed the tray he'd been carrying toward me.

Blueberry pancakes with a smiley face made of whipped cream. My favorite, long ago. I almost started bawling looking down at it.

"You've grown so much, pumpkin," said Papa Zander as I picked up a fork and knife.

"Almost a queen," added Daddy Alarik, his voice incongruously even lower than Papa Zander's.

My stomach soured and I sighed, stabbing the fork into a piece of the stack but not picking it up.

Papa Zander nudged Daddy Alarik with his arm.

"Right," said Daddy Alarik, clearing his throat. "Zander tells me you're having reservations about the princes."

"How could you just *decide* this for me without even asking me?" I said, not even bothering with pretext. My eyes pricked with tears, but I was determined not to let any fall just now.

"It, uh…" Daddy Alarik wasn't usually at a loss for words. "It was just an idea I had. I'm worried about the next heir to the throne. With my sister uninterested in having children of her own—"

"And what if *I* don't want to have them, either? You didn't even ask."

To spite my chaotic stomach, I shoved the bite of pancakes into my mouth, the tears streaming down my cheeks hot and salty as they hit my lips.

"Do you not want to have children?" Daddy Alarik asked.

"I don't know," I mumbled through bites of food. "I haven't thought about it. I just don't like everyone *expecting* things of me." I kept eating, faster, making more angry stabs at the stack.

"Like?" asked Papa Zander quietly.

"Children, marriage, the throne—all of it!" I shoved the plate forward and crossed my arms, leaning back in my chair.

"You are *destined* to rule over Nelia," began Daddy Alarik. "I know it may seem overwhelming—you don't even *realize* what kind of vision I had for my people when I was the equivalent of your age."

I glared at him. His *vision* had involved taking over the Earth by force in order to save its environment. I knew at least that much had happened before I'd been born. There was still a Nelian in a high-security Natch prison who had broken the Nelian-Earth ceasefire to wreak havoc at a Natch orphanage.

Of course, as a result, he'd busted up an abusive place that had stifled Natch abilities, which had led to the creation of Veras Academy. But that hadn't been his plan at all.

Just as this era of peace and cooperation hadn't been how the King of Nelia had seen *his* plan going before that.

If he hadn't felt bonded with Mom, who knew if things would have turned out so well?

Papa Zander studied me and I tried to empty my mind, to keep my errant thoughts from him. When that didn't seem to work, I purposely sent him an image of what I imagined the three princes looked like buck-naked and smiling seductively, and Papa Zander visibly jumped in his seat.

See? I said in my head. *A daughter wants to keep some things secret from her parents.*

Papa Zander flushed a little and looked down at the table. He and Dad Jayden shared a special bond in the pentagon of my parents' relationship, so I knew it wasn't the image of gorgeous, naked men that had sent him scurrying. Just the idea of his daughter with them.

"Daddy," I said, addressing Alarik. "How can I marry anyone if I don't feel the… pheromones? The Nelian *sense* where you just know?"

Daddy Alarik studied me. "You're half-human," he said after a moment. "You might not feel it at all. Do you think you…?" He shook his head. "If you felt it, you'd know. There'd be no denying it. No resisting it. Mother Nelia works in mysterious ways, but when she bonds her children together, it's for a bigger reason."

Like him bonding with Mom and taking a more peaceful approach to his goal of saving the Earth. Or Aunt Alanna bonding with her team of rebels who had vowed to take my parents down—turning them to our side, making it so there was less need for rebels to stand against us to begin with.

So if Mother Nelia had had plans for me to wed one of these princes for some grand, political purpose, surely, she'd make me *feel* the same type of things.

Grinning, I dug back into my pancakes.

"What is it?" asked Papa Zander, speaking aloud instead of poking around in my head. "You look happy."

I shrugged. "I'll go on these dates," I said. "And if I don't feel any special connection, well, it can't be that important to the grand scheme of things that I wed any of them."

Papa Zander and Daddy Alarik exchanged a look.

Then Daddy spoke. "Nelians find joy in each other's bodies all the time. With or without the *sense* that you're meant for one another." He didn't seem at all ashamed of speaking about this with his daughter, and in fact it was far from the first time I'd heard it. "But making love to someone you're *meant* to be with… You'd know. You'd know if you had that innate Nelian sense, supernova."

So if sleeping with the princes didn't rock my socks off… I wasn't meant for any of them.

My face flushed at the idea of sleeping with the princes so casually, and I had to think about ice cream, strawberries, fields of flowers, anything to make sure Papa Zander didn't pick up on—nope, all of those things got corrupted, too. Licking off the same ice cream cone as Prince Trey. Prince Rio feeding me a strawberry, slowly, dangling it just out of reach and making me bite for it like a wild animal. Prince Zeke sauntering toward me in that field of flowers, a lily trailing down from his lips to his neck to his exposed chest.

Papa Zander cleared his throat.

I thought you wanted me to marry one of them, I thought spitefully.

He didn't respond.

"I don't want you to focus so much on the Nelian way of coupling," said Daddy Alarik, oblivious to what had just gone on in my head. "It's quite possible that, as a half-human,

45

you don't feel the Nelian sense at all. So go on these dates, try to consider the implications of refusing—"

Papa Zander nudged him and cut him off. "That's all we're asking of you, pumpkin." He sent a roguish smile my way. "Go on some dates, like many girls your age would. And maybe you'll have more fun than you expect anyway." He sent an image of the three princes with roses in their mouths and winking at me via our telepathic bond, his squeamish-ness at the idea of me with any of them clearly tampered.

I sent an image of me sticking my tongue out at him in response.

CHAPTER SIX

Food and a new sense of focus helped get me back to myself. I'd already felt like there was this cloud of impending doom that had hung over me as my days at Veras Academy ticked away, a clear line in the sand marked "Before Graduation" and "After," where my life would break off into two. Though Nelians found their way to Earth somewhat regularly, the invitation the other way was extended to only the smallest number of Earthlings—diplomats, scientists, and very rarely, a celebrity figure. And the Veras students, of course.

The thing was, as beautiful as Nelia was, it was... Simple. Empty. A world where nature ruled and the few Nelians were simply the caretakers of their miniscule corner of a planet comprised entirely of lush, verdant plant life and small but plentiful bodies of water.

After a day or two of gazing at the stars, most humans would grow bored.

It was third period now, and the grounds were mostly empty, except for a class of elementary school Natches playing soccer for gym. Every few minutes, one kid or another would burst out with some power—vanishing, then

47

reappearing to kick the ball or guiding the ball with some unseen force—and only the ones who got caught by the gym teacher got the whistle and a point taken off their team's score.

The kids seemed to have a strategy for that. Get one kid caught while two more were manipulating the ball behind the gruff coach's back. That was actually part of the game, though —training for how to use their powers in everyday situations without causing a scene.

"I thought you had class," a familiar voice said from behind me. I'd been gazing out the floor-to-ceiling window in this hallway for longer than I'd realized.

"I'm taking off," I said. "Princess business and all that."

Sage ambled up beside me to take a look at what had caught my attention, but his gaze was drawn almost immediately behind him, so I followed his line of sight. Lacey walked out of an empty classroom, flipping off the lights and buttoning up the top of her ruffled blouse. Our eyes met and she waved in a short, jerky movement, looking immediately away. For a second, her fingers grew longer, inhumanly long, her head starting to loll forward and droop. But she straightened her back and got control over her power and its default state, snapping back into the pretty young teacher she was as she exited the building to watch her class finish its game.

"A quickie while her class is under another teacher's watch?" I asked dryly.

As if I'd pointed out the fact that his T-shirt was inside out —it wasn't—Sage did a quick onceover of his appearance for the telltale sign that had given it away. I nudged his arm with my elbow. "She's beautiful. Kind. A bit *old* for you—"

"Jayden and Zander are seven years older than Mom," he said, not bothering to give any of our fathers a title. It had grown cumbersome for him when we'd reached our teenage years. "And don't get me started on Alarik—"

"Point taken," I mumbled. "I just... I don't know... I didn't expect you to settle down so quickly."

"So quickly?" He scratched his jaw, where a thin layer of stubble was protruding. "I tapped that almost as soon as I turned eighteen."

"Ew, thanks for the image and the reminder, and that's not what I meant." Shuddering, I clutched both my elbows. "I just mean... You never even *dated* anyone before her."

"Sure, I did," he said, angling away somewhat. "I went to two dances with Pepper and one with Hazel—"

"Oh, god, don't remind me." It seemed as if Hazel somehow blamed *me* for my brother not being interested after that. Well, when she chose to bully her crush's twin sister, I couldn't say I knew what she'd expected to come from that. "I just mean... How do you know? How do you know she's the one? You're young yet."

"I know." Sage's jaw clenched.

"That sounds... *formal*," I said, struggling for the right word.

Sage turned to me. "Don't tell anyone, but—"

"Papa Zander's on campus," I said, clearing my throat. Not that he needed to be that close to reach out to us.

Sage cocked his head, then shook it off. "Well, if he knows, he hasn't said anything. I think anytime I'm with Lacey, he stays far, far away, no matter what kind of emotions he senses."

"Right," I said, not wanting that picture again.

Sage grabbed my hands in both of his. "Bry, I asked her to marry me."

"*What?* When?"

"Just last weekend."

"It's been *five days* since last weekend," I said, frowning. "Why wouldn't you tell me?"

He chuckled. "Aren't you going to ask what she said?"

I took my hands out of his and pointed to the classroom behind us. "Judging by that, I'd say she said *yes*."

The tips of his ears turned red. "Well, yes, she said *yes*."

"So why is this a big secret?"

"She wants to tell her brother first—we agreed that siblings would be the first to know." He smiled slyly. "I would have told you earlier, but I've been *busy* celebrating, and then there was this whole mess with the princes visiting and—"

"Congratulations!" I said, shutting him up before he dwelled on all that for too much longer. I swept my little brother into my arms, some kind of strange sensation floating through me that it had been a long time since he'd been my "little" brother, even if I had protected him in the womb. In any case, the realization of what he'd just told me shot through me then like a bolt of lightning.

This "After" event was happening *now*, in the "Before Graduation" side of the line. My life was changing before I even expected it to. Though the tears that prickled the corners of my eyes were joyous ones, the silly grin on Sage's face making my heart melt with happiness for him, I gave him one extra big hug, squeezing hard enough to make him pop, as one last, desperate sense of trying to hold on to things.

"Bry, glad you're happy for me," he choked out, "but I do need to breathe to make it down the aisle."

"Right," I said, letting go. "Sorry." I wiped a tear away. "I'll try my best to keep it from Mom and Dads, but Papa Zander has an annoying habit of popping up in my head when I least expect it."

"Yeah." Sage swallowed. "I think he's been more worried about you, how you're going to handle this whole prince thing, these days, so he hasn't been around, but... If he's prying in your head, he might stumble on it." He shrugged one shoulder. "Lacey will understand if it couldn't be helped." He looked at me, his expression growing serious. "How *are* you handling this whole prince thing?"

Prince thing. As if it were just another item on my to-do list. Well, he wasn't wrong.

I smoothed down imaginary wrinkles on the front of my

jeans. "It's... Well, I haven't spoken to a single one of them. I saw them in a class, then bolted for my dorm room right after and..." I threw my hands up in frustration. "But I've got it handled."

"You do?" Sage pursed his lips. "Do you need any help with this plan of yours?"

"Help like what?"

"Making sure some pompous royals with their heads up their asses don't take advantage of my baby sister."

"*I* was born first," I pointed out. "Several minutes beforehand."

Sage shrugged. "When I think of assholes taking advantage of a situation to hurt you in any way, you're my baby sister."

"I think I can handle myself." I nudged him again. "Who's protected whom since before birth?"

"Yeah, yeah." Sage stared out the window, his gaze zeroing in on Lacey patting the head of a child who'd run over from the game to tell her something excitedly. I didn't ask if they planned on having kids—if Lacey could even have them with her powers. Then again, maybe she could if she spent the whole nine months in Aunt Alanna's ability-negating presence—but when my aunt slept, Lacey's powers would return.

There was no way she and Sage were having kids that way. But I didn't want to talk about it. That was his business —and just one more reminder that the world was ready to move on, dragging me with it kicking and screaming.

"Just be careful around them, okay?" said Sage. "I got a look at them last night in the dining hall and they seemed pretty full of themselves."

"I'm with you there. I've never met a more arrogant collection of condescending assholes—"

"Princess," said a man in a baritone, if somewhat amused, voice from behind me. "You're a difficult one to pin down."

Pivoting on my heel, I came face to face with Prince Trey, Princes Rio and Zeke a few steps behind him. Trey's finely shaped lips were clamped tightly together, his blue irises sparkling with a glimmer of mischief.

CHAPTER SEVEN

"Your Highnesses," I said, suddenly wobbly on my feet, "I didn't see you there." So much for my fleeting, if not entirely dismissed, idea of seducing the princes to see if I felt any Nelian pheromones drawing me to them.

But all in all, the end result would be the same. I doubted I'd fall in love with any of them to begin with. I just wanted to show my parents that I'd tried.

"That much is obvious," said Prince Zeke with a grunt. He smirked, though.

"Yes, well…" I smoothed more non-existent wrinkles on the thighs of my jeans. Zeke's eyes in particular caught hold of the movement, his gaze lingering on my legs. I felt a flush hit me at my core. "I've been busy."

"Skipping class and generally avoiding us?" ventured Rio. Of the three of them, he'd seemed the most aloof, the most disinterested. But his eyes sparkled now with some ounce of amusement.

Before I could respond, Trey spoke up. "Yes, well, if you had made a point of reaching out to us earlier, we could have saved you any undue anxiety." He exchanged looks with Rio and Zeke, who both nodded. "We don't relish the idea of an arranged marriage any more than you seem to."

I wanted to retort—an inexplicable need to spit out that he didn't know anything about me, let alone that—but he was right. There was no point in arguing about it.

"Oh," I said simply, then decided to stop letting them lead me around by the nose. "Have you met my brother?"

"We've hardly met *you*," said Zeke.

I ignored the comment and made the introduction. "Prince Sage Haddix, Princes Trey of the U.K., Rio of Japan, and Zeke of New Zealand."

"Nice to meet you," Sage said, offering each his right hand. I was sure he was breaking a dozen royal etiquette protocols, but prince and princess though we may be, we hadn't exactly grown up learning all the Earth royal customs.

The exchange students didn't seem too bothered by it, though, each accepting the handshake with a barely noticeable reluctance.

"I'm going to serve as the chaperone for your dates," said Sage.

"You're *what*?" I did a double-take.

Sage ran a hand over the back of his neck. "Since they're official sanctioned events and all." He winced and sent me a brief apologetic look. "Besides, the princes are sure to have their own bodyguards. Mom and Dads asked—"

I slapped my own face. Of course. Hurry up and find a husband, dear daughter, but do so with an audience.

"Ah, yes," said Trey. "*Dads*? That is a rather interesting situation. You have four fathers, do you not? The King of Nelia shares his consort with three Earth commoners?"

Instinctively, I flipped a chunk of my hair forward over my shoulder to make sure my ears weren't showing. "Is that a problem?"

"No," said Trey with a smile. "Horses for courses and all. Each to their own. It's not unusual for a Nelian, is it?" His gaze lingered at the side of my head, as if hoping for a peek at the pointed ears. Then his eyes darted pointedly to the cut of my tee, the smallest hint of cleavage revealed at the dip of the

V-neck. I wanted to be turned off, but annoyingly, I was overcome with a flood of longing to check him out from head to toe.

As if I'd give him the satisfaction.

As if I'd be *able to* with my brother breathing down my neck.

"How do you want to do this?" I asked.

The three princes exchanged a look. Trey spoke. He seemed to be the unofficial spokesman for the group. "Eager to get this sorted, I see."

Rio stepped forward. "I thought we could have dinner on my yacht," he said, his hands clasped behind his back. He wasn't entirely disinterested, but there was something so formal about the way he asked, like it wasn't his idea of a good time, either.

"You have a yacht?" I asked. "On the lake?" Didn't people usually keep those confined to the oceans?

"My parents frequently have business in the area," he said. "It's very environmentally-friendly, I assure you," he added. "Runs on solar power entirely."

It was true that fossil-fuel-guzzling vehicles were no longer allowed, as they'd once been. But that hadn't been my objection.

"Sure," I said, tapping my foot. "That sounds… lovely. When?"

"Tonight," said Rio, nonplussed. "Meet me at the docks at seven?"

I examined one man after the other to see if anyone had an objection, but no one did. In fact, Trey was watching me carefully, as if this response was part of some kind of test, and Zeke was pretending to look out at the yard, but I caught his gaze flickering my way every few seconds.

"It's a date," I said, plastering on a toothy grin.

Rio reached for my hand and put his lips to the back of it. His kiss was soft, like a feather tickling me, and sweet somehow, my hand warming even as my cheeks did. I knew it was a formality, but I felt suddenly underdressed in the casual clothes I'd tossed on without putting much thought into the choice.

"Until tonight," said Rio, his voice low and surprisingly seductive.

As I watched them go, I clutched the hand he'd kissed to my chest.

"I should have told you earlier," said Sage. "About the chaperone thing. Sorry about that."

"It's fine," I said as the bell overhead rang. "If someone has to come with, I wouldn't want it to be anyone else." I sent him a sly look. "I trust you to know when to back off—or step in."

"The thing is," said Sage, though I was only half-paying attention. Hazel and Sheila stepped out of a classroom at the end of the hall almost too perfectly timed since they ran right into the princes. "I'm not the only one Mom and Dads asked. And since I have a date tonight…"

I waved him off. "Yeah, yeah. Can't keep the lovebirds apart for even one night, can I? It's fine. I wasn't expecting any escort anyway."

Hazel and Sheila were both curtseying now, Sheila rather clumsily. Hazel kept her back ramrod straight, like she'd done this before.

"Thank you!" Sage clasped his hands together. "I'll be there for the other ones, I promise. Lacey just wanted to tell her brother tonight, and she wanted me there for it."

Prince Trey's face brightened, a sudden look of realization dawning on him, and it was evident the British brat of Veras Academy must have met her sovereign's kin at some point before this. He took her hand in his and laid a kiss on top of it as Rio had with me, and my body tensed.

"I'm sure Derek can handle it just fine on his own," said Sage, his voice distant, and I whipped around to find him already several feet away, headed toward the door leading outside. "But just call me—or tell Zander—if you need me, and I'll head on over!"

"Wait, what?" I sputtered, but it was too late. Sage was stepping out into the sunshine.

Derek had agreed to *chaperone* me? When? Why hadn't he told me? And after last night, did he still even want to?

An already awkward situation was just about to get a thousand times more embarrassing.

"OKAY, SO I TAKE BACK WHAT I SAID ABOUT ENVYING YOU HAVING to date three princes," said Rajani between sips of her iced cappuccino. "This is about as romantic and enviable as dating someone on national TV." Her heavy-lidded gaze slipped pointedly around the café to the four Nelian guards just *standing* there by the front door. Then there was Derek three tables over, cradling his black coffee silently, his back to us as if he were in place as an undercover bodyguard. He'd brought along a tablet to continue his studies, perhaps as part of the "disguise."

Who was I kidding? It was more like he didn't want to talk to me.

I hadn't said a word to him, either. In fact, I'd asked Rajani to tag along at least this far in order to avoid even the *possibility* of awkward silence between us.

We did make a strange pair, though, Rajani in a skin-tight jogging outfit, her dark hair pulled back into a ponytail. I'd made an effort to pretend there was at least a chance of this date going well and had on a slinky black dress that stopped just above the knee and left a wide dip of pale fawny skin uncovered in the back. My hair had been ironed straight, my makeup almost heavy enough to justify a night at a club, though with more subdued shades of brown and rouge. A little black sequined clutch had all my essentials—my paperthin phone, some tissues, a granola bar in case my hunger overcame the dry mouth and quivery, twitchy muscles that comprised my nerves at any point.

"You eat that shit up," I said, reaching for the cup of iced tea in front of me with trembling fingers. "Bachelor shows on TV."

Rajani grinned and grabbed my free hand. "Maybe so. But I'm not sure I want to be reminded that it's all an illusion—or at least that there are dozens of crew members just out of shot watching it all go down." She lowered her voice. "It'll be fine," she said, but then she grimaced. "Awkward as hell, but fine."

We both went silent for a little while longer, Rajani's eyes drifting above the lid of her cup pointedly to Connak near the door. I focused instead on the projection TV above her head, the weather report predicting a clear, unusually warm spring night. The anchor—handsome, his yellow hair pomaded like plastic atop his tanned, symmetrical face—had moved on to a story about a farmer's market in the area, how King Alarik of the Nelians had paid it a visit, rewarding the farmer who'd produced the biggest tomato in the area with an additional government subsidy. My gaze darted down to the window instead, my stomach knowing before my brain that just now wasn't the best time to be reminded of my royal connections.

Though it was hard not to be with the guards posted at the doors.

"It's about time," said Rajani, nodding toward a digital clock projected on the wall behind me. At the same time, the whirr of an espresso machine snapped me back to the moment.

"Yeah," I said, getting up and pushing my chair back in. "So I guess this is goodbye for now?"

"You make it sound so *final*," said Rajani, chuckling. "You'll get through this." She scooped both our paper cups up and put them in the proper compost receptacle. Daddy Alarik had pushed once for reusable cups only that everyone would have been responsible for carrying around and washing themselves, but my uncles had talked him down to more biodegradable options. No more plastic, though—at least not for wasteful one-and-done deals like drinks.

"Text me if you need anything," said Rajani, slipping earbuds into her ears. "I'll be running, but I have my messages set to auto-dictate."

"I'm sure I'll be fine," I said, not totally believing the words slipping out of my mouth myself. I was about to say more, but the TV caught my attention.

"This just in. There's been a breakout at the Halfsmith State Penitentiary," said the anchor, and my ears perked up at the sound. The Natch prison. I knew of one prisoner kept there.

"The escaped inmate is the only Nelian kept in custody on Earth," continued the anchor. "Xerxes, perpetrator of the Second Hope institution incident during the ceasefire that put Earth and Nelia back on shaky footing for a time."

An image of the Nelian I'd never really seen before came on screen. Just visible from the chest up, it was clear he was stockier than most Nelians I'd ever seen, broad-shouldered but still fit. His green hair was cropped close in the picture, his smooth fair brown skin clashing with the orange of his jumpsuit. The tips of his pointed ears lined up perfectly with a pair of dark green brows narrowed in contempt over large, round, dark eyes.

Rajani was looking up at the screen, too, the Nelian guards devolving into hushed tones as they came to life and spoke to one another.

"Isn't that your aunt's ex?" asked Rajani. Not the way I'd define him first thing, but yes. That, too.

"Your Highness," said Connak, slipping in beside me. "Perhaps it's best we cancel the evening's activities."

"I thought that jail was hundreds of miles away," I said, squeezing my clutch until a sequin dug into my palm.

"It is," said Derek, suddenly at my side and actually speaking to me. "But—"

"And what was his power again?" asked Rajani, tapping a finger to her chin. "Compelling people to tell the truth? Not sure why he was ever much of a threat, to be honest."

The discussion had drowned out much of what else the anchor had to say, the whirr of that damned espresso machine not helping any.

"We can handle it, right?" I said, glancing from Connak to Derek and back. Derek's face fell just as he was hailed on his communicator device on his wrist.

I stood there awkwardly, fidgeting as Derek spoke in hushed tones to whatever member of Veras had called to check in with him.

Sighing, he ran a hand down the back of his head. "They're not too concerned," he said. "Just gave instructions to be more watchful. A strike team is going to check it out and will get back to us when they know more."

"Then let's go get this over with," I said, straightening my back and heading for the door.

CHAPTER EIGHT

AT THE DOCK, THE FOUR MEN IN BLACK SUITS AND SUNGLASSES who lined our path toward the yacht were no doubt royal Japanese bodyguards, though I couldn't tell at a glance if they were Natch or Typical. The yacht the wooden planks led to was sizable and ornate without being ridiculously grandiose, enough room to comfortably host a gathering for a small group of friends and not a raging party. The thought comforted me, that His Highness embraced a less ostentatious way of living it up, though I was quickly struck by the fact that there wasn't going to be room for half our combined guards, let alone all of them.

"His Majesty King Alarik has been in touch," said a grave voice, clipped and careful. Prince Rio descended the steps of the yacht, his trim figure complemented nicely by the slightly baggy khakis and the pale blue polo shirt he wore. I felt incredibly overdressed.

"As the criminal Xerxes has made a target of your parents before," continued Rio, "they're on high alert until they can help the authorities apprehend him. However, they feel certain that they themselves would be the primary target, should Xerxes be planning anything." He spoke to one of his men in Japanese, and the man nodded, slipping past me to pass on the instructions to Connak in hushed tones.

Rio, the man of super speed, moved slowly, almost deliberately, as he held his arm out for me. "I see no reason why we can't still enjoy ourselves. We'll be safe out on the water—safer than we could be anywhere else."

His sturdy, toned arm was warm beneath my hand, and a wild flush of heat soared up from my core to my head and down again. "Our bodyguards will be on a second boat behind us," he said. My mouth gaped open, my gaze shifting over my shoulder, where Connak and the other Nelians seemed to be agreeing with whatever Rio's man was instructing them to do.

"Come. Let me introduce you to the captain and the chef," said Rio.

Derek shifted uncomfortably behind Connak, his tablet tucked under his arm. I supposed he couldn't object if everyone else thought it prudent.

I didn't know if I relished the idea of him with Rio and me in such close quarters regardless. The steps were tightly packed, and I stumbled slightly at the top, leaning unintentionally entirely into the prince's arms. His lips parted slightly, his gaze growing wistful as we stayed with my breasts flush against his firm chest for just a beat too long than was proper before I thought to jump back. My heart threatened to drown out all other sounds assaulting my ears.

Taking my hand in his, he led me toward the front of the boat. The cool breeze off the lake was chillier than I'd anticipated, and I shivered, wishing I'd thought to wear a shawl.

Rio leaned toward me, his dark eyebrows drawing together. "Let me get you something to keep you warm."

He disappeared into the wheelhouse of the boat for a moment, and my attention was drawn to the men working below to disengage the boat from the dock. I turned out to the red-tinted horizon, the smell of water and fish hitting my nostrils as I took in a deep breath of beautifully fresh air. I'd always lived close to a lake but had never gone out on it.

The boat rocked slightly as Rio returned, a blanket in his hand.

"You look stunning," said Prince Rio, holding the blanket out like a cape for me to step into.

"I thought you princes weren't interested in an arranged marriage," I said, slipping into the blanket and feeling its warmth immediately as his strong hands helped wrap it in place around my shoulders.

"That does not mean I can stop myself from commenting on beauty when I see it." His gaze lingered on mine for just a moment and then there was a twitch in his jaw as he stared out at the expanse of the lake. If I didn't know that it ended after about a hundred nautical miles, I would have imagined it went on and on for eternity.

"Let's be off," said Rio, turning on his heel and descending into the wheelhouse. After a minute, I followed, figuring I ought to meet this captain and chef. There didn't seem to be room for many more crew than that.

The boat took off smoothly, but out of instinct, I still gripped the handrail hard for the first few minutes, watching the shore grow smaller and smaller, noticing when another boat, just as small, also decked out with plenty of solar panels, took off after us, housing Rio's guards and the Nelians, no doubt. I wondered if Derek would be on board. I supposed my parents and his couldn't have known when they'd asked him, but it was almost as good as asking Hazel or one of her cronies to come along. Just another person who thought I was destined to be promiscuous.

The wind jostled my hair, sending a chunk of it flapping over my face, reminding me that I'd decided not to care what people thought. I could have a fun time with three handsome princes. Afraid of commitment, apparently, there was no way for me to please everyone.

I finished descending and stepped inside the wheelhouse, the vacuum of the pressure practically shoving me inside.

For the second time in under twenty minutes, I stumbled right into the figure in front of me.

"We'll have to see about getting you your sea legs," said Rio, turning slightly over his shoulder, then focusing back on the wide window in front of him.

He was gripping the wheel, and as I looked around the room—my grip still lingering on his strong bicep—I realized there was no one here with us.

"*You're* the captain?"

He bit his lip, likely trying to clamp down a smile. "And the chef," he added, gazing at some of the instruments.

"'Let me introduce you to the captain and the chef,'" I parroted. "Clever."

We picked up speed a little and I held on tightly to the dashboard, widening my stance even as my skirt rode up my thighs a few inches. He could think what he wanted. I wasn't about to tumble into him for the third time.

Despite the raucous sound of the boat cutting through the water, despite the chill of the outside air, the wheelhouse seemed to grow steamier and steamier, Rio's shallow, even breaths somehow both disciplined and amorous all at once.

He fiddled with some more controls and levers and we slowed down. Turning, I saw the shoreline far off in the distance, the other boat still quite some distance behind us. When I turned back, Rio's eyes snapped up as he flicked on the cabin lights, and I looked down to realize I was still clutching and crouching, my skirt even tighter against my skin, ridden up higher than I'd realized.

I bolted upright with a start.

Rio cocked his head but didn't comment. "Just give me a moment," he said, heading toward a small set of stairs leading downward. "We'll eat on deck." His voice grew smaller as it carried up to me.

There was a rustling and a series of clanks.

I headed to the staircase, my legs still a little wobbly, even though the movements of the boat were more subtle now, just an easy, rocking sway.

"I can help." I froze in surprise. With how narrow the staircase had been, I hadn't imagined the galley would be grand. There was a bedroom area, partitioned from the rest of the cabin—and though the king-sized bed took up the majority of the space, the way the twilight streamed in through the windows made it seem as if you could be sleeping out in the open air. On the other side of a bamboo screen was a lounging area, complete with a white sofa that took up the length of nearly all the window acting as a wall. Beyond that was another door, leading out to the deck at the back of the boat, a small table and two chairs no doubt bolted down to the surface to keep them in place.

The clinking behind me made me turn, and I located the restroom and the small kitchenette beside it. Rio stepped out, two black, square platters in his hands. Somehow, he'd gotten a small dash of white powder—flour, or perhaps powdered sugar, on closer inspection—on his nose.

Before I realized what I was doing, I brushed it off him. He froze, and tucking my clutch under my arm, I grabbed both platters from him, examining the array of noodles with sliced cucumbers and a hard-boiled egg, garnished with black dots I guessed to be dried seaweed, marinated in a sauce that smelled of soy and ginger. There wasn't any steam coming off the platters, and I realized they were chilled.

"Cold udon," said Rio, scrambling to get ahead of me to open the door. "With egg, cucumbers, and ginger."

The newly night air caressed my face as I stepped out, the atmosphere hanging off the water. Despite its slight twinge of fishiness, the breeze was invigorating as I put the platters down, sliding my purse under one of the chairs and taking a seat.

Rio disappeared back inside the cabin for a bit and

returned with two glasses of a pale green liquid I recognized immediately as green tea.

From a rolled-up set of two cloth napkins, he produced two sets of bamboo chopsticks as well as two bamboo forks.

"Do you have a preference?" he asked.

I grabbed for the chopsticks and beamed. Rio followed suit as he sat down. It was cute that he'd brought two forks, as if he'd intended to mirror whatever my choice had been.

It was hard to focus on my food with this handsome man across this very short table, the two of us alone here on this boat, the guards' boat having stopped at least a half mile away behind us, giving us some space.

Perhaps the "chaperoned" dates weren't really so chaperoned after all.

"You know, you surprise me," I said, picking up my first few noodles in a small clump. "You can sail and cook…"

"Taste it before you tell me I can cook," he said, his head slinking into his shoulders just slightly, but his lips tugged up in one corner.

I did as bidden and found the taste of such a deceptively simple-looking dish powerful, my senses seeming to come to life as the sauce worked its way through across my tongue.

"It's delicious," I said once I'd finished chewing.

"Your eyes popped," he said, chuckling.

"That doesn't mean it's not delicious. What a strong flavor." I took another bite, and Rio finally started enjoying his.

"It is a simple dish," he finally said after a few bites. "I would hate to have you think this is the best Japanese cuisine has to offer."

"It's the first time a prince has cooked for me," I said. "That makes it among the best *anyone* has to offer, in my opinion." I felt like such a sycophant for saying it, but the way Rio's eyes lit up, his stoic expression melting, it seemed the right thing to say.

I gazed around the deck for a moment as I sipped the tea. "Do you do this often?"

"Cook for princesses or sail, do you mean?"

I chuckled. "Either, I suppose."

Rio studied the sky, the sparkling stars popping up against the darkness one by one as the sun faded entirely. "I often travel," he said, and I tried to stuff down the sudden feeling of envy. "And the world can be a beautiful place, but when you are royalty, it is often a very crowded, hectic one." He picked up his chopsticks and ate some more. "My father showed me how he dealt with it: A boat in every port, small enough to house just one or two. Out on the waters, the world seems distant, the noise far quieter." He chewed for a bit and finished off his plate. The bottom of each platter was covered in a small bamboo mat. "I don't want you to think we're wasteful, a boat in every port we visit—"

"Please," I said, finishing my own noodles. "One of my fathers may be Alarik, but I don't police everyone I meet over how environmentally-friendly every little thing they do is."

He studied me, his hands folded together, his elbows on the table in a very un-prince-like manner. The casualness of the gesture, though, the intimacy he conveyed so close to me, did something wild to the area between my thighs.

"I admire your father," he said. "All of them." The way he spoke that was without judgement and I appreciated it. "I just thought I should let you know that we share the boats with others, allow others to commune with nature out on the waters, make sure the boats are all properly cared for."

"I appreciate that," I said, sending him a smile. "I like knowing that Daddy Alarik's word has reached more corners of the Earth than mine."

"It would have to," he said. "This is *our* world. All of ours. We had to work together to save it—and we are in danger of slipping back into dangerous habits at any time."

Standing, he gathered our platters and chopsticks with all the graciousness of a professional butler, excusing himself for just a moment. I wanted to help him with the door at least, but he insisted I wait. When he returned, he came back with two small, round, and tall shortcakes, sprinkled with that powdered sugar I'd caught on his nose earlier, surrounded by strawberry halves and garnished with a small, double-leafed stalk of parsley. On closer inspection, I realized the shortcake was layered, cream and cake and strawberries lined up alternatively.

After picking up the fork, I dug in. "Oh, *yummy*," I said, remembering to cover my mouth a beat too late. "And you made all this on a boat?"

"It is no-bake," said Rio, more reservedly digging into his dessert. "I was not sure if you would have preferred a gourmet meal by a professional chef or—"

"This is perfect," I said.

The clutch purse I'd forgotten about vibrated from under my chair. I didn't want to seem rude, but we were all alone here and there'd been that news before we'd left. Unless it was Papa Zander, anyone needing to contact me in a pinch would have to text or call, considering I wasn't wearing an in-the-field comm device on my wrist. "Excuse me," I said, and he nodded, not a trace of annoyance on his face. I appreciated that, too.

I was hit with a tiny dose of annoyance and mostly relief when I saw it was just Rajani. *How's it going? Need a rescue yet?*

Great, I wrote back quickly. *I'll give details later—in person.*

I stuffed the phone back into the purse and under my seat again, finishing the dessert in awkward little bites. My senses seemed to grow stronger—the feel of the bamboo in my hand, inhaling the vibrant scent of the freshwater air with each breath. My heart seemed to be thudding more and more wildly as I looked across at Rio, as I could practically *feel* him sitting across from me, and a sudden thought occurred to me that perhaps strawberries were an aphrodisiac. Or was I just confusing that with the idea of strawberries and cream and sleek, slick bodies writhing together—

"Your abilities fascinate me," said Rio, putting his fork down. "Though I've yet to see them in action, I've heard a lot about them. Protection."

My ears and neck grew impossibly hot. "Well, I haven't had a lot of cause to use it outside of class."

"The benefit of living in an era of peace, one would say." Rio pushed his plate aside slightly and peered at me, his elbows back at the table. "Though I have to admit that sometimes, I am envious of some of the older generations' war stories."

"You are?" I asked. There were a lot of things one could be envious about the previous generations, but fighting one another was not one of them, in my opinion.

Rio seemed to sense my disapproval, his chest caving slightly. "Not *really*, of course. I just…" He stared around at the deck, at the boat some yards behind us. "Sometimes I would really like to stretch my wings, so to speak."

"Not a lot of room for super speed on a cramped boat?" I pushed aside my own dessert plate and leaned in closer, my forearms hugging the table, my throat growing dry as my body grew warmer, despite the nip in the air.

His eyes glistened. "No. But I would not trade this little corner of the world for anything." His fingers moved hesitantly toward my own, and when I didn't flinch, they danced like feathers across the back of my hand.

"Princess Bryony," he said in the softest of tones. I was going to melt into him. Despite my original plan that I would "sample" each one of Their Royal Highnesses, I was suddenly struck with the idea of making it happen somehow and as much as I felt a need to know, to understand what it was like to be in this prince's arms, I was also second-guessing myself.

What if I screwed it all up? More than embarrassing myself, I could bungle relations between Nelia and a country on Earth. Maybe that was just the sudden panic talking, but I pulled my hand away gently.

"Bry," I said, taking my napkin off my lap and dabbing my lips with it. "My friends just call me 'Bry.'"

"Bry," said Rio, as if trying out the name in his mouth. His hand retreated and he ran a finger along his collar, loosening the top button below his neck.

"You missed a display of my power," I said, the words tumbling out of my mouth before I could stop them. "Right before you came. A kid was getting teased on the playground at the Academy and I..." I stopped to see if he even wanted me to keep going. He was nodding, a relaxed smile forming on his face as he gazed at me.

I stumbled through the story of the kid and my protection bubble, feeling like an idiot when I mimed the movement of my arms held out in front of me in order to form and hold the sphere in place.

But he didn't so much as chuckle. In fact, he seemed riveted. "And how does that work? That bubble of protection?"

"I don't know. I just focus and it appears where I need it to be." I mimed the gesture again.

"And could it be any size?"

"Well, the larger it is, the more it strains me, but..." Despite the jelly my thighs were turning into beneath the table, I worried for a moment, the slight suspicions that they seemed too convenient, these princes' powers, too dangerous. Maybe he was asking because he needed to know—

I laughed internally. If the nation of Japan were a threat, surely, my parents would know.

"And what about smaller?" he asked. He gestured to the deck. "Could you make it small enough to encompass one or two people right here?"

He stood, and like the children and rats before the Pied Piper, I stood, too. I'd have thought *he* had been the prince with the ability to command others, but I gathered it was just some kind of animal magnetism.

He held a hand out to me, and I took it, marveling at how he managed the most princely of gestures without batting an eye. "Could you cover us both in it?"

Numbly, I nodded. "Of course." The words caught in my throat.

He led us farther down the deck to the little bit of open space on the bow. The lights back on the shore twinkled, like a little bit of the starlit universe fallen to the Earth. "Would you hit the sides of the boat?" he asked, his voice breathy as we shuffled closer to one another, the bow barely wide enough to fit two people. "With this bubble?"

Despite myself, I chuckled. "It's not like that. It... It adapts. Repels what I need it to. Or contains it."

He bowed his head closer, his free hand brushing back the length of my hair. He didn't flinch whatsoever as he revealed the pointed tip of my ear, his lips moving forward to brush the skin I knew he'd find a stranger texture than any Earthling's. "Show me."

So I did.

CHAPTER NINE

My entire body tingling, from my ear warmed by his hot breath to my toes, I focused on enfolding the two of us inside my bubble of protection. The energy radiated out from inside me, my hand slipping from Rio's as I moved to shape the bubble with small, contained gestures. The air around us took on a pinkish haze, subtle but there if you looked for it, and Rio was keenly watching it, reaching a hand toward it.

"Is it safe?" he asked, pulling his hand instinctively closer to his chest.

I nodded. "If I want it to be for you."

He clamped his lips together, watching it.

I smiled. "It *is*."

Reaching his hand above his head, he touched it.

I almost lost my footing, and it wasn't the gentle swaying of the boat beneath my feet. No one had ever really just… reached out and touched my protection bubble before. Blasted it during training, sure. Rammed against it during an episode in which they'd been losing control. But stroking it, fingers lightly dancing across its surface as if it were the gentlest of glass, the finest of jewels?

Never.

A moan escaped my lips and my knees buckled, the bubble fluttering slightly before I straightened my knees and dug in, determined not to let it fall.

Rio dropped his hand immediately and moved in almost to catch me, his hand landing on the small of my back before he realized I wasn't about to fall after all.

The small of my back grew balmy in the dipping gap down the back of my dress as his hand rested on skin. I realized with a start that somehow, this was one and the same. Him touching me, him touching my bubble. He had pierced through to the core of my desires, had caressed *a part of me* as no one ever had, just by his curious touch.

"*Sugoi.* This is amazing." His voice echoed around the space that muted all other noises, all other senses of being where we were. I flushed at the compliment, growing bolder, moving my hands in circles in an attempt to move the bubble closer, tighter.

Almost on instinct, his touch on my back turned into a grip as he shifted me toward him, away from the lowering pinkish haze around us.

My eyes were locked on his, his breath so near my skin, I could feel it.

With a start, the bubble vanished around us, all of my focus entirely elsewhere.

Well, that's something I have to work on in training.

But Rio didn't move to put more space between us even as the bubble lifted, as the quiet sounds of the bobbing tides returned to our ears, as the chilled breeze returned to ruffle our hair.

Without thinking, I moved a hand up to feel his black, wavy hair between my fingers, and the softness made my back arch, moving me more into him, my thigh grinding into his.

"Might I show you the rest of the cabin?" he asked quietly into my ear.

Flushing, I realized with a start that the other boat—the boat that could have Derek on it—was within the line of sight of where we were standing.

Nodding, I removed my fingers from his hair, but instead of being revolted by my invasion of his personal space, he took my hand in his and squeezed, leading me like just a normal person on a date with another normal person, none of the pageantry or royalty to think about.

The inside of the cabin was dimly lit, but the lighting was perfect to be able to make our way around while still being able to gaze out the long wall of windows at the sparkling water, which reflected the stars and the moon in the sky. Showing me to the couch, he asked, "Can I get you anything? Champagne? Wine? *Sake*?"

"Spritzer is fine," I said, staring down at the hands I'd threaded on my lap. My heart was pounding, echoing in my head, and I worried if I started drinking, I'd lose all sense of control.

I was meant to be here, "trying" Prince Rio on for size, so to speak. But when it came down to it, it all felt rather embarrassing.

Rio returned with two identical glasses full of fizzy beverage, and some small part of me warmed to discover that he hadn't chosen to drink himself, as if he were simply waiting for my lead.

"Tell me more about yourself," he said as he sat two spaces away from me, resting a smooth, defined arm on the back of the couch. "Anything you feel comfortable sharing."

"Such as?" I took a shaky drink. This close, it felt like I was breathing in his salty, fragrant air.

"Well, I told you about my sailing, those quiet moments of retreat." He waited for me to speak, but I found myself simply stroking the glass in my hands, the condensation cool on my fingers. "Or you could start with... What is your major, I believe it is called?"

"Political science," I admitted. "With minors in history and geography."

"A queen-to-be through and through."

Smiling shakily, I downed the rest of the glass and searched for a coaster.

"More?" Rio asked, taking the glass from me instead.

"No, thanks," I said, and my voice sounded shaky. Rio took the glasses away anyway, taking one last sip from his own and dropping them off somewhere in the kitchen.

"The thing is," I said, my body growing heavy, "I didn't pick my major. It's not that I'm bad at those subjects or that I don't find some enjoyment in them, but..."

When I didn't finish my sentence, Rio returned and finished it for me. "It is what your parents expect of you." There was more than just wisdom in his words; there was empathy.

"Yes!"

"So what would you study—if it were up to you?" Rio rested his chin on one palm, which he propped up against the top of the sofa behind him.

"Well, geography isn't too far off," I said. "But I want... I'd want to be *out there*, you know? Studying the world firsthand."

Rio's tightlipped smile was kind rather than condescending. "I am surprised the heir to the Nelian throne has never been seen accompanying her father on any diplomatic missions."

"It was a deal," I explained. "Between my parents—and with me, once I was older. They'd give me a 'normal' Earthling life, like my brother—as *normal* as life can be for the child of the founders of the nation's most esteemed Natch academy."

"So you haven't had much royal etiquette training or anything?"

"Not really," I said, chewing the inside of my cheek. "I

guess I have to admit they've been pretty lax there. In some ways, I appreciate it. In others, I feel like I'm not at all prepared."

"For three marriage proposals?"

"Yeah," I admitted sheepishly. "But it's like... They've given me so much time to have a life here, to hang with my friends, to study, to goof off... I'd feel like a selfish brat to insist on seeing the world."

"That is hardly a selfish trait in a future leader at all," said Rio.

I winced, folding my hands tightly atop my thighs.

"You do not seem to like that," he said after a moment of silence. "Any reminder that you are a princess or a leader—"

"But I'm not that," I said. "I'm a princess, I guess. But how do they expect me to lead a race of otherworldly elves? I feel more like a human than a Nelian." Subconsciously, I moved to tuck my hair over my ears.

"*Yamete*. Stop," said Rio, leaning forward and closing the distance between us. "Do not cover them up. They are beautiful."

His hand gripped mine gently, and I shivered, the area between my legs suddenly too hot, threatening to grow moist.

Rio pulled back only slightly, sitting much closer than he had before. "Then tell me about you—the human. You mentioned friends, goofing off. Is there someone?"

"Sorry?"

It was Rio's turn to look away suddenly. "Someone you are in love with. Who could make this prospective marriage situation all the more unwelcome."

"It's not *unwelcome*," I said, surprising even myself. "And there isn't anyone. Not really."

Rio's eyebrow arched at that, but he didn't ask.

"And you?" I thought to ask quickly—too quickly.

"No one," he said quietly. "I consider Prince Trey and Prince Zeke to be my closest friends—we have met at so many events over the years—but I rarely see them in person."

That was interesting. Not that I'd picked up on any animosity between them, but I hadn't realized they were that close.

"I always knew my father would find me a bride he deemed suitable," he said, his Adam's apple bobbing just slightly. "So I knew not to get attached."

I wanted to ask if that was the case for all the princes, but I didn't want him to think I was fishing for information on anyone else.

This date was about Prince Rio, and my scattershot, emotional brain could manage to focus on just one handsome man at a time. I hadn't gone this long without a boyfriend for me to fall so easily for so many, like one of Hazel's boy-crazy clique.

"Have you ever felt yourself holding back?" Rio asked, his voice falsely bright. "Knowing your fate to be predestined?"

My mouth opened like a fish's. He was reading my mind, though not literally. "Well, I... I suppose. *Yes*. I've never done more than make out with a guy before."

Open mouth, insert foot. After I'd said it, I realized that likely hadn't been exactly the question he'd been asking.

Rio's eyes widened for a moment, and then he seemed to be fighting off a closed-lipped smile. "That must have driven them mad," he said, his voice deep and husky.

"Sorry?" I squeaked.

"Having to stop at simply making out with a beauty like you."

Tugging at my skirt, I tried pulling it lower, only to find it continuously hiking up my thigh.

He chuckled. "I apologize. I do not spend enough time alone with women. If it helps, I find you fascinating beyond just your unimpeachable looks."

"Oh? I mean... Thank you. You're incredibly gorgeous, too." My mouth really had to learn to wait for my brain tonight. But it was so hard so near to him, his hand just a few inches away from my shoulder, his pheromones practically oozing off him.

His pheromones. My heart was so jittery, I wondered if this was it. If this was the Nelian sense, and I'd know if…

"Could you show me?" I asked, almost glad for my mouth working faster than my brain just then. "What you do with women when you're alone with them?" My voice was hoarse.

Rio's lips twitched slightly as he closed what little distance there remained between us. "Are you sure?" he asked, his hand moving gently to cup my chin.

Nodding, I closed my eyes. His lips pressed against mine, soft at first, but determined, almost as if warming up my mouth for what was to come ahead.

We came up for breath just briefly and then his lips were back, his tongue slipping slightly inside, brushing mine, his kiss hungrier.

He pulled away too soon, his fingers still resting under my chin. I shuddered at the loss of his lips, my hot groin growing moister just with those kisses.

He stood, holding out his hand. "Let's take this to the bed."

I took the offered appendage and stood, feeling as if I were floating, but perhaps that was just the gentle rock of the boat beneath our feet.

"Tell me when you want to stop," he said quietly.

We're planning on stopping? I wanted to ask, but all I could do was nod numbly.

"Your first time should be special," he said, as if reading my mind.

I looked around at the beautiful boat, the endless night sky beyond the windows around us. I felt his hand in mine, strong, warm, and I remembered the sensation of having him so close in my bubble, his lips on mine.

I didn't think my first time could be any more special than this.

But I knew when I looked into his eyes that as much as he

wanted this, he was worried. We hadn't known each other long and I'd gone and admitted my inexperience...

"Just give me a minute," I said as we passed the bathroom. I slipped inside and took a deep breath, letting it out slowly, trying to calm the tingling of my limbs. But at the same time, I didn't *want* to calm it. I wanted to be out there, to figure out if this was what the Nelian sense was, if I could actually be destined for Prince Rio.

It took me just a few minutes to freshen up in the bathroom, realizing I'd left my purse out there on the deck and afraid that rushing out to grab for it—to see if anyone had been calling me—might ruin this building, hot tension between us.

When I got out, I found the cabin lights off entirely, and though it took me a few blinks to adjust to the darkness, the light shining off the waters outside was more than enough to bathe the interior in its soothing, cool glow.

"Rio?" I asked, hearing nothing, seeing nothing. There didn't seem to be enough room on this boat for him to have used his powers to any advantage to hide from me.

But they sure got him to my side from wherever he'd been pretty fast.

Suddenly, arms slipped around my waist, twirling me around so that I stumbled and found myself pressed up against his chest again. My forearms were flat against what I realized was his *bare* chest, a line of sleek, sculpted trim muscles on his thin frame leading all the way down to his abdomen, his navel hovering an inch or so above his pants.

"I see you got more comfortable," I said, my mouth running away from me again.

"Is that all right?" he purred in my ear.

"Of course!" I shouted, louder than I'd meant.

I stared up at Rio, his dark eyes reflective of the silver glow outside.

His lips seized mine, one hand on the small of my back, the other clutching possessively through my hair. The air grew steamy between us, the skin of his pecs hotter beneath my hands.

His lips pulled away, hovering mere centimeters from mine, and I let out an animal-like noise, like a poor creature denied its food. His lips moved to my cheek, peppering my brow, my nose, my ear as he guided us both firmly toward the nearby bed, the back of my legs bumping up against the edge cushioned by the plush blue comforter. I kicked off my shoes.

"Your skin," he said breathlessly, his fingertip caressing me from my chin to the top of my pointed ear.

I leaned into the touch, a desire to move closer to him, to let him pet me overtaking me. "A Nelian's skin is different than an Earthling's," I explained. "Some call it rubbery—"

His mouth pounded against mine, hard, my bottom lip pinched slightly between his teeth.

"Delicious," he said softly, pulling away.

Taking hold of both of my shoulders, he lowered me to the bed, slow, taking careful measure that my head landed softly upon the plush blanket. He leaned over me, one knee on each side of my body, the bulge threatening to pop out of his pants far too tempting to ignore.

"Take me," I whispered.

Rio shook his head just slightly and tugged at the sleeve of my dress, lowering first one shoulder and then the other, wrenching the material until my strapless bra was on full display, my arms working to get out of the dress all the way.

His soft finger ran between the cleavage popping out of the bra, and I dug my hand into the blanket beside me, writhing at the far too soft play, our eyes locked all the while.

"I thought your ability was speed," I teased, my breaths coming hot and heavy between words.

The corner of his lip twitched upward. "Beauty, you do *not* want speed in the bedroom."

His lips claimed mine again and I wrapped my arms

around his back, trying to pull him closer, to take more of him, but he would not budge.

Gasping, I pulled back and started wriggling out of the rest of my dress, and he pulled back to give me space to do so, taking the dress from me and yanking it down the final few feet with the speed and force I'd been longing for.

He stepped back a moment, staring at me in my midnight black bra and matching silk panties, and his muscles seemed to harden as he took me in, staring at me as if about to devour me.

Instinctively, I squirmed, placing a forearm over my bra, squeezing my thighs together, but that just made the building tingling sensation stronger and harder to ignore.

Rio grinned. "You're just making yourself more beautiful."

Half-panicked, half-ecstatic, I writhed some more.

His mouth was on my abdomen in a flash, his kisses demanding. His hands slipped up under my back, trailing to the bra, unclasping it in one smooth motion. My arm was still pressed against the bra, though, and he lifted his head and made eye contact, as if asking what I wanted to do.

Feeling braver, I flung the bra to the cabin floor, a gentle rock of the boat timed perfectly to make me writhe once more. His greedy lips went back to work, trailing up to the underside of one breast and then the other, zeroing in on a nipple and taking it into his mouth, sucking. My groin grew moister then, my silk panties soaked, as his teeth tugged, making the nipple grow harder and harder.

Gasping, he pulled away and stood back, his thumb running a gentle path over the other areola, causing ripples in the pale brown skin as he urged it to erection.

"Beautiful," he whispered, and then he was leaning forward again, his lips back at my bellybutton, his hands taking hold of my thighs and yanking me down, lining up my ass with the edge of the bed.

He pulled back, staring at me, as his fingers trailed up to

the elastic waistband of the panties, dipping inside. An unasked question.

"Yes," I said, nodding, hardly able to get that word out from my parched throat.

He yanked them down and took me in, my smooth, waxed mons not revealing a hint of the original green there.

His kisses found the top of my folds, his tongue darting downward, sliding through the slick, slippery wetness.

Moaning, I arched my back involuntarily, panicked for a moment that my groin would knock right up against his head, but he pushed back at my thighs, directing them wider apart, stretching them. It hurt, but the pain was the good kind of pain, muted exponentially by the buzz building and building beyond anything I imagined right at the apex of my legs.

But he gave no quarter, no moment to even think about anything but forward—more, more, more tingling, more heat, more moisture, as his mouth moved up again and found my clit. He sucked on it, his tongue moving alternately out to lick it, his hands pushing into my thighs as he demanded I be his.

I was, the sounds leaking out of my mouth growing louder and more guttural.

Leaning up, he wiped his lips with the back of his hand as he stood straighter. His skin glistened with sweat and I longed to get those pants off of him, to have him inside me.

Instead, though, his hand moved to my apex, massaging the clit in careful circles, his eyes never leaving mine. I tried to maintain some semblance of control over my body, but it wouldn't stop wriggling, the boat rocking me slightly with each movement.

His finger trailed between my folds, sleek, slow, until it found my entrance, where it moved in those teasing, demanding circles just for a bit.

"Inside!" I gasped, and he didn't need to be told twice.

A single finger entered as his other hand took hold of my leg, bringing a knee up to his lips. His finger pushed, finding a little resistance at first as I felt my muscles contracting, but it moved forward, the pleasure more essential to me than any pain. My muscles finally grew slack, the rest of the finger trailing inside.

I moaned.

Just as I felt my body adjusting to the digit inside me, it pulled out again, his other hand gripping hard on my thigh, and then another finger joined the first inside me, thrusting inward.

It could have been the darkness of the room, but I felt my vision go black at the edges as my head ground back into the comforter. His fingers slipped in and out, his lips sometimes kissing my knee, his thumb alternatively moving in massaging circles around my clit as his fingers slid in and out of my pussy.

He'd been right. Though my body screamed out for him to move faster and faster, there was no way that speed could make this moment any better, this moment I just wanted to last forever and ever.

And though we were not entirely united, I found myself exhausted, orgasming at just the work of his sleek, demanding fingers.

It wasn't until I outright screamed—a breathy, throaty scream—that he pulled out and dug his hands into his pants, loosening them, his eyes not once leaving my hot, sweat-soaked form.

The fly of his pants fell and his erect member popped out, his hand moving in quick, jerking movements on it, far harder and faster on himself than he had been on me.

"Writhe," he asked of me, his voice guttural.

The boat kicked up slightly again, and I couldn't have stopped myself if I'd wanted. I writhed, moaning, imagining his thick, long cock inside of me where his fingers had been. The *slap, slap, slap* of his movement, his sharp breaths driving me back to insanity, back to the blackness dotting the edges of my vision.

I screamed again in release, and Rio let out a deep grunt all at once, his seed flying out and straight onto my abdomen.

His shoulders visibly sagging, he moved forward quickly, kissing my abdomen, wiping the semen away with his lips.

I ran both hands through the back of his hair, digging my fingers into his scalp, trying to breathe, trying to calm my beating heart, until finally he climbed properly onto the bed, collapsing at my side.

CHAPTER TEN

STARING INTO RIO'S WARM, GENTLE GAZE FOR A WHILE, I ALMOST didn't want to voice my question. But I had to know.

"You didn't go all the way," I said, my voice surprisingly hoarse. It had to have been all the screaming.

Rio's hand grazed my ear. "Were you unsatisfied, beauty?"

I chuckled, burying my cheek more into the pillow. "No."

"Your first time should be special."

I didn't know how much more special it could get than that, but I couldn't say that. I felt like if I pushed too much more, maybe I'd find out I'd been pushing him into going further than he was comfortable. Maybe *he* simply hadn't wanted to go all the way.

Maybe I wasn't hot enough to make a man want to—

Rio ran one of his feathery fingers over my lips. "I do not like the look in those eyes," he said softly. "Bryony, there is nothing more I would enjoy than having the honors. But you will thank me," he added quietly. "Because your first time going all the way really should be with someone you love."

Love. There it was. I rolled over despite myself, leaving my back to the prince. I didn't want to argue with him, tell him that I didn't know how "virginal" I still was after what we'd just done anyway, but he'd mentioned *love*.

If I argued much more, I worried I wouldn't be respecting that. I just had to calm my aching heart that was still so wild and untamable around him.

A sound like an engine whirring some distance away broke through the relative quiet of the bobbing waves, the gentle breeze.

"That will be our guards," said Rio, getting up and shuffling around the room, dressing.

Sighing, I sat up as well, searching the bed for my underwear, surprised to find my bra stuck on a lampshade some feet away in the dark.

Rio, fully dressed, his hair slicked in that intentionally messy look so people might be none the wiser, handed me my dress as I finished clasping my bra.

"If you would like, I could see what it is they need, ask for more time if possible—"

"It's late," I said, biting my bottom lip as I shimmied into the black number. Truth was, I had no idea what time it was. "And I should check in with my family anyway, after what happened."

"Right," said Rio, his lips tight, a faltering smile pasted on quickly afterward.

I wasn't too worried about anyone. Papa Zander could always telekinetically let me know if anything too important came up. Still, I made a show of heading back outside, grabbing my purse from under the table, and checking my phone. Rajani had sent me a message telling me good luck and she wanted *all* the details. No one else had sent anything.

I checked Derek's last message, which was still from last night, already read. I'd never responded to it because we'd had that fight.

The engine grew closer and then quieter as it cut out, the other boat rumbling to a stop some yards away.

One of the Japanese guards shouted, *"Denka,"* but he

didn't seem panicked, nor was Rio anything but calm as he sauntered over to the edge and raised a hand in greeting. This seemed to be a routine the prince and his guards expected. I wondered how many other women he had brought here for some of his *solitude*.

The prince and his guard exchanged more words in Japanese, and Rio nodded. Connak clutched the edge of the guards' boat, looking ill, his muscles tense as he tried to remain upright. I chuckled slightly, the smile falling off my face when I saw Derek through their boat's wheelhouse, papers spread on the table in front of him. His eyes met mine and they quickly moved away, as if ashamed he'd been caught looking at me.

Sliding my phone back into my purse, I took a look at myself and found one of the sleeves of my dress too far down one shoulder for it to have occurred any other way than it had.

Turning on my heel, I gazed back at the shore, crossing my arms tightly across my chest.

RIO HELD MY HAND AS HE GUIDED ME OFF THE RAMP AND BACK onto the pier. "So, have I made a seawoman out of you?"

Tucking my hair back over my shoulder after it'd blown about in the slight breeze, I beamed. "Maybe. But I'd like to actually try sailing on an *ocean* instead of a lake."

"That would be amazing," said Rio, his voice brightening. "Will you let me take you there someday?"

My heart fluttered. I wanted to say *yes*. But I hadn't even dated any of the other princes yet. It'd be foolish to commit to a second date with one now. "I... We'll see."

Rio stepped closer, moving a strand of hair off my shoulder to trace a finger across the tip of my ear. "I had a wonderful time," he said.

"Me, too." My gaze drifted over his shoulder to the

second boat docked now, the Nelian guards making their way off. Derek's head bobbed slightly as he looked my way, his jaw clenched as he made a point of turning his back on me.

His shoulders were stiff, his back straight. And then suddenly, they loosened, his arm darting outward.

"There's a kid drowning!" he shouted. "Down the beach!"

What was anyone even doing swimming this late at night? Rio and I both jogged up beside him, Rio's bodyguards and my Nelian escort all gathering to see.

Many, many yards away, there was something that seemed to be a stiff arm extended upward, a small body barely moving in the lake water, as well as a shrieking woman at the edge of the beach leaping in.

I whipped my arms out in front of me, but my protection bubble couldn't reach that far.

"*Denka*," said one of the bodyguards, almost as if he knew Rio might try something and intended to stop him.

"May I?" Rio asked, bending slightly.

Confused, I was about to ask why. But that person drowning out there didn't have an extra minute for me to wonder.

I trusted him.

I nodded and then he had me in his arms in a princess carry, my head falling fast against his chest with such pressure, it was like we were flying across the beach, the sand whipping up so fast, it almost scratched my skin.

But then we were there on the beach. Right by the screaming woman, who'd just set out to swim after the child.

My head dizzy from the whiplash, I nonetheless flung my arms out as Prince Rio set me down again on the sand, my bubble of protection soaring outward onto the lake and finding the child. Enveloping her, the bubble pulled back toward the shore, picking up the woman—the mother, most likely—as it made its way back to shore.

I put them both gently on the beach, some distance from the water. The bleary-eyed woman, confused and dizzy, her wavy, brown hair sticking like glue to her sallow cheek, nonetheless rallied quickly as she turned to her daughter and began shaking her. "Kristy!"

By now, Derek, Connak, and the rest of the guards had arrived the old-fashioned way, even the taciturn imperial bodyguards out of breath.

"Let me," said one, his accent lending a gravity to his words.

Shell-shocked, the mom stepped aside as the bodyguard began CPR on the girl.

"Hisashi knows first aid," explained Rio. "He will save her."

He seemed so sure.

The next minute felt like eternity, but after a few more pumps to her little chest, the girl shot up, spewing water everywhere in front of her, coughing and trembling in her mother's waiting arms.

"Thank you!" the mom whispered without even looking up at any of us. "She wasn't supposed to be out there. I told her it was time to go and..." She choked on a sob. "Thank you."

———

AFTER WAITING FOR PARAMEDICS TO TAKE THE CHILD AWAY, WE headed back to the pier.

"That was a memorable way to end the night," said Prince Rio.

"You saved her," I said, in awe of how fast he'd acted—at how fast we'd been together, like shooting stars across the sand.

"*You* saved her," said Rio. "And Hisashi," he added, nodding at his bodyguard. Then he took my hand and kissed the back of it like a prince out of a fairy tale. "You are a hero."

"*We* are," I said, my skin tingling.

We didn't get to say much else, as I felt positively self-conscious about the crowd gathered around us—not just the entourage we'd brought with us, but people from downtown wandering nearer now, some taking photos even, shouting questions about what had happened.

As the crowd grew, Connak drove up in the car he'd used to take me downtown. Cars, though metal and unnatural to Nelia, ran on solar energy in the years since Daddy had come to Earth, and he'd insisted on a select group of his guards learning how to handle them.

Derek rode separately. Rajani was due to jog back from the café earlier, so I didn't see her until I got back to school.

She harangued me for all the details, and I did tell her, but the whole mess of conflicting emotions and the rush of adrenaline left me feeling queasy.

As we finally went to bed and I sat in the dark, the scent of Rio now washed away after my shower, it almost felt like it had all been a dream.

I didn't regret it. But it felt... unfinished. And then there were Derek's judging eyes, and I shouldn't have cared, but I did.

Burying my nose into my pillow, I stifled a scream. Things had been much simpler last week, even with the specter of graduation hanging over my head.

I wasn't sure when I fell asleep, but I woke up, my vision bleary as sunshine filtered through our curtains, Rajani shaking my shoulder.

"Are you still coming on the field trip?" she asked.

"Field trip?" I echoed, my voice cracking. "It's the weekend."

"That's why it's extra credit. Your aunt and uncles? Holding a training session? On Nelia?" She stared down at me as if I were clueless. "High school and college students only?"

I blinked and checked my phone. Seven in the morning. I probably had only gotten a couple of hours' worth of sleep.

"I don't know if I should," I said. "I still haven't checked in with my parents about their mission—"

"They're fine." Rajani, fully dressed herself, was tossing clothes at me. Blearily, I studied what she was throwing at me. Exercise clothes. Sweat-slicking gray leggings and a navy tank, as well as a sports bra and a pair of cotton panties. "They made an announcement when they got back at six this morning," she continued. "They haven't found the fugitive, but they're tracking his movements with Professor Wade's super brain and computer or something and, look, do you want Hazel and her bimbos to show us up or not?"

Groaning, I started peeling off my sleepshirt. "It's an ability-less retreat," I said, knowing Rajani's metal exterior gave her an advantage against Hazel's stone-inducing breath. She was one of the few who could withstand Hazel's halitosis, as we jokingly called it, which made engaging in combat with her something of a breeze.

"And you think she can take me?" said Rajani, her fists pumping in front of her as her whole body bounced like a boxer's.

"What side of the bed did *you* wake up on?" I asked, standing to finish getting fully dressed. I grabbed a ponytail holder from my nightstand drawer and drew my red hair back into a bun. "The bloodthirsty one?"

Rajani stopped punching the air but kept bouncing, grinning. "I thought if I showed off my moves, a certain Nelian guard might take better notice of me."

"So you and Connak are going to be a thing now?" I scanned my phone—no new messages—and put it back on the nightstand. There were no satellites orbiting Nelia, so there was no phone service.

"We're not a thing *yet*," said Rajani, snatching her water bottle from the top of her dresser, along with her gym bag full of snacks and towels for both of us.

I grabbed my own bottle and we headed out, Rajani locking the door behind us and slipping the key into the gym bag. We stopped at the dorm floor bathroom briefly, a bunch of other bleary-eyed women taking showers and freshening up before apparently heading on the field trip as well. Thank Mother Nelia that Hazel and Sheila were in the other college women's wing, but it was little surprise to find Pepper there in the mirror, slathering on layer after layer of mascara even in her gym clothes.

"You do that much longer and you're going to add five pounds to that svelte figure," said Rajani in her best high-school-mean-girl impression. Hazel's crew still brought that out in Rajani on occasion. They made it hard for it not to.

Pepper held the mascara wand out some feet from her dark eye. "You're lecturing *me* about adding weight, metal muscles?" Undeterred, she went back to applying the mascara. Against her dark skin, the dark lashes were making her eyes more cavernous.

"At least my ability is actually *useful*, twinkle fingers," snapped Rajani, heading out with the gym bag slung over one shoulder.

"Sorry," I mumbled, trying my best to not muddy the waters. We were adults, for goodness' sake. "You look nice today."

Pepper tossed her head, the small braids gathered into one, long ponytail behind her head shifting over her shoulder as she did. She studied me as if waiting for the punchline.

"See you in a couple minutes," I said awkwardly, heading to the door.

"Wait!" said Pepper, and even the two other girls left in the bathroom stopped to look. Pepper put a cover over her wand and leaned against the bathroom sink. "Did you go on a date last night? With one of the princes?"

"Yeah." I shifted uncomfortably under her glare, trying to take control of the moment by crossing my hands over my chest. "Why?"

"Which one?"

What did that matter? "Prince Rio," I said.

Pepper nodded thoughtfully. "Pick him. Or don't pick any of them. I don't care."

My mind froze as I tried to process what she'd said, feeling suddenly judged by the onlookers behind Pepper. "Excuse me?"

Pepper whirled back toward me. "Prince Trey is Hazel's," she said matter-of-factly. "And Sheila and I have a thing for Prince Zeke." She pulled a tube of lipstick out of her cosmetic bag and started applying it in the mirror. "Jerry likes Rio, but if the man isn't gay or bi, I'm sorry to say my friend doesn't have a chance."

"Are you serious?" I asked.

"I am." Pepper puckered her lips, then sent me a scathing glare. "Are you?"

Was I serious about dating the princes? About being asked to marry one? I had no idea. But if Hazel and her ridiculous crew of bully wannabes thought they had chances with goddamn *princes*, they were more immature than I thought.

"Mind your own business." I stormed out of the bathroom, eager to unload the confrontation on Rajani, but as I neared the grand foyer that would lead to the back yard, the anger began to flee. Telling Rajani right now would just make *her* angrier and start this whole thing that couldn't be stopped.

I took a deep breath as the group headed on the trip came into view. There were about two dozen of us milling about outside, including Hazel and the rest of her group, who were trying their best to seem aloof and wickedly fashionable even in their gym clothes, Hazel's blonde-and-black, frizz-free ponytail pulled high atop her head. Rajani was talking with some of her fellow pre-med majors, and I just stood in the middle of the grass, not wanting to bother her. Derek was standing against the big oak tree, reading a book, not even bothering to look up as I approached. My feet carried me toward him, ready to hash it out in the relative safety of numbers, when a familiar voice called out to me, and I turned to find Mom standing next to Sage and Lacey, her hand entwined through his.

I pivoted and headed on over. Mom was practically bouncing on her heels and I gave Sage a questioning look. His cheeks darkened and his stance grew just slightly fidgety.

Mom hugged me and kissed me on the cheek.

"You're in a good mood," I said, feeling a small trembling tingle from Mom's powerful lips. A kiss on the cheek wouldn't boost abilities for more than a second, though.

Mom grabbed both my hands in hers. "How did your date with Prince Rio go?"

Was that what had her so excited? I opened my mouth, not sure what to say, but there must have been something written on my face—could have been the heat crawling up my cheeks—because Sage and Lacey exchanged a knowing, amused look and Mom got even happier, if that were possible.

"That's great!" she said, based on nothing but my reaction to her question, practically wringing my hands.

"It—It was fine," I said. "We had a great time, but—"

"So good news all around," said Mom, beaming at Sage.

"You know," I said, letting my fingers slip out of Mom's grip.

"They told me this morning," said Mom. She scowled, but her eyes were still sparkling. "I should have known your twin sister would get the news first. My baby's getting married!" She grabbed Sage by the cheeks and kissed his brow, then did the same to Lacey, leaving both a little stunned, but the nature of Mom's abilities made her lips rather loose regardless.

"What'd I miss?" asked Rajani as she appeared behind me.

Mom got this wide, cartoonish grin on her face as she grabbed Sage by the shoulders, practically shaking him. But she didn't say anything.

Her jaw dropped. "Your fathers don't know—oh, well, Zander does now."

Sage bit his lip, apparently having a conversation in his head with Papa Zander.

"Mom, how did the search go?" I asked, as much to keep abreast of everything as to give poor Sage and Lacey a break from all the attention. "For that fugitive?"

"Don't you worry about that," said Mom, her words coming out rapidly. "Your instructors and I are handling it. I just want you to go on a few more dates and have some *more* fun."

"*Mom.*"

"Maybe there'll be dual wedding bells soon enough!"

"*Mom!*"

"Dual wedding bells...?" said Rajani, her mouth opening agape as she took in Sage's and Lacey's intertwined hands.

Mom laughed. "All right, all right. I'll let you be. Pick up should be anytime now."

As if on cue, a portal ripped open in the air some feet away from us like a tear of paper, the crackling blue shimmering in the air revealing dense forest and the hands of two Nelian portal-creators keeping the pathway open.

"Did you pack everything you need?" Mom asked Sage and me in turn.

He nodded and I pointed at Rajani's backpack. "Roomie's got it covered."

"You all take care of yourselves and have a great time!" Mom started walking away. "Derek, honey, your mom and dad are still in the field."

I turned without meaning to to see Mom talking with Derek, son of her best friend, practically a second son to her among the many, many children she'd taken under her wing.

But my eyes zeroed in immediately on the bulky, tall figure making its way toward us, his fiery-red hair grazing his shoulders like a mane. His bulging chest muscles were covered in a tight black tank top, his thighs practically popping out of the black gym shorts he had on underneath.

Prince Zeke.

He planned on joining us?

Other students were already climbing through the portal one at a time, ready for a training session in the Nelian forest, my aunt Alanna no doubt just near enough to start causing everyone to lose their powers in her vicinity without affecting the portal-creators' work.

Well, everyone but me. Professor Wade had studied the issue and he wasn't sure why, but Aunt Alanna's negation abilities didn't affect my own protection ones.

I turned on my heel.

So this prince of illusions thought he could handle a fight without his abilities?

I swallowed. Okay, he was definitely buff enough to handle a fight without making an opponent imagine he were somewhere else.

"Did you know he was coming?" whispered Rajani into my ears.

I shook my head just slightly.

"*Kia ora*, Your Highness," grunted Zeke in Kiwi accent.

I shifted just slightly and wriggled my fingers at him. "Hi." *Were we supposed to go on a date already?*

Behind Zeke, several men in workout attire and sunglasses hovered, their heads moving just slightly this way and that. His bodyguards.

"I thought we'd count today as our date if that's all right with you," said Prince Zeke, conspicuously looking me from head to toe, his eyes lingering at this curve and that. "I had a hankering for a workout, so I thought I'd take a tumble with you."

Derek passed by our group on his way to the portal just then and visibly flinched.

"Yeah, sure," I croaked, swallowing, suddenly feeling far too hot in the rugged prince's presence. Judging by the moisture building between my legs, my sweat-wicking workout attire was already being put to good use.

CHAPTER ELEVEN

ONCE EVERYONE WAS THROUGH THE PORTAL, WE FOLLOWED THE Nelian guards who'd come to serve as our envoy and made a short hike toward a familiar cabin. Some distance away from the heart of Nelia where most Nelians dwelled, this cabin allowed Aunt Alanna to visit her home planet without causing her fellow Nelians the inconvenience of losing their abilities in her presence—and for about an hour even after.

Rajani was half-devoted to checking out Connak a few yards to our front and half-devoted to nudging my arm every time Prince Zeke looked my way. The man was quiet, but his wide eyes spoke volumes, the way they took in our surroundings—the chirping birds, the breezy air, the lush vegetation. Every so often, he'd stop to brush his fingers over a plant you couldn't find back on Earth, his narrowed brow and rigid stance almost reverential. I had to focus forward not to find myself turning into a puddle during the trek through mostly uneven terrain. I hadn't realized I'd find his quiet sense of wonder so sexy.

But there was no way this date would lead to anything of the sort that Prince Rio's had. Not with upward of forty people as witnesses, between the students, the Nelians, Zeke and his guards, and my aunt and uncles, who were waiting for us up ahead. So much for my "try them all until you buy them" strategy to decide which, if any, I could possibly see rearranging my life plans for.

Uncle Bo was the first to pop out of the forest clearing, making a beeline for his not-so-little sister and giving Sage a slap on the shoulder. He was so obviously Lacey's brother, with the same blond hair and cream coloring, though his beard was flecked with white as well as gold. Lacey's mouth gaped open, her posture slumping and a slight moan escaping her lips precisely as virtually everyone else in the class grew more rigid, leaning subconsciously away from the source of their discomfort but plowing ahead anyway.

We were within Aunt Alanna's sphere of influence, and everyone must have felt the sudden indescribable loss of a part of them. But that was why they were here. To practice fighting without their abilities—without even being able to subconsciously reach for them. Veras Academy shaped students to be ready for anything.

"Welcome, extra credit class," barked Uncle Monroe. He was jacked, his hair cropped so closely as to be almost bald, his skin leathery and practically screaming ruggedness, though his confident stance and handsome features made any sign of aging more like a battle scar hard-earned.

Zeke stepped forward with the rest of the class, and I noticed he didn't flinch once from the loss of his powers, though this was surely the first time he'd ever experienced it. I half-expected him and his entourage to introduce himself to my aunt as party of importance, but they moved on silently toward the clearing that had been created around the cabin, the Nelian-made vines bending and guiding trees and bushes this way and that, the spindly growths somehow looking like spiderwebs.

Inside the clearing stood Aunt Alanna, as beautiful and unaging as ever. Her skin was lighter than Daddy Alarik's, taking after my grandfather, her long, green hair as smooth, straight, and as shiny as any model's. Her pointed ears poked out of the hair without any attempt to conceal them. Beside her were her other two husbands, Uncle Rhett and Uncle Caspian. Rhett was twirling a *bo* staff, his lean muscles moving like water with the smooth movements, his usual Asian-American cowboy look hard to drop even in workout clothes since he'd pulled his black-and-silver hair back in a small ponytail. Caspian was talking to Alanna, both laughing. He had to have dyed his wavy, black hair because the only sign that he was quite a ways past thirty were the wrinkles around his eyes if I looked close enough, the rest of his smooth, brown skin virtually unmarred. He spoke in Spanish to Alanna, and she spoke in stilted Spanish sentences back to him.

"Listen up," barked Monroe, brushing past the group of students to act as our primary instructor. "Today we're going to get through two sessions." He held up two fingers. "One without weapons this morning. Then lunch. Then one with weapons this afternoon—non-lethal weapons only," he added for emphasis, pointing to a pile of wooden sticks and *bokken* wooden swords martial artists typically only used for practice.

"Pair up!" shouted Uncle Bo, moving out into the middle of the clearing alongside Monroe.

I turned to Rajani and she gave me a wide-eyed look before chuckling, making her way over to Derek, perhaps to stop me from making that choice, as she'd know my other pick would have been him.

I hadn't exactly told her all the details about our little blow-up.

"Princess." Zeke shuffled toward me, his arms crossed. "I *did* say this could count as our date."

"Right." I nodded at him, taking him in from top to bottom. A small part of me was worried I was hopelessly outmatched. The other part of me wanted to be wrestled to the ground, onlookers or not.

"Start with basic pinning maneuvers," said Uncle Rhett,

practically reading my mind and weaving through the group that had broken off into pairs. I caught Derek's eye as he faced off with Rajani, and he turned away, swallowing.

"No shots above the neck or to the groin," continued Uncle Rhett.

"That hardly seems fair," grumbled Zeke. "I can work magic on some of those locations."

Raising an eyebrow at him, I widened my stance.

"Begin!" said Uncle Monroe.

Zeke didn't move, instead walking around a few feet in front of me, and I responded in kind, the two of us moving in a circle. All around us, other students were already growling or grunting, one pair even already rolling on the ground.

"I hear your date with Rio went *really* well last night," said Zeke.

My face flushed, but I only fell behind in my steps for a second. A few pairs behind Zeke, Pepper and Jerry were locked in a grappling stance, their hands threaded together, their faces contorted. Pepper looked my way and narrowed her eyes, allowing Jerry to push forward and pin her to the ground.

I felt almost as smug as if I'd pinned her myself.

Zeke's leg swept out and caught me by the ankles—not too hard, but enough that I lost my balance, stumbling toward him and gripping on to one bulky forearm.

Grinning, he didn't offer much resistance as I leaned into the hold and tried pulling him off-balance, yanking his arm over my shoulder.

He did stumble, but then he shifted the arm, gripping it around my waist and yanking me toward him, our abdomens flush against one another's.

My breaths were shallow, perspiration glistening across my body, as his warm breath caressed the top of my head.

"I've got quite a few more moves than my mate," he whispered huskily. "If you'll let me show you them."

His grip went loose and he stepped back. There were

others making noises all around us, my uncles and aunt shouting instructions here and there, but it all rang empty in my head as I focused on the man leading me in another slow circle in our small corner of the clearing.

"Stunning," said Zeke, and his shining eyes darted quickly toward the forest pushed back by the vines. "This place," he clarified. "Peaceful. You spend a lot of time here?"

"Not really," I admitted, the rumbling thunder of a distant waterfall my parents had brought me to once before somehow louder in my head than all the sounds of students fighting around us. "But yes. It's beautiful."

Zeke lunged again, this time yanking me by the arm and somehow twirling me without putting too much pressure on my limb, pinning me, my back to his abdomen. His grip was loose across my stomach, but my mind still swam and I found it difficult to extricate myself, even if that was the entire point of the assignment. "So tell me about yourself, princess."

"First of all, it's 'Bryony,'" I said. "'Bry' would be even better." I used his smug decision not to pin me down too hard to slip down to the ground, crouching, then crawl between his legs to get behind him. Popping up, I plastered my stomach to his back before he could do so much as turn three-quarters of the way around. He chuckled darkly.

"I love tea, reading on occasion, and vegging out in front of the TV," I said. "I'll take a long walk on the beach, but there isn't as pleasant a shoreline on the Great Lakes as there might be on the ocean." Digging my heels into the dirt, I tried throwing him off-balance, hooking my leg around one of his calves. He stumbled but didn't lose his footing, instead managing to throw *me* off-balance as he turned. His hands slid behind my back as he *lowered* me more than body-slammed me to the ground, as gently as if I were the princess who couldn't sleep because of a pea beneath her countless mattresses.

"I doubt an enemy you face will offer such little resistance," said Uncle Caspian as he passed by. Both Zeke's and my heads turned toward the disturbance. I'd almost tuned out everyone around me. Uncle Caspian's teeth gleamed as he grinned. "But A+ for form." Chuckling, he moved on.

Zeke had me pinned now on the ground, his hands clutching my wrists above my head, his body glistening with sweat. The heat between us drove me wild, his lips so close, I could practically taste them.

"Full name's Ezekiel, but no one calls me anything but 'Zeke,'" he said, his voice catching between breaths. "I like looking at nature, beautiful women, and especially a beautiful woman all fine and dirty at home in nature." Leaning forward, closer to my ear, he whispered, "And I turn into putty around gorgeous women who are far more intriguing than I ever expected."

Rather than shift my head just slightly to plant a kiss on his rough, stubble-covered chin, I decided to show him a surprise, all right.

I formed my bubble of protection, projecting it between us and repelling him upward, soaring several feet through the air.

"You didn't know that she doesn't lose her powers around her aunt, did you?" asked Rajani, practically bouncing in her spot on the picnic blanket next to me. "She's the *only* one. That we know of, anyway."

"No," said Zeke, taking a drink from this thermos, his eyes not off me for a second. "I wonder why that is."

Shrugging, I took another bite of my lettuce-wrap chicken sandwich. "My biology teacher, Professor Wade, has studied it extensively. Best we can guess is it's some kind of result of the mixture between Earth and Nelian blood. It's not even being related to her because Aunt Alanna can take Daddy's powers away, too."

Shirking, I winced at the word "Daddy," but Zeke simply clamped his lips together.

We ate for a little while in silence, my gaze wandering in order to keep the pounding of my heart in check. This was ridiculous—I wasn't going to lose my head this much over multiple men like Mom and Alanna had. Yet the tingling permeating my body wouldn't be swayed, not when I took note of Derek some distance away, holding a book in one hand and a sandwich in the other. On the other side of him, Hazel and her crew were shooting daggers at me, but I had no idea what they expected. I was *supposed* to be going on these dates with the princes. And I wasn't even alone with him.

"I thought we were here to practice without abilities," said Zeke, zipping up his lunch bag.

"We are," I said. "But we're also here to learn how to take an opponent off-guard. You're the only one participating who didn't know I'd still have my powers." My shoulder bobbed up and down nonchalantly. "You can't blame me for taking advantage of that fact."

"Maybe not," he said, his accent able to make any little thing he said sound sexy. "But that won't work twice."

I bit my lip to refrain from telling him it would work as many times as I wanted it to, even *if* he'd be expecting it. But I laughed.

"Okay!" shouted Aunt Alanna from near the cabin door. "Break's over! Time to pick up a weapon."

Everyone got to work putting away our reusable lunch bags, letting the biodegradable napkins flutter off into the forest. Rajani gathered our stuff into her bag and wished me luck, setting off after Derek, who was the only student left sitting when he was supposed to be picking up a staff or sword.

"What do the Nelians need weapons for?" asked Zeke, drawing my attention back to the hunk standing beside me.

"Don't recall being told they used them during their invasion of Earth."

He spoke so bluntly, not even dodging the issue. I liked that about him.

"Well, I don't know about swords and staffs," I explained, picking up a *bo* staff for myself. Zeke followed suit. "These are more my uncles' things."

"That's right," said Zeke. "They *all* married your aunt, eh?" He smirked.

Okay, maybe he was a little *too* much of a straight shooter. I led him away to the edge of the clearing, right near a path in the forest, away from prying eyes.

"Yup," I said matter-of-factly.

Uncle Caspian shouted at everyone to take their places and ready their weapons. Then, with a flick of his arm, he told us to begin.

I didn't wait this time, shooting my staff out and forcing Zeke into a defensive position. Just in time, his staff caught mine.

"They do need weapons, though," I said, nodding toward the small group of Nelian guards who patrolled the length of the forest's edge as we all got our workouts in. Twirling my staff, I managed to make Zeke stumble, no abilities necessary. "But they usually prefer bow and arrow."

Panting but as handsome and rigid as ever, Zeke twirled his entire body away from the pressure of my staff, catching it on the opposite side and forcing me to dig my heels in. "Oh, and why is that?"

"How big are animals in New Zealand?" I asked.

"How big are—what?" He chuckled, giving some ground, and I pushed back. "I don't know. Big as the ones around here, I reckon. We don't have bears or probably any mammals you think of. Our bats and birds can have pretty large wing spans, though."

"Well, the boars here are about the size of elephants."

A thrust of my *bo* staff forced his to the ground too easily as he stumbled from my news.

"Wild boars?" said Zeke, the *bo* slipping from his fingers. "That's what they have to fear on this planet? Elephant boars?"

Aunt Alanna passed by, regarding us. "Point Bryony. Start again. And yes, you absolutely should fear the giant boars of Nelia."

Zeke chuckled slyly and we got back into starting position as Alanna moved on her way. "So have you ever fought one of these creatures?" He struck his *bo* staff out, catching my staff and spinning it in a circle. I gripped my staff tighter and fought back.

"I have not," I admitted. "But I've seen them, and they're no laughing matter."

A cry pierced the air a few groups away and I turned, giving Zeke the perfect opportunity to get my staff down. But my attention was focused on the heated argument drawing half of my uncles toward the scuffling partners, and even some of the Nelian guards patrolling the border into the forest. Pepper was on the ground, a red welt on her cheek as she screamed up at Jerry, who held his wooden sword up above him as if ready to strike his already fallen opponent. She kicked a scattering of dirt up at him and he screamed, looking away.

"You blinded me!" he shrieked.

Alanna moved over to see what had gone wrong.

"Amateurs," said Zeke, drawing nearer to see what had caught my attention. The scent of sweat and dust wafting off him somehow became an invigorating odor as it hit my nostrils.

"They're not exactly combat-experienced," I agreed. Neither was I, but I didn't fly into a rage when things didn't go my way. Pepper got to her feet and brandished her wooden sword like she wanted to clobber her out-of-commission partner, stopped only by Uncle Caspian and Uncle Bo stepping into the fray. Behind them, Hazel and Sheila had paused their bout, chuckling at their own friends.

Zeke raised an eyebrow. "I'd hate to be partnered up with any of *those* lovelies."

I snorted.

"What?" he asked, his eyes sparkling.

"Before we came here, Pepper warned me off marrying you. She wanted you for herself."

Zeke's head cocked. "Is that a fact? And how did she suppose I'd be sweeping her off her feet? Against my father's wishes?"

"I don't know," I admitted as Uncle Monroe barked for the rest of us to get back into position and keep it up if we wanted any of that credit. My gaze darted quickly toward Rajani and Derek, reminding me that Derek was only a few fractions of a point short of closing in on valedictorian. I needed to focus.

But my grip was still weak, my attention still elsewhere, as Zeke knocked my staff to the ground, allowing him to step closer again. "And how did you respond?" he asked. "When she demanded you back off?"

"I told her to mind her own business."

A lock of Zeke's fiery-orange hair slipped over his shoulder as he leaned in. "Glad to know you don't give up so easily," he whispered.

I was about to respond when another cry—this one much more shrill than Pepper's—rang out, the thunderous rustling of the forest behind us drawing everyone's attention. Hazel and Sheila clutched each other's hands, their wooden swords on the ground at their feet as they stared into the parting forest all around them. The Nelian guards who'd been patrolling there were still over by Pepper and Jerry.

The ground actually shook as the rustling grew louder.

"Pull back!" shouted Aunt Alanna, running to put herself between the edge of the forest and the nearest students. Uncle Caspian ran after her, but she was determined to get the frozen Hazel and Sheila to pick up their feet already instead of huddling together, their legs shaking.

"Dammit," I muttered, tossing down my staff. I was the only one who could rely on powers right now.

"Bry!" I heard behind me from multiple directions, the closest a deep, guttural bellow.

The beast broke through the forests, shredding through the vines like paper, its tusks moving this way and that as it shook its head. Its breath was visible as it snorted, digging its hoof into the dirt.

And still, Hazel and Sheila just shrieked. No running. No getting ready to fight. They totally flaked.

"Move!" shouted Aunt Alanna, but there was nothing much she could do.

CHAPTER TWELVE

I SKIDDED TO A STOP A FEW FEET AWAY FROM THE BOAR, projecting my bubble of protection over Hazel, Sheila, Alanna, and Caspian. The boar charged at them and the sheer weight of its bulk against my bubble sent a painful grunt out of my mouth as I stumbled, my arms out in front of me, holding on to the bubble with sheer grit.

A strong pair of hands gripped on to my shoulder, an abdomen against my back as if bracing me, and I felt a sudden burst of strength as the invigorating odor of dust and sweat assaulted my nose.

Aunt Alanna sent a careful look my way, then reached Hazel and Sheila, unharmed, urging them to move back toward the cabin, where the others had gathered. Already, Nelian guards were back up in position, but I had to manipulate my bubble of protection to allow them passage in order to strike at the boar, and I wasn't used to this level of manipulation. A pocket here, tightening the bubble there around my uncles and aunt, who'd finally gotten the idiots to start running, another pocket there for Connak to squeeze through. My legs were positively shaking as the boar got angrier and angrier, headbutting against my pink bubble.

"You can do it, Bry," whispered Prince Zeke in my ear.

"I've never seen a finer, more capable woman." His hands shifted down my arms, clutching my forearms to help keep my arms up.

I *did* summon the strength, letting the Nelian guards through to start ripping their arrows at the creature, covering the retreating figures.

An arrow struck the boar in the flank and it cried out, its breath growing more harried as it ran toward us.

"Bryony!" shouted Aunt Alanna.

The boar was headed straight in our direction.

"Shit," muttered Zeke, and though I saw a flurry of figures headed our way, including Prince Zeke's own guards, out of the corner of my eye, it was too late. They were too far, and I was too weak. My protection bubble was weakening and in the wrong position, forming an unintentional barrier between us and the beast and virtually everyone else on the other side.

I tried to let my bubble drop, to redirect it, but my legs were jelly as I fell back into Zeke's arms.

"Fuck!" said Zeke, and I wondered if he'd tried using his powers to confuse the creature. It wouldn't work around Alanna. "Hold on, Bry," he said, tapping my arm quickly as if to wake me. "Just hold on!"

With a grunt, he rolled us both sideways, into the cluster of vines, out of the path of the charging boar. My protection bubble flickered and snapped, allowing countless figures to head toward us, but the creature turned with a thunderous screech and made its way toward us first.

"Get up!" shouted Zeke, dragging me to my feet. We both stood, but I was weak, stumbling.

Zeke tightly gripped on to my waist with one arm.

Another screeching squeal sounded behind us and I turned slightly, catching sight of another boar responding to its friend's cries.

"Zeke!" I shouted. We were trapped. Arrows shot off around us, but they weren't flying far enough.

"Hang on!" said Zeke, reaching for a dangling vine above

us. With a mighty roar that almost sent the boars stumbling, he started climbing, one-handed, lifting both of us up.

I knew that despite his unbelievable strength, he couldn't do it alone, so I willed myself to find the strength, clutching on to the vine above us with both hands, letting him get a better two-handed grip. The two of us shimmied upward and upward, our abdomens flush against one another's, trying to reach a height above the creatures mere yards away now.

With a crash, the two beasts plowed into one another, neither willing to slow for the chance of spearing their prey. They shook the vine we were climbing and it snapped, the two of us flying backward, landing together with a painful thud on the back of one of the beasts.

I tried to push myself up, but I crumpled down and Zeke pushed me flat, gripping the creature with his other hand by the sheer body hairs. "Just hold on," he said through gritted teeth, and it was clear as the squealing creature took off that we were in for a bumpy ride.

THE BOAR DIDN'T SLOW, ANGRY AND WOUNDED, MOVING ON AND on through the forest, far away from the cabin and the group of anyone who might help us. It took me a while to recognize the thunder of the waterfall growing closer, finally eclipsing the sound of the boar's own hooves. I clutched on to the wispy boar hairs as tightly as I could, feeling Zeke's comforting grip on my back as we bobbed and moved forward. The gaseous smell of the boar beneath us wasn't helping matters, as I was about to be sick.

At last, after what felt like forever, the beast started slowing. The waterfall grew more thunderous, water droplets splashing across our backs as we neared the basin.

"I think," said Zeke between breaths, "it's stop—"

But the boar, not oblivious to us being on its back like I'd suspected, came to a screeching halt, bending forward and flicking us both into the basin of water.

I barely had time to think and throw up a bubble of protection to soften the impact as we slammed into the water. We floated along the bubble's surface, the water not reaching us, but I was dizzy and I struggled to hold on to it.

Zeke got his wits about him after a beat, righting himself and turning toward the shore. Both boars were drinking, ignoring us, their grunts echoing even over the roar of the waterfall. Behind us was only cliff face.

"Can you—" Zeke took a look at me. "Bry, let go." He closed the distance and grabbed my hand. "Let's swim for it. Toward the waterfall. I've got you." He bent slightly so I could fall on top of him.

The moment his arms wrapped around my shoulders, the bubble collapsed, sending us both into the water. The stream was strong, but Zeke was stronger, projecting us forward with a sturdy butterfly stroke. In almost no time at all, he brought us to the very edge of the waterfall, onto the dark rock offering a walkway around and behind the raging waters.

One of the great beasts lifted its head just as Zeke pulled me to his feet. Zeke turned his free arm toward it and bared his teeth, his pinched expression belying his efforts, no doubt, to project an illusion toward the beast.

I rested a weary hand on his arm. "You won't have your abilities for another hour."

"Even at this distance from the princess?"

I nodded. "Natch and Nelian lose their abilities as long as they remain in her presence, and for an hour or so afterward." I didn't bother to explain that her negation abilities didn't work when she was unconscious or sleeping, and he didn't think to ask how she managed to travel back and forth between the two worlds if portal-projecting Nelians couldn't somehow use their abilities on her.

"Everyone except you," he pointed out.

I nodded.

Taking my hand, he led me behind the waterfall, out of sight of the great beasts who loved to torment any and all beings they stumbled across.

The rocks were wet and somewhat slippery, but I managed to find my footing, my sneakers offering the grip-page I needed them to. We needed to get all the way across the waterfall and to the other side, then wait for the boars to leave before we tried heading back toward the cabin. The force of the falling water was mighty, the splashing soaking me through to the bone. Zeke's workout attire clung to his skin, revealing two taut nipples on his broad chest, and every line, every muscle along his front and back. His long, orange hair clung desperately to his skin, and I found myself reaching over to wipe a clump of it off his brow.

He yanked me to him, chest to chest, his breaths so shallow, his mouth so near, I could hear him clearly over the thunder of the waterfall.

We lingered there for a time, and I knew if I didn't step back, I was definitely going to kiss him—if he didn't kiss me first.

"Look!" I said as I put the slightest of space between us. Behind him, at the center of the waterfall, there was a sort of path. A cave through the rock, but it didn't remind me much of a cave. Rather than dark rock, it glowed incandescent blue, the pathway lined with moss and grasses.

"Maybe it's a way out," I shouted over the waterfall.

Zeke grabbed my hand again and led me forward.

Though the ground was still moist, our feet slinking slightly in the dirt, the farther we moved, the drier the little grove became, the softer the thunder of the waterfall behind us.

But then it all came to an end, the mossy pathway opening up to a small grotto, no path to lead us farther.

"Damn it," swore Zeke, but he stared ahead for a moment, his green eyes seeming to reflect the blue light all around us. "I couldn't project an illusion this beautiful."

Taking in the space, I had to agree. Though the moisture still clung to my skin, the temperature was just right in here, the blue glow seeming to almost float off the mossy ground, twinkling on the cave's ceiling like stars in the sky.

When I turned back, Zeke was staring at me, his hand going to my elbow, directing me to face him. "Bry," he said, his voice husky. "Rio really likes you."

"Oh!" That was the last thing I'd expected from him just then. "That's... I... I think he's amazing." I bit down on my lip, unable to look him in the eye. It was the truth, but judging by the fluttery sensation in my abdomen, the tingling between my legs, there was no doubt I thought Prince Zeke was amazing, too.

"I told myself to back off," said Zeke, taking hold of my chin and forcing me to look at him again. "Out of respect for a mate. But I don't want to."

Before I could even think of how to respond, his lips seized mine.

I pushed into the kiss, my hand slipping from his and grabbing him by the back. The fabric was wet beneath my hand, and I pushed it aside to slide up and feel the warmth of his moist skin. The muscles were rock-hard beneath my touch.

Zeke came up for air and chuckled. "He said you tasted different."

Gasping, I wondered what else Prince Rio had told him.

"And delicious," he added, going back in for another kiss.

My groin pushed instinctively into his and his hand fell from my chin, his whole body thrusting forward as he gripped me by the back. We kissed and kissed, his lips exploring more of my face, my neck as I smooched his stubble, his salty sweat as appetizing as candy on my tongue. Like music, we timed coming up for breaths with peeling one another's tops off, leaving his broad chest bare, a trail of soft fire tracing his pecs leading all the way down his abdomen, disappearing beneath his workout shorts. I stood there in my black sports bra, my sloppy bun long since knocked out, my hair probably wild and frizzy and a mess to look at.

Zeke took hold of a lock of it and let it slip between his fingers, like a gentle rain. "I thought Nelians all had green hair."

If he looked close enough, he might see my roots. "There's a thing called hair dye."

Out of habit more than anything, I moved to shift the hair back over my ears. Even when in a bun, I'd managed to cover the tips of it.

He seized my wrist and stopped me, the corner of his lip twitching. "You look gorgeous as a redhead," he said. "I was just curious. I didn't think your mother had red hair, either."

I appreciated him not telling me to let my hair be its natural color, even if his attention was directed now to the tip of my ear, his fingers tracing it softly.

I shivered, his gentle touch so reminiscent of Rio's.

"Rio told me you're a bit, *inexperienced*," he said.

I glowered at him. Rio *had* said they were close, but it sounded like he'd gone and bragged about what had happened. Then again, I'd shared most of the details with Rajani myself.

"Is that a problem?" I asked, tossing my head back.

"No." He grinned and kissed my forehead. "Not for me. But I thought you might want to take it slow."

He spoke as if this were the start of something, as if we'd have time later to pick up the pace. I placed my hands on either side of his face and kissed him full on the lips. "I'm ready. I'll go as far as you're willing to go."

He deliberately raised his eyebrows. "You might regret saying that, love."

"Try me."

He yanked me toward him again, his hard cock grinding tightly into my abdomen. "Will do."

His hands moved as one beneath my sports bra, rolling it up. I raised my arms above my head so he could get it off, and the moment it hit the ground, he took both of my breasts in his clutches, squeezing, pushing them upward, his thumbs pressing savagely against my nipples.

I cried out, stumbling a little, and he softened his grip somewhat, but I leaned forward and bit his earlobe for good measure.

Grunting, he sucked a nipple into his mouth, pinching it between his teeth just hard enough to hurt slightly, my nails digging into the sleek and hard skin of his back. He moved to the other nipple and I shrieked as his teeth clamped down on it, but I found one of my legs wrapping around his torso, grinding my groin against his thigh.

His hands slipped down my leggings, the tightness of the material forcing his appendages to meld with my skin. He massaged my thighs as he nibbled my lip, his touch progressing to the sleek, moist area between my legs. His fingers caressed my clit, making me moan and lean even harder against him, the dance of his fingers over my apex less gentle than Rio's, more *greedy*, more needy.

He directed me backward, his bulk pushing against me until my back slammed up against a moss-covered wall. The kisses never stopped the whole time, his fingers dipping down between my folds and teasing at my pussy.

Whimpering, I grinded the back of my head against the wall, trying to anchor myself before I floated off.

I reached for the hem of his shorts and yanked down, revealing just an inch more of the fiery orange hair at his groin.

Zeke stepped back and kicked the shorts and shoes off, revealing his full, throbbing member, his wide, bare feet padding against the mossy stone as he stepped back toward me. I took the opportunity to peel off my own workout pants, kicking my sneakers to the side.

Zeke took me in from head to toe, then grabbed hold of both of my arms possessively, yanking me forward so his lips could smash against mine.

His hard erection dug into my bellybutton and I ground forward into it, feeling the area between my legs grow sleeker and sleeker.

Zeke took hold of his cock and fixed its tip to my clit, directing it in little circles that made my knees buckle. He caught me by the upper arm with one hand and directed his cock lower, through the folds of my pussy, the massaging back-and-forth leaving a trail of throbbing slickness in its wake.

His tongue grazed my forehead, his hand shifting through my hair and yanking it back until my face lifted to meet his. His lips hovered mere centimeters above mine. "Do you want me, baby?"

"I do," I said, my voice hoarse.

He swallowed visibly, then lunged for my mouth, his kisses ravenous, his nibbling enough to make my lips swollen.

All the while his cock traveled between my folds, caressing my clit and just teasing at my entrance, never quite piercing inside like my whole body ached for.

Gasping for air between his sucking motions, I collapsed back against the stone, allowing Zeke's massaging thrusts to send me to a euphoria a hundred times as dazzling as the illusions he'd shown himself capable of producing back in class. He ground harder through my tingling folds, and my mind grew blank as I rocked in time with his movements. His possessive grip on my hair wouldn't let my head fall back for more than a second before it was turned back toward him, his lips skimming every part of my face. His warm breath simultaneously soothed me and caused me to break out in shivers.

It didn't seem possible that every pulsating stroke could build the hot and feverish euphoria building inside me, but it did, growing only greater and greater until everything but this moment simply ceased to exist.

And then he froze, a guttural growl releasing from

116

between his lips as his cock shuddered between my folds, and I cried out, the sound echoing off the cavernous walls.

Before I was ready, he pulled back and gripped his cock at the base, turning slightly, shooting his seed off to the side.

Panting, I watched him and he watched me, his chest rising and falling.

Before I could say anything, ask why he, too, had held himself back from going all the way, his lips were on mine more gently now, caressing them softly.

He stroked my cheeks with tender fingers. "Let's rest," he said, kissing me on the forehead. "And then when you think my abilities may have returned, we can see if they'll work on those monsters out there."

I kissed him back, then let out a deep breath, feeling my whole body relax against him, soaking up this moment.

After a while longer of this euphoric, quiet tranquility, he barked a laugh. "You were right."

"I was right?" I asked, breathless.

"My homeland's mammals have nothing on those."

———

CURLED UP BESIDE PRINCE ZEKE IN THE BEAUTIFUL BLUE GLOW OF the cavern, I was able to calm my rapidly beating heart and wonder at the beauty all around us. Even though I knew I was currently in Nelia, I felt a million miles away from it all. Nothing bothered me in that moment.

Every so often, Zeke raised his hand above his head, trying to test his abilities, no doubt, and then he gave up, wrapping that arm back around my naked figure.

And then, after a while, the shimmery blue cavern ceiling above us disappeared with the movement of his arm, replaced by a mountainous valley at twilight, the sun setting just over the peaks.

I clutched Zeke's chest tighter. "This isn't the first time I've seen this place... You created this scene in the classroom for us."

"It's one of my favorite places back home," Zeke admitted. "I get some peace and quiet, some alone time." This was becoming a pattern with these visiting princes. With a flourish, the illusion vanished and the cavern ceiling reappeared. Zeke squeezed me to him and kissed my cheek. "But I'd rather show you the real thing. Someday."

I opened my mouth to speak, but I didn't know what to say.

Would I only be able to see it if I chose to marry him?

Was I leaning in that direction now?

Stuffing down all thoughts of Rio and—Derek, why I had to think of him just then—I simply nodded. I wanted to see it. In this moment, I wanted to be with Zeke.

I was beginning to understand why Mom and Aunt Alanna simply hadn't been able to choose.

"They must be worried about us," said Zeke, getting to his feet. He offered me a hand and I took it. The two of us picked up our respective items of clothing and put them back on. Out of the corner of my eye, I watched him slip his damp workout clothes back on, then run a hand roughly through his shaggy hair. He looked as hot getting into his clothes as he did getting out of them.

He held a hand back out to me, his chest puffed out, a silly grin on his face. "Let's see what those mighty pigs fear, shall we?"

The walk back through the cavern and out behind the waterfall went smoothly, the thunder of the fall almost louder than I remembered as we stepped back into its domain. When we reached the very edge of the falls leading back to the forest, Zeke put a finger to his lips.

The two boars we'd seen were sleeping in front of the water basin, their bulk shuddering with great snores.

Zeke crept quietly, keeping as far from the monsters as he could. The soft earth beneath our feet aided in our near-silent movements, but just as we managed to make our way into the forest, my damp sneaker slipped across the top of a rock I hadn't seen. I tumbled forward and a branch snapped beneath my feet, the loud crack echoing out over the sound of the waterfalls.

Both boars' heads snapped up almost immediately.

"Oh, shit," I mumbled.

Zeke jumped right into action, both arms out in front of him as the boars spotted us and scrambled to their feet. The beasts' eyes narrowed in tandem, one stomping its front foot.

All of a sudden, the forest around us was replaced with a desert as far as the eye could see. The giant boars looked around, letting out little squeals.

Then out of nowhere, a giant bat—at least twenty times the size of the boars and as wide as a skyscraper is tall, wingtip to wingtip—soared down from the skies, letting out a great screech. It had brown fur over a monstrously round belly, its sharp, vampire-like teeth on display beneath a pig-like snout.

I screamed and threw a protective bubble over our heads, but Zeke simply laughed as the bat swept down and the boars turned tail, running off in the opposite direction. Slowly, the desert smoothly melded back into forest, and the bat from the depths of hell dissolved into nothing but air.

Right. The illusion. I lowered my protection bubble, my chin trembling as I tried to flash Zeke a smile.

"Sorry about that," he said. "I'm used to practicing illusions around those who seem to know what to expect."

"I knew it was an illusion. I just…" I tucked a strand of hair behind my ear. "I wasn't expecting *that*."

"*That*, love, was a lesser short-tailed bat." He scratched the side of his nose. "Might have exaggerated it a bit."

"A *bit*?" I rolled my eyes at him but accepted his proffered hand, and we both trudged through the forest back toward the cabin.

CHAPTER THIRTEEN

WE MET UP WITH THE SEARCH PARTY HALFWAY, NATCHES AND Nelians fully powered because Aunt Alanna had apparently gone to the heart of Nelia to get out of their range. Zeke's bodyguards practically searched him over for scratches, which made the often sour-faced man chuckle. I was really seeing a lighter side of him after this whole ordeal.

My uncles and brother checked in with me and explained that everyone else had gone back home, Rajani protesting all the while.

They didn't mention Derek doing the same, which wounded me somehow, like a sharp kick to the gut.

But I didn't ask about him.

The two Nelians along who could produce a portal opened the way, sending us and the humans in the search party home. Zeke and I were back in the Veras Academy yard before we could manage to exchange another word—unless we wanted it overheard by a horde of onlookers.

That didn't stop him from making his way to me and kissing the back of my hand, the only princely act I'd witnessed of the man yet.

"Until later," said Prince Zeke.

Flushing, I could almost tune out the crowd gathered around us. But toward the door leading to the college wing, there was Hazel and her cronies lobbying an icy glare my way, Pepper for once leading the charge. Running out of the door was Rajani and Derek, the former nothing but relief and the latter's expression moving from relief to tight-lipped disapproval pretty fast. And from the grand entryway of the Academy came Princes Rio and Trey and their entourage of bodyguards. I didn't have time to read any of their expressions before I was hugged from behind.

"We were so fucking worried!" said Pop Nash, practically squeezing the air out of me. "Don't ever do that again." He loosened his hold somewhat but stood there with his arm wrapped over my shoulder. "Hello, Prince Ezekiel. Thank you for taking care of my daughter."

Zeke arched an eyebrow. "Oh, she took care of *me*."

"Why am I not surprised?" Pop Nash didn't seem to pick up on any of the innuendo, thank Mother Nelia. He patted my hair as I slunk into him, just wanting to vanish from the sight of all these onlookers.

Like a jolt out of the blue, Papa Zander spoke in my head. *"Pumpkin! You're okay! I couldn't hear you on Nelia and when they told me what had happened, I—"*

Between that and the crowd and what I'd just been through and the fact that Mom and Dad Jayden were on their way toward me now, too, my body decided that apparently, after the exhaustion of the ordeal and everything good and bad that had come with it, now was the perfect way to give me the only exit I had:

Passing out in my pop's arms.

THE QUIET REPETITIVE BEEP OF MONITORS ABOVE MY HEAD WAS the first thing to register as I strained to open my heavy eyelids.

"Her eyes are moving," said a familiar voice. Rajani. "Should we get Professor Wade?"

"Not yet," said another familiar voice. One that made me freeze on this cushioned slab on which I found myself. Derek. "He said he'd be back to check on her, but his kid is sick and his husband is at work. He said Bry just needed to rest. We can get Jayden if need be."

I almost didn't want to open my eyes, but I didn't think I could outlast them until they left. I could practically *feel* them leaning over me with bated breath.

"Hey," I said to Rajani, who was leaning over me. Derek sat a few feet back in a chair, an open old-fashioned book on his lap, even though the overhead lights were rather dim. He pushed up his glasses and looked back at his book pointedly.

"How are you feeling?" asked Rajani.

"Sore," I said, sitting up and cradling my head. It throbbed with the echo of a headache. "But okay."

Rajani sat beside me on one of Professor Wade's infirmary beds and gave me a side hug. "You've been out for hours. It's... What time is it?" she asked Derek.

At least he was talking to *her*. "Three in the morning. You just missed your parents—well, some of them. We sent them on their way. They've got their hands full tracking down that fugitive."

Right. Xerxes, the Nelian held in Earth custody, had escaped, and here I was off having wild dates with princes. My chest tightened.

"They're sleeping in shifts," added Rajani. "But I should go tell someone you're up..." She got to her feet and patted my hand. "Maybe you should just spend the rest of the night here, just in case." She beamed. "We all still got extra credit, but you got, like, *all* the extra credit possible. You saved those ungrateful dimwits."

I chuckled dryly. "I would have done it for anyone."

"Well, *anyone else* would at least have been grateful about it." Rajani tossed her hair over her shoulder in her best impression of Hazel. "*'I bet she thinks she's even more special now, doesn't she?'* Derek had to literally hold me back from socking her."

Derek coughed into his fist at that and Rajani looked between him and me. "Right…" she said. "So, why don't you two have a chat? I'll, uh, well, I can wait a few hours to check in with your parents if you want."

"Why would—?" I said at the same time Derek said, "What are you implying?"

We both stared at each other and then went silent. I bit my lip.

Rajani patted my shoulder and whispered, "Whatever's going on between you two needs to end now. He was worried sick about you, you know."

I should hope so, even if he *did* think I was promiscuous.

Neither of us spoke to one another after Rajani left, the *beep, beep, beep* of a nearby machine the only thing filling the silence. My nails dug into the cushion of the infirmary slab as I checked over my shoulder to find none of the other beds occupied.

"So…" I said, clearing my throat. It was clear he wasn't going to be the one ending this tension between us anytime soon. "*All* the extra credit? Does that mean I widened the gap between you and me for valedictorian?"

Derek slammed his book closed and tossed it on the table beside the bed. "I don't care about that."

"You *always* care about that. That's like the only thing you consistently care about."

"You could have died," he said, clasping his hands together between his legs. "Or been hurt."

"And would you have regretted what you said to me?" My voice was hoarse. Even as I spoke, I knew I was being bitter.

"*Bryony.*" His eyes finally met mine, the piercing hazel boring through his glasses.

"What?" I answered sharply. "We apparently haven't been on speaking terms. What am I supposed to think?"

"I'm sorry," he said. "And yes, I *would* have regretted it. I would have regretted the fact that my best friend, my... Thank you for thinking so little of me."

He'd gone suspiciously quiet after calling me his "best friend."

"What is this really about?" I asked, my voice barely squeaking out of me.

Straightening in his chair, Derek took a deep breath and then let it out. "I've had a crush on you since we were five, Bry."

Five? *Five?* "We're almost twenty-two," I pointed out. "And you never—not *once*—gave me any hint to suggest—"

"Of course I have!" Derek threw up his hands. "This whole competition to get better grades, that just started as me trying to get you to think of me as your equal."

"What are you talking about? Of course I think of you as my equal. You're *smarter* than me in some ways. More driven, certainly. You know exactly what you want out of life and I..."

Derek took hold of both of my upper arms, his glowing gaze burning into mine. "You're heir to the Nelian throne. You barely have to study to pull off good grades. Your powers are so special that not even Princess Alanna's negation can take them away. And now... Now you're being courted by three of the most handsome princes on the planet." His hands slipped back to his lap, his eyes darted downward. "I'm not good enough for you."

A chill wracked over my body at the absence of his touch. I reached over to cradle his cheek. There was the slightest hint of dark stubble there, which was surprising, as he usually groomed quite fastidiously. "Don't say that," I said. "And don't act like my marriage to someone else is set in stone."

Derek leaned away from my touch. "Things didn't look too casual between you and Prince Zeke after that crisis."

My back straightened. I wouldn't let him shame me, even if... Even if his words made more sense now. He'd been jealous, plain and simple. "They went well with Prince Rio, too," I said boldly.

"And you haven't even dated Prince Trey." Derek scoffed. "Not that three men fighting over you won't be hard enough, but once he gets to know you, he'll love you, too."

My mouth gaped open as Derek's eyes met mine. I didn't know where to start. Clutching my hands together, I squeezed them between my thighs, determined to calm the tingling going wild at the way his chest rose and fell with deep, savoring breaths.

"You love me?" I asked, realizing he counted himself among the "three" he considered currently in love with me.

"With all my heart," he whispered, taking my hand in his.

"But you... You plan to travel the world after graduation," I said. "You've always planned to leave me."

"I planned to get out of your way," he said, clearing his throat. "I knew a childhood friend would never be enough for the Queen of Nelia—"

"Why would you think that?" I demanded to know, my heart beating wildly, and not just with desire. We could have had so long together, him and me, but no, we'd just been friends—tongue-in-cheek rivals for the best grades, friends with different plans for the future.

He'd never given me hope that our futures could entwine in any possible way.

"Daddy's partner is an Earthling," I said, "and he shares her, and she's almost never on Nelia."

"But you're being courted by princes for alliances—"

"But if I'd been dating you for ages, they probably wouldn't have even suggested it!" I pulled my hand out of his and clenched it into a fist. "You're so... You're so..."

"Stupid?" he offered.

"*Stubborn*," I finished for him. "How dare you decide who's good enough for me? Without even asking me?"

Derek went quiet for a few moments. "You're right. But it doesn't matter now. It's too late."

I opened my mouth. I wanted to tell him it wasn't too late, but my mind was reeling with the possibilities—with what he'd just admitted to me.

"Derek, you hurt me," I said. "Implying there was something wrong with me."

"I'm sorry," he said quietly.

"My mom and dads and my aunt and uncles—"

He cut me off. "I know."

"I know your mom and dad are *normal*, so to speak, that my relatives are an exception to the rule. But I don't look at my family with disgust."

"I don't, either. Bry. You know I don't." His hand covered mine. His skin was rough, his touch gentle. My heart was thundering at the simple connection between us. As if we'd never touched before.

But this was different.

"Bry, I said those things, and I'm sorry," he repeated, sitting taller. "I have no excuse. I just have a reason: I was afraid I'd lose you. I told myself I wasn't good enough for you and then at the first sign of you potentially choosing someone else, I balked." He slumped, removing his hand from mine. "What an idiot I am."

"Don't say that." It was time to rip the bandage off. "Especially since... you were right," I admitted. "I guess I do take after my family."

Derek's mouth parted slightly, but he waited for me to go on.

"I... do love you. I don't think I've ever properly realized it before, but I do." I clutched my hand to my chest, thinking it over. "But I'm so confused, Derek. I really connected with both Rio and Zeke. I... don't want to dismiss the idea of marrying a prince."

I expected to see Derek's brow furrow or for his posture to

slink. Instead, when I looked up, I found him smiling, his eyes boring into mine.

"You love me?"

"Yes, but—"

He cut me off with a kiss, his book on the stand beside me somehow cluttering to the floor.

When your best friend kisses you, you're not supposed to feel an invigorating of your senses as a weight in your chest lifts. You're not supposed to grab him by the back of the head and kiss back, craving more of him than is already in your hands, hunting for more of his touch.

But that was what I found myself doing, some hidden part of me breaking loose, blurring the boundary between lover and friend.

Derek pushed me back on the infirmary bed and crawled on top of me.

"Wait!" I said, putting a palm on his chest.

He stopped, his lips parting, his skin visibly hardening as he drank in the sight of me.

"You didn't hear me," I said, trying to put mind over matter. "I like Rio and Zeke. More than *like* them, I—"

Derek covered my lips once more. "I heard," he said, his voice richer, huskier. "And I don't mind."

I arched my back, falling into his kisses again. "You don't mind?" I asked.

"I love you, Bry. I'm with you, however you'll have me."

His fingers slipped up the spaghetti-strap pajama top I found myself in. My pussy buzzed with anticipation and I yearned for more of his touch.

"But I—"

"Let's talk later," he said, his kiss sweeter, softer now. His face hovered over mine. "If that's okay with you."

Biting my lip, I nodded.

It was like I'd opened the floodgates. His cock flush against me, his thighs gripping either side of my own, he rolled my pajama top up. I helped, getting myself out of my clothes. I was naked underneath, a few circles on my skin from where Professor Wade must have attached his monitor electrodes, visible even in the dim lamp glow of the dark room.

Derek rolled off his shirt, his eyes never once leaving my breasts, and though I'd seen him shirtless before, there was something about the way his chest rose and fell that accentuated those lean, defined muscles like nothing else.

My hands were running across them before I even realized I'd reached up, the soft fuzz across his pecs at odds with the rock-hard muscle beneath.

His bulge grew harder beneath his pants, his thighs shifting just slightly to grind it against my pelvis in a way that lit a fire between my legs.

Moaning, I leaned back with the rocking movement, my eyes closed.

His lips found my breasts, his tongue teasing at one nipple, sucking, flicking.

He seized me by the sides and with a sudden roll, I found myself on top of him, the weight lifted, but my buzzing pussy not satisfied without grinding as hard as I could against his groin.

His package was bursting at the seams of his workout pants, and his eyes rolled up just slightly, a lament escaping his lips.

"What about protection?" he asked. "I didn't think to bring any. Can't say I was expecting this." His voice grew almost wistful.

Did that mean I'd found one prince—albeit not a literal one—willing to go all the way, virginal or not? Or perhaps he suspected I was no virgin after my royal dates.

Maybe it was because I knew him better.

But now, here, my mind still abuzz—I'd skirt the definition of the v-word again.

"I have a better idea," I said, gripping the hem of his pants and pulling down, shimmying backward to allow his entire member to spring free.

It was thick, practically straining at the skin, a long, bulging vein wrapped up and around the stalk. I wasn't sure I could fit that in my mouth, but my thighs grew wet with sleekness that craved his cock in one way or another—and I needed it *now*.

I took the tip between my lips, massaging it with my tongue, and his breath hitched, a low growl escaping between his teeth. Then I slowly took the head in, sucking, the salty sweat like nectar.

"*Bry*," he said softly.

My tongue worked around the stalk as I relaxed my throat and grasped more and more inside me. His cock pulsated inside me, responding to my tongue and the way my lips wrapped around, sucking, quivering, taking almost the entire thing in until I swore I could fit no more. My hands dug into his thick thighs as I inhaled the scent of him, sweat mixed with old books and a touch of an animalistic-like musk. Or maybe that was just what I associated with him, what I *consumed* of him as my throat grew hoarse, his member shuddering.

And then with a deep, throaty growl, he lunged forward into my mouth, his cock erupting until the back of my throat was coated with his sleek, salty semen.

We stayed there together, as one, as long as we could both manage, and then finally, my need for air overcame the pins and needles between my legs and I let his member slide out from between my lips.

Wiping my mouth with the back of my hand, I swallowed and stared up at him, his heaving chest moving in time with my own.

"Bry," he said softly, his hand moving down between my legs, teasing at my slit.

I collapsed on the bed beside him, the long but thin cushions meant only for one patient at a time. But we managed, spooning into one another, my bare breasts against his warm skin, my cheek against his clavicle as his hand went to work, sliding beneath the elastic of my pajama shorts. It moved slowly, teasing at the clit, then traveling down between my labia, the moist sleekness of my folds making his fingers glide without resistance.

My breaths grew shallower as I moaned, burying my lips against his skin to keep from crying out and waking up the whole school.

And then there it was, his fingers dipping just inside me, the pressure against my apex so intense that I had to scream —at least a little. I buried my face harder against his skin, nipping at it as I orgasmed.

Chuckling, he pulled his fingers out, sliding his digits softly up my abdomen. He shifted to get more comfortable and wrapped his arm around my back.

"Thank you," he whispered, kissing the top of my head.

"It couldn't have been *that* great." I didn't want to admit I hadn't really known what I was doing. He certainly seemed to have. My body still shuddered at the echo of his touch.

"Oh, it was," he said, his voice sultry. "But more than that... Thank you. For forgiving me. For accepting me, even if just for one night."

I opened my mouth to tell him he was wrong, that I hadn't meant for this to be some strange, hazy infirmary-based one-night stand.

But I wasn't ready to decide. Derek was home, but he was also someone with dreams—dreams that would take him away from me.

And Princes Rio and Zeke, as new to me as they were, as mysterious as they still might be, had opened themselves up to me in the short amount of time I'd known them—more than I'd ever dreamed possible.

And there was still one more date, the matter of Prince Trey.

I could make my decision later. For now, I trailed a finger through the soft curls on Derek's chest, focusing on the man in my arms right now, until I finally drifted off to sleep.

CHAPTER FOURTEEN

WHEN I WOKE UP, MY PAJAMA TOP WAS LYING ON TOP OF MY chest along with an infirmary blanket and Derek was nowhere to be found.

There was some shuffling off in another room and I blinked my bleary eyes until I saw Professor Wade tinkering at his computer, sunlight streaming in through the window across from me. I slipped on my pajama top and got up, finding my sneakers next to the table beside my bed.

"Professor Wade?" I asked. "Am I good to go?"

"Oh. Bryony." Professor Wade pushed his glasses up and looked up from his computer monitor. "How are you feeling, kiddo?"

As one of my parents' friends and a founding member of Veras, Professor Wade sometimes seemed to forget I was an adult. "Fine," I said. My stomach rumbled and I put a hand to it, my cheeks flushing. "Hungry."

"Head on down to the dining hall." He picked up the comm bracelet he'd left beside his computer keyboard. "I'll let your parents know you're up."

"Are they still on their mission?"

Professor Wade grimaced. "We're not having much luck. Your mom and Nash swapped with Roulette and Darien."

The latter two were Derek's parents and their return perhaps explained his absence from my bed this morning. Unless it had just been a matter of keeping our rather intimate night a secret from Professor Wade. "Jayden's still here, consulting with Alarik and Zander."

"It's fine," I said. "Don't bother them. They need to find that fugitive." Mom and Dads hadn't told me a *lot* about their conflicts with Xerxes, but if he was the only Nelian in Earth custody after the invasion, I knew it couldn't be great.

Professor Wade put his comm down warily. "I'll let them know as soon as they check in."

"Thanks." Padding out into the hallway, the buzz of kids from the nearby elementary school division pierced through the relative quiet I'd experienced in the infirmary. Heading toward the dining hall, twice I had to flatten myself against the wall to let some giggling, running children pass.

"Slow down!" I shouted, standing in for the teachers who'd lost track of them. "No running inside!"

The second time, a familiar blond head stopped in his tracks and turned around, a giant grin appearing on his little face as he looked up at me.

It was the kid who'd had a power meltdown on the playground the other day. His friend hovered behind him, leaning halfway in the direction of the dining hall, bouncing. But the little boy shuffled awkwardly, his hands behind his back.

"Thank you," he said softly. He gestured for me to come closer so he could whisper something to me. I did, leaning over. Instead, he kissed me on the cheek.

Giggling, he ran off with his friend, and I stood, rubbing my cheek, sort of shell-shocked.

"I hear you're a charmer," said a baritone voice with a London lilt. "But I didn't realize my competition extended to the second grade."

A rush of adrenaline flooded my body as I turned on my heel, a prickling sensation on the back of my neck.

Prince Trey stood there, all charm and grace, thrusting his

chest out as he made unwavering eye contact. He looked good even in "casual wear," though there was a stiffness, a complete lack of wrinkles, in his clothes that still made him seem "more than" everyone around him. His green plaid shirt was open, revealing a skin-tight gray T-shirt that practically popped at every angle of his muscles. His jeans were dark, and though not too tight, they clung to his thighs and calves in unmistakable dips and curves. As he ran a hand through his wavy, blond hair, I caught a whiff of lemongrass.

"Prince Trey," I said when I realized more than enough time had passed since he'd addressed me to make this astonishingly awkward. Though children still meandered in the halls around us, there was no sign of any of his guards or the other princes or anyone we knew at all. I felt strangely vulnerable, though that might have had to do with the fact that he was incredibly handsome and he knew it.

That was the kind of attitude that was infuriating and sexy all at once.

"I was on my way to get news of your condition." His gaze trailed down to my stomach, and I realized with a start that I was wearing a wrinkly, sloppy pajama top and pajama shorts with my feet in still-dirty sneakers.

My casual clothes were definitely not in any way, shape, or form indicative of my royal status.

"I'm fine, thank you." My stomach rumbled. "I was on my way back to the dorm to shower and"—my head grew fuzzy at the fact that I'd just spoken about showering to this prince, and his eyebrow arched perceptively—"change," I finished lamely.

"Well, do not let me detain you." His head tipped back slightly. "I'm glad to see you recovered. Yesterday must have been *exhausting*." His smirk gave extra meaning to the word.

Stupid princes and their stupid tell-all friendship.

I tossed back a lock of hair over my shoulder. "Riding a giant boar of Nelia and swimming in a waterfall can do that to a lady," I said, not rising to the bait.

He shook his head just slightly, his eyes sparkling as he held back a laugh. "I'm sorry to have missed it. If you're feeling well enough, I thought we might have our date today."

Chewing my lip, I nodded slightly. I supposed it couldn't be helped that the princes had things to do and places to be—that they wanted to get their formal dates with me over with and then…

Then, I really had no idea what would happen. But perhaps some time apart, to think it all over, to let me feel their absence before I committed to anything life-long, would be best. Did they really need to be "exchange students," lingering in the hallways? They were all slightly older than I was.

Besides, I didn't have to worry about Prince Trey. It was clear he was capable of charming the socks off a lady if he wanted to, but that just meant he was less likely to get attached.

I felt lighter for a moment. We could have some fun.

"Sure," I said. "What did you have in mind?"

"There's an amusement park outside of town."

I cocked my head. Amusement park? Jollity Land? It was a no-frills, ride-focused place, but it was the biggest park of its kind for hundreds of miles in any direction. Well, there wouldn't be time for any *playing around* with him. But it was just as well. Three men in my headspace was two men too many as it was. "I didn't take you for the amusement park type."

He leaned in closer, one forearm resting on the wall behind me, practically forcing me to flatten my back up against it. "You will find I'm full of surprises."

My throat went dry as my beating heart nearly caught in my chest. "What time?" I asked through the frog in my throat.

"Perhaps the afternoon is best. Say 2:00?" He leaned back.

"Sure." I moved to head down the hallway when an announcement blasted out over the intercom. "Grades nine through university," came Dad Jayden's direct, no-nonsense voice, "report to the dining hall in twenty minutes. No exceptions. Lower school students report to the back yard. Repeat, grades nine through university…"

"That sounds ominous," said Trey from behind me.

"You should check in with your security detail," I said, my Veras Academy instincts kicking in as I turned to head toward the dorm. I'd need to take the world's fastest shower, but I'd get it done.

Separating the kids from the older Natches usually meant an important message had to be conveyed in two very different ways: Be aware and report to a teacher versus get ready to fight.

We'd never actually *had* to fight before.

If we did, I'd be ready.

"HERE," SAID RAJANI AS SHE CAME BACK TO THE TABLE WITH A croissant and a banana in hand. She practically bounced as she moved. "I rustled this up from the kitchen since you missed breakfast."

Derek looked up sheepishly at that from the projected book screen in his lap but didn't say anything.

"Thanks," I said, practically ripping off the banana peel to quell the rumbling of my stomach. I shared a smile with Derek, glad to have him back at my side, and squeezed his knee as three of my dads walked to the back of the room, where there was a large wall on which an image could be projected. Roulette and Ice-Blast, Derek's parents, joined their huddle, and the five of them whispered as the room grew more and more crowded and everyone else trickled in.

I stuffed the croissant in my mouth, chewing as fast as I could as I observed the rest of the room. All three princes were present, congregated toward one wall, their guards spread out around them.

My brother was nowhere to be found, but if the kids were outside, Lacey was likely with them—which meant Sage probably headed outside for the kid-friendly lecture.

Hazel and her cohorts got up from the table at which they'd seated themselves and managed to bully their way into making some space at a table full of young teenagers that was nearest the visiting royalty.

Prince Rio raised a questioning eyebrow and Zeke shifted in place, looking over their heads, but Prince Trey put on a dazzling smile and made eye contact with each in turn, practically causing them to melt into their benches.

No wonder they thought they had a shot.

"Listen up!" said Papa Zander, and all the flutter of conversations went quiet. None of us had grown up with Zander being a known and wanted outlaw, but his demeanor still carried some of the righteousness and confidence of someone who demanded to be paid attention to. "I'm sure you're aware, but there's a security threat to this institution."

An image of a Nelian appeared on the wall, the same mugshot I'd seen on the news, his cropped, green hair clashing with the top of his orange jumpsuit. Daddy Alarik looked at the image and his posture stooped, his chin trembling slightly as he looked away.

A strange, almost phantom-like sensation washed over me, seeing him in pain.

This threat meant more to him than I'd realized. His connection with his subject gone rogue…

"This is Xerxes," said Papa Zander. "He's a Nelian who's been imprisoned on Earth for the past twenty-two years." He rubbed his chin thoughtfully as he stared at the picture. "He escaped two days ago and is thought to be working with Natches, whose identities and abilities are largely unknown."

He threw up a shot of what looked like security camera footage of a brick wall. A man covered head-to-toe in black, his face obscured by a ski mask, approached the wall and with a flash of light, it melted, turning into goo. Xerxes walked slowly out of the hole shortly thereafter, clearly having waited for him.

"There's this Natch, suspected to be a man around six-feet, two hundred pounds, who can melt rock. Perhaps more." Dad Jayden pointed to the figure in the mask. He clicked a button on a remote and two more figures in all black appeared on the screen. "Another man and a woman, their powers unknown if they're Natches, drove an armored vehicle through the fences to pick him up. We've found evidence that they were contracted to help, not supporters of Xerxes in any way, but as to whether or not they're still with him, we can't be sure. Xerxes himself cannot create a portal or summon vines. His ability is one-of-a-kind among his people. He forces people to tell the truth."

Hazel snorted so loudly, everyone in the room turned to her. She shrugged, her friends all devolving into giggles.

"Do not make light of this ability," said Daddy Alarik, stepping forward. "It may not be dangerous on its surface, but we suspect it has been used to blackmail powerful people, who arranged for this secret Natch strike team to stage his escape."

Rajani raised a hand in the air and spoke once Dad Jayden had nodded at her. "But how was he given access to these people in order to get whatever information he's blackmailing them with?"

Papa Zander grimaced. "We're working on uncovering that, too, to find leads as to who might know where they went next."

Roulette spoke up, her bright-red dyed hair one of the inspirations for my own look. "Xerxes has been spotted in several states since the breakout," she said, clicking a few buttons on a remote and showing more security footage as well as some photos clearly shot on phones. Xerxes, now dressed in khakis and a black T-shirt, his muscles practically bulging out of every inch of the fabric, came out of a store, his arms loaded with food he no doubt hadn't paid for. In another, he was simply walking down the street, rushing with some purpose. He was always alone, no sign of his Natch companions.

"Every time he's spotted," said Ice-Blast, a slight trace of a Puerto Rican accent in his words, "we send a team, but he's no longer there. He appears to be alone, but there's something… purposeful about the way he's caught on camera." He scratched his salt-and-pepper beard as he studied the images, clearly lost in thought.

"We don't know what his end goal is," said Daddy Alarik. He nodded toward the kitchen, where some of his guards had gathered, including Connak. Rajani grinned broadly and I suddenly realized why she'd been so giddy when she'd brought me my breakfast. "We're monitoring the situation on Nelia, keeping a close eye on past accomplices of the Nelian traitor, but we're certain no one has used a portal to move the man to his home planet." He went quiet at that, his Adam's apple bobbing visibly. Was he *actually* certain? He didn't seem to be.

"Which means," said Papa Zander, crossing his arms tightly, "he needs to stay on Earth. But whether he hopes to eke out some kind of life here or he has something more nefarious in mind, we can't yet say." His eyes darted pointedly to me, and though he didn't speak in my mind, he sent some kind of sensation that made the fine hairs all over my body stand on end. "We just need you all to be aware that there's a chance he'll show his face here or anywhere in town. He'd be an idiot to come to the place that's most prepared and able to deal with a threat like him—especially if he's working alone after the breakout—but there's still a chance."

"Princess Alanna has been sequestered to her home," said Dad Jayden. "She has a personal connection to him that might make her a target, and we don't want the sudden loss of anyone's powers to occur during an inopportune time. Her husbands are keeping her well under guard, along with a few more from Nelia."

Sheila snorted at the word "husbands," although it wasn't news to her. Hazel's eyes darted wickedly toward me, as if she knew I could sense her wanting to bully me about my "strange" family.

As if we were still kids and this would bother me.

Still, I slouched somewhat until Derek dismissed the projection of his book and squeezed my hand.

"Be on the defensive, but report to an instructor should you see any sign of him," said Roulette. "On campus or off," she added, turning her head toward Derek and me and smiling coyly. Almost as if teenagers caught in a compromising position, we both instinctively dropped our hands. I hadn't realized anyone could see that we were holding them under the table.

"Do not try to engage," continued Ice-Blast. "Unless absolutely necessary."

"I have a question," said Hazel, her hand pointlessly up in the air since she wasn't waiting to be called on. "If his abilities are to make people tell the truth, why can't one of us with more *useful* abilities take him on?" She glowered in my direction pointedly. Like my abilities weren't useful.

"You're still students," said Papa Zander. "Don't underestimate a clever, skilled fighter."

Hazel turned her nose in the air, both her hands atop the table in front of her.

"Any other questions?" asked Dad Jayden. When no one else moved to speak up, he added, "Dismissed."

It was Sunday, so everyone was in more of a hurry to get back to whatever it was they'd been doing than they might have been if this meeting had interrupted a class. Princes Rio and Zeke slipped through the crowd, their guards walking ahead of them and providing a wide berth. I caught both of their gazes in turn and blushed each time at the intensity of their stares.

"Do you want to study for our political science test tomorrow?" Derek asked of the table.

140

Rajani let out a deep breath. "Oh, please. We're a week away from spring break. My mind is already getting ready for vacation."

I chuckled. "I don't think that's how it works."

She shrugged and watched Connak as he consulted with my dad. "I need to find out what *he's* doing."

With a start, I suddenly knew. After yesterday's date with Prince Zeke had gone entirely off the rails, I'd almost forgotten about our escorts. "Didn't anyone tell you?" I asked Derek. "I have my date with Prince Trey this afternoon."

Derek's gaze darted obviously toward the last prince remaining. The prince seemed to be attempting to exit the dining hall, but he was being accosted by Hazel and her group. Hazel kept twirling a lock of her striped hair around her finger, her lips poutier than usual. His smile looked genuine but strained. Almost as if he'd had a lot of practice paying polite attention, but she was wearing even that thin.

"And Connak is on guard duty?" asked Rajani. "Rats."

"I assume so." I looked to Derek. "Are you tagging along?"

"Sage asked me to take his place last time," said Derek, pushing glasses up his nose. "But I bet your parents would be mad if he ditched you twice." He took a deep breath, then squeezed my leg. "You have a nice time. I need to study more than you do anyway."

Maybe he'd been serious about not being upset about "sharing" me after all.

Then again, Prince Trey was the least likely to be added to my growing list of serious suitors. The fact that he could tolerate Hazel alone was enough to ensure that getting serious with him was bad news.

"So I suppose you don't need a friend along this time to wish you luck," said Rajani, her daze darting toward Connak. "Guess I better actually study while you're off banging princes."

Heat pricked my skin. I hadn't even told her everything that had happened with Zeke yet.

She smiled wickedly. "A lady knows," was all she offered for that little bit of mindreading she seemed to have done.

Papa Zander walked over to me as the last of the dining room crowd dissipated, even Prince Trey seeming to make his excuses with a bow of the head and maneuvering around Hazel and her friends. The prince quickly made eye contact with me and smiled, and Sheila and Hazel followed his line of sight, scowling in tandem at me before turning on their heels.

They *did* know I was at least expected to have a formal date with the prince who'd caught Hazel's eye, didn't they?

"Feeling better?" Papa Zander asked.

I nodded, tracing a finger over the surface of the table. "How's the tracking going?" I jutted my chin toward the remaining projections on the wall.

"Your mom, Nash, and Chastity are working with my people," he said, referring to the two founding members of the Renegades still part of his strike team. "We'll catch them. But I want you to be on your guard."

"Prince Trey is taking me to Jollity Land," I said, waiting to see if he had any objections. "And then I… I guess I'm supposed to make a decision."

Papa Zander put a hand on my shoulder. "You don't have to rush into anything. These dates are just supposed to be introductions, a chance for you to get to know them."

I hoped he wasn't probing in my mind just then, but if he had been, he'd be turning the same shade of red I felt I must have been.

"Just keep an eye out, okay? And this time, stay within sight of your security detail."

"*Please*. Like I *coordinated* with the boars to get separated last time?"

He smirked. "It seems to have worked out for you and Prince Ezekiel fairly well."

"*Papa*," I said threateningly.

142

He gave my shoulder a playful pinch. "Only guessing, pumpkin. And you may have just confirmed I should stay far, far away from those thoughts." He turned over his shoulder. "Jayden. Alarik. Our baby girl's growing up—"

I covered his mouth, ruing the day I'd ever let any of my dads talk me into dating their handpicked suitors.

CHAPTER FIFTEEN

Relaxing in the luxurious cushioned seat of a blue-lit limo, I was regretting letting my dads pick out my suitors far less. Cars all ran on solar panel electricity, and though Daddy Alarik had *encouraged* the smart use of vehicles appropriate to the size of your party, which minimized production of unnecessarily large vehicles and encouraged modification of existing ones, well, we had quite a group along with us, between Prince Trey's navy-suited bodyguards, my Nelian escorts, and both Sage and Lacey. Sage sat kitty-corner from me across the large, cavernous space, giving my date and me as much privacy as possible. Or carving it out for himself. Lacey's brow was furrowed in a headache caused from literally holding herself together no doubt, and Sage kept his hand threaded through hers, bringing it up to his mouth to kiss it every few minutes.

"I hear they're to be wed," said Prince Trey beside me. "The schoolteacher and the student."

"She was never *his* teacher," I made sure to point out. Though Dad Jayden kind of had been Mom's at one point—after she was already an adult.

Prince Trey beamed at me, his lips tight as if suppressing a laugh. "It still makes me randy."

"Gross," I said, crossing my hands tightly across my chest. I'd changed yet again after the morning meeting, this time into tight jeans and a flowery short-sleeved blouse, along with a navy sunhat I kept on my lap while in the car. My phone was in my jeans pocket, thin enough not to make it bulge. I'd left my purse behind. It was sunny and just warm enough to make the amusement park an ideal suggestion, though we were bound to find that half the city had thought the same. But based on this cramped vehicle alone, it was clear Prince Trey and I were never going to have a moment without witnesses.

It was just as well. I wasn't sure I was comfortable alone around his Natch ability to command people, though he hadn't misused it since his little demonstration in my biology class, as far as I knew.

Prince Trey crossed his leg, resting his ankle on his knee as he put an arm across the back of the bench behind me. That scent of lemongrass floated toward me, threatening to turn my muscles into jelly. Despite myself, I found my breath growing just a little more shallow at the proximity and had to purposely lean forward slightly so I didn't fall back into his touch.

"Is there anything you want to make sure we do?" He leaned slightly toward me and whispered, his voice cracking. "Just the two of us?"

When my thoughts jumped immediately to the two of us alone somewhere in a bedroom, my muscles stiffened.

Prince Trey chuckled. "In the park," he added, but he'd known what he'd been doing. "Any rides that tickle your fancy?"

"I'm not sure," I said, clearing my throat. "It's been years since I've been here."

"Fortunately for you, I know all the best rides." He winked.

We pulled off the interstate and we all jostled somewhat,

Prince Trey moving closer to me, his side coming into quick, brief contact with mine.

My heart was practically beating out of my chest as I stared up at him, his breath minty cool on my forehead.

"What's this?" asked Sage from across the limo and I jumped, putting a bit more space between me and the prince again. I looked out the window to see what he was asking about and found the limo pulling into the sole hotel attached to the amusement park property.

A hotel. Had he booked the two of us a night in a hotel?

I swallowed, a lump suddenly caught in my throat.

Prince Trey straightened. "We always use a hotel's services whenever possible as a base of operation." He leaned to his other side as one of his bodyguards whispered into his ear. "My men will split into two, one group monitoring our safety remotely, ready to spring into action should something go wrong."

Okay, I felt stupid now.

He leaned back toward me and whispered, "Were you hoping for something else, princess?"

"'Bry,'" I said, forcing myself to sit up straighter rather than melt into pieces of goo. "Or Bryony."

I didn't comment on anything else he'd said.

Trey leaned back and nodded, clearly studying me. "They told me you were nothing like the princesses we've met before."

They? I squeezed my hands together between my legs. Rio and Zeke, of course.

There was a flurry of activity just then as some of Trey's guards got off, along with a couple of Connak's Nelian guards.

I piped up. "Connak?"

He bowed slightly at me from his seat near Sage. "They have video equipment and are monitoring outside threats." He tapped an ear piece that dangled from his ear. "Prince Trey's men have lent us these contraptions to keep in touch."

The limo had virtually emptied out now, leaving just Sage, Lacey, Connak, another Nelian guard, and two of Trey's bodyguards along with Trey and me.

"You'll hardly know they're there," said Trey, bumping his arm against mine. "My team and I do this all the time," he added. "We'll be perfectly safe."

"Of course," I said, my fingers crackling with pink aura. It wasn't like we were expecting a threat.

But it wasn't like there were often fugitives with ties to my family on the loose, either.

Brushing aside that strange inkling of being watched, I stared out the window of the limo, my hands clutched on my knees as the entryway to the amusement park grew nearer.

The driver parked the car and got out to open it, then everyone poured out. I was the last to leave, and Prince Trey held his hand out toward me, the vision of a prince even in his casual clothing.

I took his hand. It was soft, yet sturdy somehow, its warmth offering me a chance to stand on steadier feet.

The sun shone strong overhead, so I slipped on my sunhat before sliding my arm through Trey's proffered one.

"In London, there's a Ferris wheel that gives you a view of the entire city," he said as we made our way past the line to a security entrance. Trey's guard exchanged a few words with the man there and showed him some papers he slipped out from the interior of his coat. The employee waved us through.

"I know," I said. "Well, I've seen it. In pictures."

"But you've never been?"

"No," I admitted somewhat sheepishly. "I haven't traveled much. Mostly just to Nelia."

Trey looked out at the crowd around us, at the merry-go-round greeting us and the nearby gift shop. "Well, I have been almost everywhere there is to be, but I have never been to Nelia. Have to admit I was rather jealous of Zeke." His gaze slipped slyly toward me. "In more ways than one."

I straightened my back. Prince Trey couldn't help himself

from flirting. He'd even do it to someone as heinous as Hazel. It couldn't mean much then.

"Well, I have to admit I'm jealous of anyone who's seen the world," I said, changing tracks. "My best friend wants to travel after we graduate, but..."

"You don't intend to join her?"

"Him," I corrected. "Well, Rajani's my best friend, too, but she has plans to go straight to med school."

"Him." Prince Trey led us closer to the merry-go-round, the dulcet, tinny tones of a familiar melody playing as the horses and other animals moved up and down and round and round. "Derek Ramirez?"

I slipped out of Trey's arm as we came to a stop in front of the fence surrounding the carousel. "So you know."

"We wondered whether there were any impediments to you making a royal match."

I chewed on my bottom lip and didn't answer.

Trey's fingers brushed gently on my chin then, lifting my face to meet his. "But you didn't answer my question. Why not travel then?" His smile was strained, almost pained, but not fake. "With your best friend?"

"I..." I shrugged. "I promised my parents I would focus on Nelia after graduation. On learning how to govern, I suppose. On getting to know my people there."

"And you can't spare a year to get to know your Earth world a little better first?"

My eyes wandered in an effort to calm the beating of my heart. Trey was too suave, too skilled, and I had enough rattling around in my head just now. Back at the gift shop, Lacey grabbed the sleeve of a sweatshirt hanging on a rack at the front of the store and stretched it out, Sage regarding her as if he couldn't believe how lucky he was. I turned on my heel to give them some privacy and looked at the line forming for a roller coaster some distance behind Prince Trey. "Let's go," I said, gripping Trey's hand.

Trey's broad smile dropped when he saw where I was

leading him. He gestured over his shoulder with his free hand, back at the carousel. "You don't fancy starting off a little smaller?"

I laughed, but when I saw the way his pasted-on smile had grown unnaturally still, I grew serious. "Do you not like roller coasters?"

Trey's mouth opened, then shut. "It's not that I don't *like* them, so much as they don't particularly like me." We'd reached the end of the line now, so we still had some time to change our minds, but I didn't want to make him too uncomfortable.

"Did you plan to work your way up?" I asked. "Steel your courage?" Unless he'd planned on directing me to all the rides that stayed a few feet within the ground the entire day.

He stiffened and gripped my hand harder. "I don't need to. It's fine."

I felt bad for teasing him. "Look, we don't have to—"

"It's fine," he said again. His shoulders seemed to relax somewhat.

"You can always step aside and watch," I whispered, leaning closer to him as people started joining the line behind us as well. "There's a chance to leave the line before you get on."

"I'm not going anywhere." Trey sounded more confident then. Looking into his shining blue eyes, I really believed him.

"I won't think any less of you," I added as another cart filled up and the line moved a great distance.

"But I might think a bit less of myself," he said, and I was surprised to find him admitting such a thing. He seemed so confident all the time—invulnerable. "Nothing ventured, nothing gained."

I squeezed his hand to give him courage.

"You know," I said, trying to keep my voice quiet, though it wasn't too hard to go unheard with the clinking of the carts as they made their way up the track, "I'm surprised you just don't demand things your way."

149

He took an uneven step forward. "You think so little of me? That I'm entitled?"

"Entitled?" I laughed. "I couldn't say. Confident, sure, a bit of a playboy, but—"

"*Playboy*?" he said, loud enough for several other people around us to look our way.

Giggling, I shushed him, trying to get him to lower his voice.

Some time passed before he spoke again. "I'll have you know that women throwing themselves at me and making a point of sleeping with as many women as possible are quite different characteristics," he said in a hushed whisper. His lips tickled the edge of my ear, making me shiver. "And I always believe in being polite to a lady, even when such attention is unlooked for."

Attention like that of Hazel? I wanted to ask. But I mentally slapped myself, straightening my back as the *whoosh* of the roller coaster soared overhead. "I meant... Well, your abilities..."

I hadn't seen them in action since that display in the classroom. When he'd teased poor Professor Wade.

Trey let out a deep breath and straightened. "I'm quite careful not to use that unfairly," he said. His brow narrowed as another set of carts came to a stop and the group got off, all smiles and yells of exuberance. "It took quite a lot to learn that. I couldn't help myself as a child. I didn't understand."

I wondered if there was something in his past I'd have known if I'd researched him at all, something about his ability to command making a seventy-year-old governess perform a pirouette for him because he'd demanded she put on a show.

But the way he was rubbing his face now, his gaze far-off, made me worried it was something far less amusing than that.

"I'm sorry," I said. "I... didn't think that through. I didn't really think you'd bully me into doing something without asking."

"Bully?" His eyebrows arched as we moved forward and another group got on the carts. We were just a few people away from the front now, sure to get on during the next change-off.

"Well, I mean, commanding someone without their permission—not that there'd really be an instance where people would *grant* you permission, I'd wager."

"There are," he said, growing stiffer. "Friends asking for it on a lark. Guards during a drill, for more efficient command on the field." He suddenly relaxed, a grin taking over his handsome face. "In much more… private settings."

My toes curled inside my sneakers, and I felt my palm grow clammy in his hands.

Somehow I felt like I'd walked right into that one. But I grew bolder with my teasing. "I thought you weren't a playboy."

He didn't even flinch, his voice growing deeper as it grew quieter. But I heard it despite the sudden *whoosh* as the cart made its way down the first dip in the coaster.

"I only invite women who fascinate me to find out what I mean," he said.

I couldn't find the words to tease him.

A few minutes passed and before I knew it, the roller coaster carts emptied, and sure enough, it was our turn to get on. Though first there was some confusion, the group ahead of us held up by one cart's riders being slow to get off. Trey changed tracks and led me to the very back cart, away from the throng, apologizing to a redheaded woman and her friend lingering behind us, whom we practically bumped into on the way. I took off my hat and sat on it, feeling the rim squish slightly under my butt, and something… bonier.

"Forgive me," said Trey, and I realized with a start that he'd been trying to snatch the hat out from under me before I'd sat down. "I was only going to say we could have one of my men hold it." Slipping his hand out and leaving the hat where it was, his touch sending an unexpected rush straight out from my abdomen, he craned his head to see. It took some doing, but I could spot the few men in suits around the ride's exit area. Connak and the other Nelian guard were much easier to spot some distance back, drawing stares even without their bows and knives. Instinctively, I brushed my long, dyed hair forward to cover my ears as the bar holding us in place came down.

Trey clasped his hands together in front of him and seemed to move his mouth in silent prayer.

"It's okay," I said, taking hold of his bicep.

Before he could respond, the youthful ride worker began his safety speech as he double-checked the bars, instructing us all to keep our arms inside the vehicle. He chuckled a bit when he saw Trey hunched over in silent prayer. "You okay, buddy?"

Trey stiffened at that and opened his eyes, looking for all the world like he'd been asked to strike a pose.

"Well, if everyone's *sure*," said the worker. He patted the side of our cart. "We're off!"

The cart was excruciatingly slow to get going, as much to build the tension as build the momentum, I suspected.

The corner of Trey's mouth twitched up just slightly, and I reached for his hand. My stomach was fluttering, feeling heavier than usual. As we crested the top of the first hill, I looked down over the park. The guards were all still where I'd seen them, turning their heads this way and that. I couldn't find Sage and Lacey at all, but I supposed Sage had gotten it into his head to turn the excursion into a date when he'd brought his fiancée with him.

What I didn't expect to see were four very familiar figures leaning on the fence near the giftshop.

They weren't wearing school colors, but there was no mistaking Hazel, Sheila, Pepper, and Jerry, all standing there and staring up at me like I was part of some show.

What the hell…?

But I didn't have time to comment on it out loud because

our cart was already moving down in a rush, the people in front of us screaming as if their lives depended on it.

I turned to Trey, my mouth open in a yell of my own, and I realized he was screaming the loudest, his eyes lighting up as the force of the air whipped back his hair, which looked perfect even as it fluttered this way and that. We made a turn and I slammed into his side. He wrapped an arm around me on instinct, it seemed, more than anything, and we took another ascent at a faster pace than we had before. Lingering at the top, my stomach feeling like I'd somehow left it down there below, I took in the entire park, and the town around it, the distant highway, everything as far as the eye could see. My pulse was racing, my senses heightened. I felt on top of the world.

"Enthralling," said Trey, loud enough for me to hear despite all the rumbling murmurs and clanking of the cart below us.

He was checking out the horizon behind me, but then I realized with a start that his blue eyes were boring right into mine. "Thank you for convincing me to give this a try," he said.

I couldn't respond, though, because we were headed down, faster than it seemed possible, then racing for an upside-down flip, and I could feel my entire body on pins and needles.

We made one loop and I felt for a second like I might be sick, but almost as soon as the feeling came, it was gone, jerked right out of me as we raced ahead again for a second loop.

At the top of the second loop, someone from the middle of the carts let out a scream that curdled strangely as a loud, ranging clang of metal pierced the air, the scream becoming a shriek filled with terror.

My blood went cold, and my hands struck out in front of me on instinct, but my brain was slow to catch up with what was going on as the cart righted itself, a woman hanging out of the cart a little unnaturally, her auburn hair flying high above her into the wind. Half her body was in the air, one of her hands gripping the bar that was supposed to restrain her, but just barely.

"Everyone! Hold on to the bars!" shouted Trey, his brows drawn together, his hands gripping the bar in front of him as if for dear life.

I realized with a start that I was gripping mine that hard, too—everyone on the carts was. But most importantly, the woman who'd been thrown loose was now gripping the bar with both hands, in far less danger of tumbling out.

But she was still pale, her eyes wide, her chest shaking.

I wanted to move my hands again to throw out a bubble of protection and realized with a sudden rise of panic that I could *not* let go of the handlebar if I wanted to.

"Trey!" I screamed, nodding toward my hands.

He caught on quick just as we made another rapid turn. "Bryony, you're in control!"

I didn't hesitate this time, flinging out my power toward the woman the second my hands peeled free, cocooning both her and the other woman she was with in my pink glow just as we rounded the corner and their bodies flung hard against my soft cushion, their hands still gripping on to the bar for dear life. Their muscles clearly strained with the effort as we rounded the corner and neared the end of the ride. One screamed in pain.

I nodded at Trey.

"Everyone, let go of the bars!" he said, and most of the cart found themselves befuddled and examining their hands as if wondering if they had ever truly been in control of them.

I was most focused on catching the women, though, as both went tumbling entirely into my bubble of protection. Finding myself releasing a hitched breath, I slowly lowered them down into the bushes behind the carts, far out of the path of danger. Their handlebar stuck up awkwardly, the joint holding it in place warped, whether from some natural wear and tear or something else, I couldn't be sure.

My mind came back to the moment and took in the buzz of shouting below us among the squealing brakes of the carts, and we all came to an abrupt stop, not a sound uttered from those of us on the ride.

More screams rang out and a couple of suited bodyguards were joined by two Nelians and a legion of amusement park security, all running toward the roller coaster to check on us and to the women behind us in the bush below, clearly dizzy but struggling to their feet.

"Well," said Prince Trey before his men could get to us. "I don't think I'll try that again after all."

He smiled broadly at me, and I laughed.

CHAPTER SIXTEEN

THAT RIDE WAS SHUT DOWN WHILE THE PARK CONDUCTED A safety check and an investigation. The women were unharmed but in shock and had been taken to the hospital, too clearly stunned to even realize who had saved them or how.

I squeezed Trey's hand through the inquiry in a conference room of one of the nearby staff-only buildings, feeling sorry I'd ever teased him about his ability. His command had been enough to save the red-haired woman before I could think to act.

"It looks to me like an accident," said a police officer, dismissing his projected notebook screen with a wave of his hand. "And that those women were fortunate the two of you were on the coaster at the same time."

"There was no evidence of tampering?" asked one of Trey's guards.

The police officer shook his head. "Nope. Park thinks the bolt wore down and some of the metal cracked. And believe me, an amusement park of this scale admitting liability isn't something they do lightly. Insurance agents are already on their way." He nodded toward Trey and me. "I'm sure you could both get a slice of the pie when it's all said and done. Everyone on that cart can."

Trey shook his head. "So long as those women are taken care of, I don't need anything."

I nodded. Danger was something I trained for. Even if it wasn't supposed to come from unexpected quarters like this.

The police officer and the guard exchanged a few more words and then my brother got up from the corner and patted my back. Lacey was still in her chair, looking sick. "If you're sure you're okay, we're going to head back."

"We should all head back," said Trey.

Sage bit his lip and looked at his fiancée. She looked about to hurl—or in her case, turn into a pile of goo. "She really needs to rest," he said.

Trey flagged one of his guards, who walked over to him. "Why don't we get you a room at the hotel?" he proposed.

"We have class tomorrow," said Sage, but part of him relaxed at the suggestion, drawing in a deep breath. "Lacey has to teach. Lacey!"

He ran over to her and put a hand on her arm, but it was growing limp, stretching outward.

"Shit," I said, getting to my feet. Throwing a bubble of protection around her, I nudged her back together and she smiled at me, righting herself back into one piece. "Thank you," she said. "It's just... It's been a long day." She laughed dryly as she sat up straighter, and I let the bubble fall, cautiously. "I don't know why I'm exhausted. You're the ones who went through all that."

Sage shushed her soothingly.

"Yeah, let's all get rooms," I said, rubbing my cheek. "Connak, can you let my parents know?"

He nodded and poked at the Veras-issued comm device on his wrist.

"Did they ever find Hazel and her friends?" I asked.

The corner of Trey's mouth twitched. "It was quite a coincidence they were here."

"When an accident occurred?" I shook my head. Some-thing pricked at the back of my neck, but there didn't seem to be any reason for it—or opportunity. I would have noticed if they'd been on the roller coaster ahead of us. Wouldn't I have?

Thinking back to how I'd wound up spending the entire wait in line flirting, though, maybe not.

But whose power would they have relied on for *that* to happen?

I hadn't realized Sage had been listening. "Connak found them and sent them home," he said. "I just confirmed with Professor Chastity that they're back. They admitted they found out where you were going on your date and decided to tag along, but they claim to know nothing about the accident, of course. Hazel threatened to sue the school if they accused her of anything."

"So it really was just an accident?" I asked to the room. Was it?

Sage helped Lacey to her feet and nodded. "We think so." He cocked his head. "Are you worried about the fugitive?"

That explanation hadn't even dawned on me. "No," I said, scratching the back of my head. "But how is that going? Mom back yet?"

"Yeah. They're all at the Academy," said Sage, waddling toward the door with Lacey, who looked about to throw up. She didn't get out much because of her powers, at least not without Aunt Alanna around to hinder them. Maybe floating on a euphoric high of a wedding announcement had made her bolder, but it hadn't paid off at all.

It was late. Between the police officers, the medical team, and our own security detail, we'd spent most of the day in this staff room. We'd even been brought a lackluster dinner here, though our efforts in saving those women had gotten the overpriced park food fee waived.

Trey's hand slid through mine. "Before we head to the hotel, will you go on one more ride with me?"

I checked the clock on the wall. "Park's about to close."

His sapphire eyes sparkled. "I arranged something special. My favorite ride."

"So it's not something that goes upside-down, I gather?"

"No. But it does go rather high."

"Okay," I said, swinging his hand slightly. "If for no other reason than to say we had a proper date."

"I don't know," said Trey, leading the way down the hall, two of his men and Connak and his Nelian guard falling into step behind us. "I have to say this has been the most exciting date I've ever been on. I only wish those poor people hadn't had to have been so terrified for it."

"They'd be dead without you," I said softly.

"Without *you*." He nudged my arm, then just *looked* at me. I felt laid bare beneath his eyes. "You're smashing."

A tingling sensation trickled up my skin, my face growing warm. We just walked for a bit, out into the slightly chill night air, the few people we met along the way heading in the opposite direction.

"The park is about to close," said a voice over the intercoms. "Please make your way to the gate and thank you for joining us at Jollity Land."

"I feel like we're doing something we're not supposed to be," I said, letting Trey lead me even so.

Trey picked up the pace, daring me to keep up. "That makes it even more exciting, doesn't it?"

Without the massive crowds in front of us, it didn't take long at all to run to our destination: the giant Ferris wheel with enclosed cabs for every group.

I stared up at it, craning my neck, but this close, I couldn't see the top. "This remind you of home?" I asked, remembering he'd talked about the London Eye.

"Yes." When he stared up, it seemed like he was gazing into the cosmos, his face almost growing slack. "But I always want to go on Ferris wheels wherever I roam. I can see the lay of the land from up there. Get a new perspective."

"Your Highnesses," said a park employee, snapping me back to the moment. He was an older man with wispy gray-and-black hair and a knowing smirk on his face, like we were a couple of teenagers sneaking around who'd been caught red-handed. With the guards behind us and the employee in front of us, this was hardly time to get all doe-eyed.

Trey led me to the open cart the employee gestured to and we sat inside, one on each side. There were no seatbelts or bars this time, just the bar the employee snapped shut on the outside of the cab.

He saluted and winked, and then went to operate the machine. The cab shook to life and I instinctively grabbed the back of the seat.

"You seem more scared of this than the roller coaster," said Trey, his head tipping back.

I settled back into my seat and straightened up. "Maybe the ride shook me more than I thought."

Without saying another word, Trey got up and crossed the short distance between us, slipping in beside me and placing his hand over mine.

My heart thundering, I turned to gaze out the window, the sparkle of solar-powered lights spread out before us. The higher we went, the broader our view. I could see the lake, the town—even Veras Academy.

When we got to the very, very top, the Ferris wheel went still, shaking after an abrupt, clunky stop. I jumped in place, looking around for the new threat.

"I should have warned you," said Trey quickly, taking my hand up to his mouth and pressing his lips to it softly. "I asked for a few minutes here at the top." The cabin lights flickered off overhead. "In the dark," he added, and as my eyes adjusted, I could see him wince. "Bad idea?"

Knowing this had all been planned relaxed me considerably, but I still found myself in need of an anchor. I flung my cheek to his shoulder, keeping an eye out the window at the twinkling lights on the horizon.

It was like we were floating here, in the dark, just watching it all.

Trey stroked my hair softly, then landed a kiss atop my head.

"Rio and Zeke are besotted with you," he said quietly. "So I thought it best to ignore the fact that you had caught my fancy."

I shifted my head back to look up at him, the area between my thighs growing hot to find his lips parting slightly, his breath so close, I could feel it. "I didn't think it'd be difficult," he said. "I didn't like that my parents had insisted on this potential engagement. And we hardly knew each other."

This conversation was setting off so many alarms in my head.

Deciding between three men was enough. Why was I feeling so attracted to a fourth? Was falling in love with so many really a genetic trait?

"But I know full-heartedly why they both fell for you," he whispered. He hesitated, then his lips seized my own.

When I leaned up into the kiss, his arms shifted to embrace me.

Gasping, he pulled back. "You're clever, strong—more lush than anyone I've ever met." His fingers brushed aside my bangs, dragging slowly across the surface of my skin. "And your skin feels—"

"Rubbery," I said, cutting him off.

He laughed a little under his breath. "I was going to say soft." He planted his lips atop my forehead. "Unlike any other's."

"Trey, I… I like Rio and Zeke, too." I flushed, wondering how much I really liked them. I'd spent two beautiful, harrowing evenings with them. Hardly enough to start considering which one to marry, but that *was* what was expected of me regardless. "And there's someone else…"

"The best friend," he said resolutely. Like he knew better than I had.

Pulling back, I massaged my temples. My little plan to have some "fun" with each of the princes was really back-firing on me.

"They told me you're still a virgin."

I stared at him. I wasn't going to comment on how he knew since it was clear the princes spoke frankly with one another, however embarrassing that might be. "Am I? Technically?"

He shrugged. "That's up to you to decide."

Sighing, I stared back out at the night sky, thinking.

He spoke. "I just want you to know that I want you to be comfortable should you and I—"

"Shut up and kiss me," I said, sliding in closer beside him and putting my hands on his shoulders.

He didn't need to be asked twice.

His hands slid up my back and into the roots of my hair, taking hold of me as his mouth claimed mine, his tongue slipping through at just the right moments to stroke against my own trembling organ.

I gasped, coming up for air. "Show me how you use your abilities in the bedroom."

He smirked. "We're not exactly in a bedroom here."

Growling, I took hold of his upper arms. "I don't care."

His throaty laughter rang out in the small space. "We hardly have time to do this properly, but I'll give you a show."

Before I could say anything more, he put a finger to my lips.

"You're going to start doing everything I command," he warned. "But I'll always let you say what you want. If I command you to do something you don't want, just say, 'no,' and I'll undo the command."

My mouth grew dry with anticipation, my insides vibrating. I shouldn't have felt thrilled at the prospect of doing everything he said, but here I was, at the top of a Ferris wheel, ready to hand myself over to this prince from across the pond.

Trey leaned back, his arms on either side of the top of seat.

"Kick off your shoes," he said first.

I complied before I could even blink, my feet fortunately able to kick out of my slip-ons with a bit of assistance from the toe of the other foot. I raised an eyebrow at him, wondering how tame this was going to be.

"Take off your blouse," he said.

There we go. My hands moved as if someone were controlling them, the blouse rolling up and over my head, fluttering to the floor. I hadn't even bothered to unbutton it.

"Unclasp your bra," he said.

I reached behind my back and did that, the bra sliding slightly forward off my shoulders, but when I felt my limbs return to my own sense of self again and I moved to slip the bra the rest of the way off, Trey spoke.

"Stop!"

I did, the straps of my bra dangling forward, my hand clutched over the front to keep the undergarment in place.

The corner of Trey's mouth twitched. "When we're playing, I prefer to be in control," he said, waiting just a moment to see if I would object.

The area between my thighs was trembling.

"Come here," he whispered, his deep voice practically getting stuck in his throat.

I shuffled across the small space and stood before him, my breaths growing shallow.

He put one hand on each side of my bare waist, the warmth of his fingers making me stumble as the cab swung slightly in the breeze.

"Show me your breasts," he whispered.

I dropped the bra immediately, then hesitated, hovering over him as he shifted his palms upward to take hold of my mounds of flesh.

Then his tongue was on my nipple, teasing it before

163

moving to the other. My knees buckled and I tumbled forward.

Gasping, he pulled back. "Remove your jeans."

I did, and when the button caught on my hips, he quickly moved in to unlatch it for me, pulling the fly down so I could step out of the jeans without ripping them to get them off in my haste.

His hands clutched either side of my waist again, slipping inside the elastic of my underpants.

"Remove your knickers," he said, taking his hands away.

I stood still, the need to do something overtaking me, but my limbs hesitant, confused.

"Remove your panties," he clarified.

I did, and I stood there in nothing but my sock feet.

I stared down into his eyes, wanting to put my knee on his lap, wanting to dig into those pants to feel that expanding bulge skin to skin, but I stood there, awaiting to see what puppetry he'd have for me next.

"Lie across my knees," he said, "your stomach down."

I did, my mons grinding against the thick denim of his pants. Part of me wanted him to be naked, but another part of me was overwhelmed by the thrill of doing this where we might be seen—of me being the only one taking the risk.

I clearly had been neglecting my sexual drive.

His smooth, warm palm caressed my butt cheek, teasing at the top of the slit that split my ass in half. I let out a little giggle at the ticklish touch, but his finger moved quickly down, teasing at the wrinkled flesh below. I gasped.

"Tell me, 'I've been naughty,'" he said.

While my mind was about to ponder why he'd wanted *me* to tell *him* he'd been naughty in this position, my lips were already forming the words, "I've been naughty," in the huskiest tone I'd ever spoken in.

His palm slapped hard against my butt cheek.

I squeaked.

The cab's lights flickered on and a grinding noise filled the air as the cab started shaking.

We were on our way *down*.

I squirmed, the pressure against my clit making me weak in the knees.

Trey's hand smacked my ass again. "Stay put," he said. Then he hesitated again, perhaps to see if I would object, but I didn't, the flush of blood heading to my forehead like something out of the wildest sex dream.

My nose hovered over the plush bench seat to the side of Trey's thighs, my nostrils taking in the scent of sweat in the air, the faint scent of lemongrass.

He smacked my ass again, and then his fingers darted to the crack between my cheeks, bypassing my most illicit of areas to circle down at my clit.

I writhed at the pressure, little moans escaping me in the harsh light as the cab made its slow, slow descent downward. My stomach felt like it was being left behind and I burst into giggles, covering my mouth.

Oh, god, though, if anyone sees us and it gets back to anyone I know…

But I hardly had time to object as Trey's handiwork grew more intense, two of his fingers sliding up and down through my folds, his erection growing harder through his pants against my groin.

Two fingers slid inside me and I *yelled*, the sensation too much for me to keep quiet.

Trey chuckled darkly, but his hands kept exploring, coming to know me intimately, thrusting deep inside.

"Stay quiet for a minute," he said. "The only word you can say is 'no' until I say otherwise."

My moaning went silent, and my hands went to my mouth, stifling the need to giggle as I felt the cab slow down.

We were at the bottom. *Oh my god, we're at the bottom.*

Trey knocked on the window of the cab. "Can we have another go?" he asked. "Just one more time around."

My heart was thundering in my ears.

After half an endless minute, the cab shuddered back to life and shook, bringing us slowly back upward.

After a short while, he spanked me again. "Speak if you want. Say whatever you want."

I found myself giggling before I could say anything. I rolled over. It must have been more than a minute because I no longer felt I *had* to stay put. "Did anyone see me?"

Trey's teeth gleamed in the dim flickering overhead lights. "The windows start up here," he said, pointing about halfway up his arms. "I don't think they had a clue."

Though they had to wonder where I was in that case.

"Shall we go again?" he asked.

"Are you *asking* me?" I pointed out.

His head tipped back, his fingers trailing up my thigh. "Turn around and let me spank you."

CHAPTER SEVENTEEN

PRINCE TREY ARRANGED FOR ME TO HAVE MY OWN ROOM IN THE hotel. Part of me thought—hoped—he'd invite me to share his instead of simply kissing my hand and winking before heading down the hallway, but during a cool shower and a bit of time to myself, I realized I was in quite over my head.

Four men. Three princes. My parents expecting some kind of formal answer, at least about whom I might continue to date with marriage in mind, if any of my fellow royals.

Each man had seized a corner of my heart. It was too soon to be thinking about marriage under normal circumstances, but this was far, far from normal.

I wouldn't *have to* marry whomever I chose, but I would be shutting the door on the other men.

I scrubbed my hair harder, practically ripping it at the roots.

All I did was disappoint myself, it seemed. I never wanted to think about life beyond Veras Academy, and here I was, expected to make a major decision about my life beyond the Academy in a matter of days.

And then there was the fact that my pussy practically *throbbed* with the need for fulfillment. For all the playing around I'd done with each of the four men, I was no closer to figuring anything out about my future than I had been before all this.

My mind was so occupied with my thoughts that I barely remembered putting on the hotel-issued robe and sliding into bed, but I couldn't have been lying there for more than a second before my phone rang.

Who actually *called* me?

Rajani, apparently. Though I noticed as I went to answer it that she'd left half a dozen messages I hadn't noticed.

"Finally!" she practically screamed over the phone. "The incident at the park is all over the news and you just go silent on me?"

I spoke aloud to the TV and asked it to turn on, scrolling through the channels with a wave of my hand until I got to the news. Almost as if on cue, the stoic newscaster switched from a story about summer beach safety to one with the headline, "Nelian Heir and British Prince Save the Day. Jollity Land Horror Invokes Heroics."

There were blurry images of the women we'd saved being slowly lowered to the bushes, clearer pictures of Trey helping me off the coaster once we'd stopped, my face flushed red but with an unrestrained smile as I gazed into Trey's eyes. I hadn't even noticed people snapping pictures.

The newscaster spoke about what happened and why "the two royals" might have been spotted together, speculating about a Nelian-United Kingdom political alliance.

Chewing my lip, I lowered the volume and turned my attention back to Rajani, who was going on about a mile a minute.

"Hazel is furious," she said, alerting me to pay better attention. "She said she was questioned by, I quote, 'those Nelian thugs on *Princess* Bry-Bry's orders like a common criminal.' But as much as I hate them, they have to have had nothing to do with it, right? I'm not doubting motive. I'm doubting ability. I mean, the *dream team*'s powerset doesn't *seem* to have anything that would make a roller coaster bar snap."

A message flashed across my screen from Derek, and I quickly responded, realizing I'd left him hanging. *I'm absolutely fine*, I wrote back. *Sorry I didn't get in touch earlier. Resting at the hotel. Be back tomorrow. Missing morning classes.*

"I mean, I don't know," I said. "I saw them there and thought it was weird. Can anyone blame me for having them looked into?"

"*I* certainly can't. Those brats don't exactly need a reason to bully someone they don't like. And there's the whole 'stay away from our princes' crap."

"Putting strangers in mortal danger is a step beyond *bullying*," I pointed out.

"Maybe they counted wrong. Thought you'd be the ones seated where those women were."

My blood ran cold. We *had* switched to a back seat. "And put *their prince* in mortal danger? Even Hazel has more sense than that." I was starting to convince myself the more I spoke. Everyone *had* said it was just wear and tear on the metal. A coincidence.

Just like the boars going nuts yesterday and that little girl in need of a rescue on Friday. Cripes, that all felt like ages ago now.

The image on the TV switched to another story, about the fugitive Nelian, last spotted in California, clear across the country from where he'd started. A clip played of Daddy Alarik giving a news conference earlier in the day. I turned up the volume.

"The Nelian government is taking full responsibility for tracking this criminal down. We're just glad to see there have been no reports of harm come to anyone. But I must reiterate: Do not engage. Call the authorities if you spot him."

A reporter asked him, "About your daughter, Your Majesty? What do you think about her heroics?"

Daddy's eyes seemed to sparkle as his lips turned into a slight smile. This was the Daddy I knew, the one who wasn't so stiff and serious all the time. "I always knew she was a hero," he said.

"And do you have a comment about her being spotted with Prince Trey of the United Kingdom?"

"No more questions," said Daddy into the mic, quickly walking away from the podium.

"Bry?" asked Rajani in my ear.

"Sorry. Daddy was on TV talking about the fugitive."

"Yeah," said Rajani, her voice dropping an octave. "They're trying to seem calm and collected, but everyone knows something's up."

My spine went stiff. "What do you mean?"

"Everyone's fine," she said. "It's just the instructors are always whispering in the halls. They send teams out and they come back grumpier than ever. Students are sticking to their dorms. Even Hazel and her cohorts haven't been lingering much out in the hallways. Have you talked to your parents?"

"While we were being interrogated about the incident."

"Interrogated?"

I shrugged, though she couldn't see me. "They just wanted to know our version of events. But the fugitive stuff didn't come up when I was on the phone with them."

"Hmm," said Rajani. "Well, *anyway*, enemies and mortal danger aside, how did your date with Prince Trey go? Have you made a decision yet?"

"Jani, I can't *decide* whom I want to marry after three dates."

"I don't know how this royal stuff works," she said, clearly a little miffed. "But you have to at least have an idea if you want to see one of them again."

I groaned. Back to all that. "I want to see them *all* again."

"You little minx." She sounded terribly amused. "Save some for the rest of us, why don't you?"

"I thought you had a thing for Connak."

She *tsked*. "I was looking for a *little action* with Connak. I

170

don't know how a life with a Nelian would work if I become a surgeon on Earth."

She was dancing a little too uncomfortably close to the question bothering me.

"But I'll have to speak to them all," I admitted. "I don't know how long they can stay here. I'm sure they have loads of political stuff to do. They're not actually going to enroll in classes or anything."

"None of them are the heirs to the throne like you are," she said. "I'm sure they can reschedule whatever they have planned if it means spending more time with you."

"Maybe," I said. But I couldn't exactly ask *all three* to stay longer, could I?

Everyone knew the Nelian king shared his consort with three other men. But would other Earth royal families even consider letting their sons share a bride?

It was ridiculous of me to even be thinking about it. I felt so selfish.

And what would Derek think?

I checked the clock. It was past midnight, and the activity of the day—in all sorts of ways—hit me like a brick wall. "Jani, I'm going to turn in. I'll see you tomorrow?"

"All right," she said, clearly disappointed I hadn't yet recounted any details about my date with Prince Trey. "Hey, Bry?" she asked right before I was going to say *goodbye*.

"Yeah?"

"Don't let what anyone else thinks stop you from pursuing your heart," she said. "All that matters is what you and the man—or *men*—you want to be with think. Royalty or not."

"Thanks," I said, feeling a soothing sense of warmth flood over me.

"If you want to thank me, put in a good word for me with Connak—"

"Yeah, yeah," I said, snickering. It didn't take me long to fall asleep after I'd shut off the TV and the light.

THE RIDE BACK WAS BLISSFULLY UNEVENTFUL, AND EVEN FAIRLY quiet, everyone no doubt exhausted from the events of the day before. Trey kept my hand in his and I didn't have the heart to pull away, even if it meant I hurt him when I met with all three of them. For now, I wanted to relish this feeling. This bliss.

Lacey seemed absolutely exhausted, Sage's brow in a perpetual furrow. As we drove into the Academy grounds and piled out of the limo, Sage pulled me aside. "We're going to Aunt Alanna's." He nodded at Lacey, still seated in Prince Trey's rented limousine. "Trey said he'd have his man offer us a lift. Lacey needs a break from her powers."

"Of course." I gave him a quick hug. "Thank you for coming yesterday."

He squeezed my elbow, his posture slumping. "I'm only sorry I proved useless when you were in danger."

"Don't say that." I play-punched him on the arm. "I'm the one who protects, remember? Literally. I wouldn't want you to put yourself in danger for me."

Sage glanced over my shoulder pointedly and I turned to see what he was looking at: Princes Rio and Zeke coming out of the front door of the Academy, speaking with Trey, their faces brightening in one another's presence, Trey slapping Zeke on the back and smiling broadly at Rio.

"You can't always be the one people rely on," said Sage quietly. "You deserve someone looking out for you too."

I opened my mouth as I turned back to Sage and shut it. I didn't know what to tell him because I didn't know what to tell myself yet.

"Don't push yourself," said Sage, heading back toward the limo.

I didn't get to ask if he was referring to physical exertion or matters of the heart before he climbed inside the vehicle, shut the door, and left.

My heart aflutter, I walked toward the front door of the Academy, knowing I was about to pass all three princes and entirely unsure what to say to them. The grounds were deserted, but I knew a class period was about to end, and the corridors would flood with students soon enough.

All three men stopped talking, Rio's laughter cutting out last as I neared. Then they turned toward me.

The only other people around were Trey's guards, who were some feet away lingering near the driveway, consulting with someone over the phone. Connak and his Nelian guard had said their goodbyes to me and were headed to a spot in the yard where they expected to find a portal to Nelia in a matter of moments.

Everyone else was out of earshot.

I clasped my hands together in front of my thighs, shuffling one foot on the ground.

"Bryony." Rio spoke first.

"Bry," added Zeke.

"Princess Bryony of Nelia," said Trey.

Then they all got down on their knees in front of me.

"Will you marry me?" they asked as one.

I hadn't ever dreamed that when someone asked me that question, I'd retreat, backing up and staggering away, my jaw cracked open in shock because words had simply failed me.

CHAPTER EIGHTEEN

THERE WAS AVOIDING A DIFFICULT DECISION AND AVOIDING people involved in that decision entirely, and I sadly fell into that second category.

It was Tuesday and I hadn't wound up attending any classes after my rude, if instinctual, retreat to my dorm room after being asked to wed not one, not two, but three princes. I hadn't known what to say. I couldn't choose one of them so easily, not after one date.

I thought none of them had *wanted* to marry me just because our parents had suggested it.

Which led me to believe that our dates had gone so well that… That… I shivered as the thought of each one of them flashed through my mind. I'd had mind-blowing dates with each of them. How was I supposed to choose?

And Derek… I simply couldn't fathom picking just one.

But now the princes probably all hated me after my reaction to their proposals. Mom had stopped by to check in on me and I'd practically gone catatonic when she'd tried to talk to me about it—I supposed word had gotten around somehow. So she'd let it go. Even Rajani had tread on careful ground last night.

But today… Today was a new day.

I was so determined to pretend that today was just another day that I'd been up and ready for class bright and early. Here I was in political science, trying to pay attention, but my thoughts drifted every few seconds.

I know we're royals, but they can't be serious. Proposals already? They don't even properly know me.

My heart thundering, my groin throbbing, I knew *one way* I really wanted to get to know them.

But that didn't have to involve formal proposals.

"*Bry,*" whispered Rajani.

I snapped up. Everyone in class was staring at me. Pepper and Hazel were over in the corner just about shooting lasers at me with their minds. Professor Kouta, our instructor, shook his head and repeated the question.

"What year did America ban the production of single-use plastics?" he asked. "Bryony, are you all right? I know you've been through a lot lately."

Pepper didn't even try to stifle her giggle.

"I'm fine," I said. "Um, 2025," I answered, not certain I wasn't off by a year or two. I knew these things, but right now, I couldn't care less about keeping track of all the tiny details.

"Professor?" asked Hazel, her hand above her head. "Can I ask why single-use plastics were banned instead of more pointless things like, say, amusement park rides?" Her brow narrowed as her eyes rested on me.

Like I had anything to do with inventing roller coasters.

"Well," said Professor Kouta, scratching his cheek with his left hand, a glint of light bouncing off his wedding ring, "you have to look at the effects single-use plastics had on the planet, far, far worse than any individual ride, which relies on solar-powered-produced electricity these days. Put into wide use in the mid-20th century, in fewer than a hundred years, they were polluting our water sources, our..."

Staring out the window, I found my attention drifting once more until the bell rang overhead.

"Don't forget about your essays," said Professor Kouta as everyone started exiting the classroom. "They're due before spring break. Drop them off digitally before no later than Friday." He looked up. "Miss Haddix, a moment?"

Rajani and Derek lingered at the door, their tablets clutched to their chests, but I waved them on. Hazel and Pepper were already in the hallway behind them, Sheila meeting up with them, their clique noticeably devoid of one member. Sheila whispered to Hazel and she glared at me through the open classroom door, clearly wishing her abilities involved smiting someone with a look.

"Miss Haddix, you missed yesterday's test," said Professor Kouta, oblivious to where my mind was.

I had? Oh, right. I'd known all about it last week when my life had seemed headed in an entirely different direction. "I'm sorry," I said, and I was. Going into shock over proposals didn't exactly make for the best excuse for missing a test.

Professor Kouta crossed his broad arms and leaned back against his desk in the corner of the classroom. "It's twenty percent of your grade. I'm sure you'd have no trouble retaking it, but I don't know if it's fair to give you more time than your classmates to study."

"No, that's fine," I said, swallowing. "I mean, I can take it right away if you'd like."

Professor Kouta's eyes narrowed a moment. "Okay. We can schedule it after your classes. Meet me in the library at... What's a good time for you?"

"Six," I said, allowing myself some time to grab food. Although with the way my stomach was acting up, I wondered if I'd ever manage to get much food down again.

"All right," said Professor Kouta, shuffling some papers on his desk. When he spoke again, he was already in the classroom doorway, clicking off the lights with a wave of his hand. "Miss Haddix? Are you sure you're well?"

Still, my eyes couldn't pull away from the window, where I realized with a start that I was looking at a Nelian portal ripping into existence some distance away in the yard, behind the giant oak tree.

"Yes," I said in answer to his question. Out of the portal stepped a guard, his posture stiff, his expression clearly agitated. He whipped around and spoke to someone still in Nelia on the other side of the portal, his lips curling. I couldn't quite make out his face from here, but from that profile… Connak?

And then one of the princes' bodyguards—I wished I had gotten to know them, I couldn't remember whose, so many of them had brown hair—appeared from the direction of the guest wing of the Academy, heading toward the portal with bold strides. His sunglasses seemed unnecessary in the overcast light, but they did seem to complete the guard look. As his arms swung in time, his jacket kept riding up his sleeves, like it was a bit too small for him.

The portal shut closed as quickly as it had opened, Connak whirling around to the bodyguard, his back to me. No one followed him out of the portal.

"Miss Haddix?" repeated Professor Kouta.

I finally turned around. "Right, thank you," I said, scrambling out the door so he could lock it, dashing down the hall to the open part, where sunlight streamed in through the floor-to-ceiling windows. But by the time I got there, zipping around a few wandering students, there was nothing by the oak tree to see.

"Bry!" Rajani jogged up to me from wherever she'd been waiting. Her mouth lingered open a second and then her eyes drew together as she studied me. "What happened? You look like you've seen a ghost."

I did? Smoothing my hair down with my free hand not clutching my tablet, I thought back to what I'd seen.

What had I seen? A Nelian guard coming back from Nelia in almost precisely the same place they always did. A prince's bodyguard conferring with him, just as they had during all my dates. It was probably a security thing.

177

Nelians usually used Veras Academy as their springboard onto Earth. I'd just never seen a portal that far off behind the oak tree before. Out of sight. But could I say I'd ever really paid such things any mind?

"I'm…" I let out a wry chuckle and shook my head. "I have a lot on my mind."

"I know," she said, her face brightening once more. "And I have a proposal for you…"

My face must have darkened at the word because she winced.

"Poor choice of words," she said. "But you'll want to hear me out."

RAJANI AND DEREK WAITED WITH ME IN THE LIBRARY AFTER WE'D grabbed some sandwiches for dinner. It was quarter to six, and I figured I ought to get some cramming in for the political science test I'd missed.

Though Derek's honor as a student, of course, wouldn't let him help me study, not when he knew what was on the test.

Rajani had fewer qualms. "Don't focus so much on the first publicly revealed Natches," she said, reaching across the table to swipe at my tablet. "I thought it would be a big deal, but it was, like, one question."

Derek cleared his throat and Rajani shrugged her shoulders apologetically as she slunk back into her seat. "Have you asked them yet?"

"I haven't spoken to any of the princes since yesterday." I looked to Derek to see what he thought of that, but his expression remained unusually guarded. He hadn't asked me about the proposals once all day, though I knew there was no way he hadn't heard about them.

A few tables over in the library's group study area, a table of teenage girls were all huddled around one of their phones, the books they'd taken out from the library open and neglected as they giggled over something on the screen, the soft sound of tinny music reaching all the way here.

"But you asked their people?" Rajani said, clearly exasperated.

"Their people?" Derek repeated.

"You know, 'have your people speak to my people,'" she said. "The bodyguards they lug all over the place!"

"I don't know if they qualify as their personal secretaries or anything. But yes, I went to the guest wing of the Academy and spoke with one of the men there."

"Which one?" Rajani asked.

I shrugged. It hadn't been the one I'd seen conferring with Connak at least. "Whoever was standing in front of the door leading down to the guest rooms."

"Oh, that's really specific." Rajani rolled her eyes. "And what did you tell him?"

"That my best friend has this crazy idea that the princes might want to drop everything they have planned next week and join us on our trip for spring break." I shook my head just slightly. "In so many words."

Rajani tossed a look to Derek, clearly looking for sympathy, but his lips were sealed. She spoke anyway. "Well, if that's not a lack of appreciation for my brilliant idea, I don't know what is."

"Sorry," I said, an itch creeping up the back of my neck. "It *is* a good idea."

"Get to know the princes better, spend some time letting off steam?" Her brown eyes twinkled. "I'd say it was fairly generous of me to allow them along, especially after you poopooed the idea of me trying to score with Connak during our time off."

"You're right," I said, folding the cover back over my tablet as I spotted Professor Kouta making his way toward me. "What I really need is more time." Biting my lip, I caught Derek's eyes and he nodded slightly. "Your idea gives me plenty more time," I said to Rajani. "And you can bring Connak—if he's interested."

"See? It'll all work out," said Rajani, standing and packing up her things. "I need to get going. Some of us have *plans* for the evening."

"Plans?" I asked. Derek looked as puzzled as I felt.

She tucked a curl of dark hair behind her ear. "I *may* have asked Connak if he had the night off, so to speak, and he may have said *yes*."

That news hit me like a bag of bricks. "When did this happen?" Connak had spent more time with me the past few days than Rajani.

A guy a few tables over hushed us and I winced. We *were* in the library, even if talking was allowed in this section.

Rajani giggled. "Last night, when you were cooped up in our dorm room." She smiled broadly. "I wanted to tell you earlier, but I was trying to play it cool. Casual. Just like I promised him this date would be."

Connak would know if he was destined to be with Rajani, even if she, as a human, couldn't feel the same way. *I* might not have had a good grasp on whether or not I felt the Nelian sense with anyone, but I knew a full-blooded Nelian certainly would.

But that didn't stop them from having liaisons with other people who interested them.

As long as Rajani understood that, well... "Have fun," I said.

"Miss Haddix?" asked Professor Kouta, approaching the table. "You ready?"

"Good luck," whispered Rajani.

Derek opened a book from the top of the old-fashioned stack he'd taken down from the shelves. "You've got this," he whispered huskily before turning to the written words.

I felt better knowing he believed in me once more.

I followed Professor Kouta into a small, quiet study room, where one wall and the door made entirely of glass, which allowed for easy visibility. In the room two doors over, I caught a glimpse of Sheila leaning back in a chair, a stylus between her lips and the open notebook and book app screens floating in front of her being ignored. She sat up straighter as I passed by and leaned forward, her forearms on the table as she stared me down.

My stomach rumbled, the sandwiches sitting uneasily against my nerves, as Professor Kouta held the door for me and flicked on the study room lights.

"Forty minutes, same as everyone in class yesterday," he said, tapping on his nearly translucent tablet. My own let out a little *ding* as I took a seat at the table, the test appearing on my screen. He sat in the corner, making adjustments to his comm on his wrist. He waited until I'd grabbed my stylus from where I'd tucked it in my tablet case. "And begin."

Despite everything swimming around in my head, part of me hoped that as soon as I picked up a stylus and started reading the test, I'd be able to focus, just as if it were any other test before my life had been turned into such a circus. Sadly, that was not the case. I *tried*, and I knew I got some questions right, but every few questions, an image of one prince or another on his knees would pop into my head, and I'd have to re-read the test question over again before I lost focus completely.

I didn't know how much time had passed, but it felt like I'd run out of time before I'd reach the end of the test. Professor Kouta flicked at a tablet in front of him, the only sound the tap of his finger on the screen, the slight in-and-out of our steady breaths. Eventually, tired of the words getting muddled every time I read them, I skipped ahead to the last question, which would involve a short essay. I needed to get at least that done; it probably counted for most of the test. I was about a quarter of the way through it when the lights overhead began to flicker.

Neither Professor Kouta nor I were especially startled by this.

Then the lights went out and the professor put his tablet down on the table, glancing overhead. "The backup power should kick in." His lips pursed as he flicked through his screen, the bright light the only thing illuminating the study cubby. "There wasn't a storm tonight."

My stylus dropped to the table, the situation suddenly feeling very *wrong*, a prickle running up the back of my neck.

Murmurs from outside penetrated even the glass wall. With a loud *thunk*, Sheila raced past our room as if there were a rabid dog on her tail.

Professor Kouta and I both stood and made our way to the door, the professor out first, raising his voice as he approached a cluster of students gathered toward one of the wide floor-to-ceiling windows overlooking the back yard of the Academy. "Everyone, settle down. If there's lightning, it's best to get away from the windows."

But there was no sign of lightning at all, just a crackling glow in the dusk out in the yard, a portal to Nelia opened.

"Bry," said a husky voice with a slight accent from behind me.

Prince Rio had appeared from somewhere in the library, his entourage of bodyguards nowhere to be seen. He wore workout clothes, a too-tight gray tank top and a striped pair of dark running pants.

Despite the spectacle of whatever was going on, my face flushed and I crossed one leg over the other as he approached.

"What is happening?" he asked.

"I don't know," I admitted. "The power is usually never out for this long—"

The door to the library flung open, Professor Chastity an easy-to-discern silhouette in the dimness. "Everyone! To the nearest shelter! Now!"

Shelter?

I spun around. Where were Rajani and Derek?

Rio grabbed my hand, but I pulled away. I wasn't going anywhere without my friends.

"Back of the library!" shouted Professor Kouta, joined by the librarian on duty in attempting to herd the crowd away from the window. "The basement!"

Some of the students obeyed, but most lingered. Even those walking away kept their heads turned, watching the portal outside expand and crackle, a lightning-like flash of energy breaking off from it and striking somewhere across campus with a loud *crack*.

Screams rang out across the library.

"Come on!" shouted the librarian, an older Natch woman whose abilities escaped me. "Go!"

"Let us retreat," said Rio, moving to grab me and carry me as he had when we'd saved that girl from drowning.

"No," I said, putting a hand on his chest firmly as the wave of students pushed past us. My eyes were scanning the crowd, looking for Derek and Rajani—but they were nowhere to be found. Not even Sheila was among them. They must have left the library before all this.

Rio frowned, and I looked into his eyes, all awkwardness I felt around him forgotten. "I need to find my friends."

Nodding, he gestured in front of him, offering to pick me up once more.

"Bryony. Your Highness," said Professor Kouta as he realized whom I was standing with. "Come on." We were the last students still lingering on this side of the library.

"What's going on?" I asked, spinning on the professor. He shook his head, his eyes meeting Professor Chastity's over at the doorway.

"Just follow the other students to the tornado shelter," he said, typing into the comm on his wrist.

"That's no *tornado*," I started, but Rio had me in his arms once more, tucking my head against his chest as he zipped us through the library. We moved around Professor Chastity in the open library doors before she could so much as blink, down the hall and to the doors leading to the back yard.

My hair still ruffled in the air as if being blown by the wind as Rio lowered me to my feet.

"I apologize," he said. "But I thought you would prefer not to stand there arguing with either of them."

I leaned up on my tiptoes and kissed him on the cheek. "You thought right."

He got the door for me and I rushed through, though that was laughable, considering the speed of the man beside me.

"Yes," he said as I went through.

"Yes?" I said, looking over my shoulder as he followed me.

"Yes, I will gladly follow you anywhere. On your beach trip and beyond."

My chest tightened as my skin flushed. This hardly seemed the time. "Rio, I invited everyone."

"I know." The corner of his lip twitched. "We all do. We all agree that it's up to you which, if any, of us you wed. Were it not for our families—"

But whatever he might have said next was cut short as the portal, about twenty yards away, kicked up, another crack of light shooting outward and toward the school.

I'd never seen a portal act that way before.

"What are you doing here?!"

Turning, I found Mom running toward me, her Veras team suit on.

I ignored Mom's question. "What's going on?"

Mom spared a glance toward Rio and put a firm hand on my arm. Around us, incomprehensible conversations carried over the wind as Dad Jayden and Pop Nash conferred with Professor Wade. They were all suited up, their form-fitting navy battle suits acting like a second skin.

Like they'd been anticipating some kind of attack. Or they'd been in the middle of one.

"Did you come through the portal?" I asked.

Mom nodded. "Please, get inside! Both of you!"

I yanked my arm out of her grip. "I'm not a little kid, Mom! Tell me what's going on!"

Mom blinked in the crackling light of the fritzing portal, her hair blown across her face. "*Please*. Just go inside." Her voice was breaking.

I opened my mouth to speak when the portal made a cracking, sizzling sound again. And through it stepped two figures. Princes Zeke and Trey.

"How…?" I asked, my gaze flicking to both my mom and Prince Rio.

Connak stumbled out after them, leaning on the shoulder of Normak, his father, clutching his side, as if he'd been wounded.

And then out stepped *Derek*.

I took off toward the growing crowd stumbling out of the portal, my fists out in front of me, ready to protect anyone from another snap of light from the wonky portal.

But just as I neared it—after I felt a *whoosh* of air and saw Rio appear beside his friends before I was even halfway there —with a crack louder than any of the ones that had appeared before, the portal was gone, collapsed into itself.

The air rang out with the slight hiss left behind from the portal's presence, which soon reverberated into nothing but the chirps of crickets in the twilight.

The others approached, their feet rustling the grass.

"Bryony," snapped Dad Jayden. "You're all right?"

My eyebrow quirked. "Why wouldn't I be? What happened?" I looked to the princes for answers, instead settling on Derek.

Derek would tell me. Even if no one else could be counted on, he could.

Derek grimaced. "They took Rajani."

CHAPTER NINETEEN

THE ACADEMY'S POWER RESTORED, I SAT WITH ALMOST ALL OF the Veras Academy staff plus Derek and the princes and their guards in a classroom turned hastily into a war room of sorts.

The few staff missing were attending to the other students, particularly the youngest ones.

Almost no one had gotten hurt when the abnormal portal had appeared. No one except Connak—and probably Rajani.

My limbs were shaking even as I sat still, my mind racing for this meeting to be over with, just so I could get out there and *do* something, be useful.

Derek rested a hand on my thigh on one side, Zeke on the other. Their eyes met across the top of me and instead of their faces contorting into any sign of jealousy, Derek simply swallowed and Zeke nodded, some kind of unspoken understanding passing between them. Neither moved his hand, and their warm, comforting presences made my limbs still as I took a deep breath, trying to calm my nerves.

Connak was in the infirmary being treated by Professor Wade while his father stood at the head of the classroom conferring with Dad Jayden. At last, Dad Jayden turned to the rest of us.

"Rajani Hunjan was taken to Nelia by a rogue group of

Nelians still acting in support of Xerxes." The door to the classroom burst open and Daddy Alarik and Papa Zander rushed in, Papa's eyes scanning the classroom until he found mine.

"You okay, pumpkin?" he asked in my mind.

I didn't have the heart to respond in words. This fugitive had taken my best friend.

Roulette bounced on her feet in the front of the classroom beside my mom. "That fucker was on Nelia all along then?"

Papa Zander turned to her. "We finally caught up to the 'Xerxes' who's been caught on camera making his way across the country." The way he said the fugitive's name, like it left nothing but distaste in his mouth, put me on high alert. "It was a Natch who could shapeshift. He was hired by the senator who organized Xerxes' breakout."

Daddy Alarik grimaced. "We've had a rather productive *talk* with Senator Nelson. Appropriate punishments are in place, and rest assured, any scandal he was attempting to prevent is now at great risk of being leaked regardless. It turns out he'd been sending trusted aides to try to talk to the man—try to find weaknesses in *my* armor, so to speak. Instead, the fools got commanded to spill their secrets, and Xerxes manipulated the situation to his advantage."

It was all well and good to know that Veras and the Renegades had been hard at work pinpointing the *why* and the *how* the fugitive had made his escape, but right now, I couldn't have cared less if the U.S. President herself had sprung him loose. I wanted to know what had happened to my friend.

"Why did they take Rajani?" I asked loudly.

The entire room turned to me, my dads exchanging a silent conversation between them. But I knew Zander could only talk to Jayden among them telepathically.

"They were looking for you," said Pop Nash, the only one of my dads who could understand the urgency I felt in the situation, the need to *act* without thinking every little detail through. "Xerxes went to jail knowing Aurora was pregnant, and with you all over the news as of late—I guess he got it into his head to take our kids."

I tensed and Zeke rubbed a palm against my back. "Sage?" I asked.

My dads looked at one another, and Mom stepped forward.

"He's safe," she said. "Your aunt and uncles are keeping a careful eye on him and Lacey. Alanna could very easily be a target of Xerxes, too."

Normak spoke next, his mouth in a grim line. "The Nelians who assisted Xerxes more than twenty years ago... We thought them rehabilitated. As a people, we were not used to this kind of..."

"Treachery," Daddy Alarik finished for him.

"Crime of any sort. We fought the wild boars, not each other." Normak swallowed.

"But you did fight the human population," muttered Roulette beside him. No one commented on it.

"Xerxes made his way here and found my son with the Natch girl," explained Normak. "He saw Connak in the footage of Princess Bryony on her dates, apparently, and he demanded to know where she was."

"Long story short," Nash said, cutting in, "we popped in from our own Nelian portal, not too far from his. The two portals kind of collapsed into each other?" He looked to Dad Jayden for confirmation and the Veras team leader nodded. "Causing all that wild reaction. They led to different points on Nelia, but they both came here."

"We stepped through," said Mom, "but Xerxes acted fast, grabbing Rajani as a hostage. He took her through the portal and the princes followed—"

Zeke's hand stopped moving across my back and I turned to him. "How were you two there?" Some of their body-guards hugged the wall behind them. "Without your guards?"

Zeke and Trey, both in workout clothes like Rio, were

covered in bits of dirt, light scratches from branches or something of the sort dotting their shapely biceps and chiseled cheeks.

Beside me, Derek squeezed my thigh. "I ran into them in the hall after you left to take your test."

"We had a talk," said Zeke, his accent making the simple sentence seem far more menacing than it was.

Prince Trey sat up straighter in his seat, his features softening. "We wanted to know what he thought about your idea of us tagging along with you on spring break."

"And whether he would count himself among your suitors," finished Zeke.

My face flushed as I avoided the stares of everyone in the room—including all of my parents. Roulette made a soft little gasp, though, her head cocking. I wondered what she thought of her son being asked by a couple of princes if he wanted to date me. I wondered if her mind jumped immediately to the type of love my own parents shared and what she'd think of her child being in such a relationship.

As if I would never make up my mind.

"In any case," said Derek, pushing his glasses up his nose with his free hand. "We were near the door to the yard when the portals started crackling. We didn't think much of the first portal at first, didn't realize who'd stepped through—"

"But then we heard the screams and the lights went out," said Trey. "We ran out to help. Saw your friend being carried away."

"Trey yelled out for him to stop," added Zeke, "but the bastard had already gone through the portal by then. Instead, all he succeeded in doing was making the rest of us stand still in our places."

Trey directed a burning stare toward Zeke, his lips mumbling something I couldn't quite hear. Maybe the princes weren't as well-trained in combat as Veras Academy students. I could hardly blame him. We'd had a pretty peaceful few decades.

"I headed after them to follow them through," said Trey, "after releasing everyone from my command. Zeke and Derek caught up to me. When we made it through and we found him and a few others." He nodded toward Normak.

"The prince commanded us to halt," said Normak, eyeing him suspiciously. "We couldn't move. My comrade and I kept the portal open. My son stumbled in after and explained the situation, and the prince let us go."

"We weren't in the same portal that asshole had gone through," said Derek, squeezing his hand into a fist. "This was the portal Veras had used to get back—unaware of the situation. It had collapsed into Xerxes'."

"My other comrade took over keeping the portal open so I could attend to my son," said Normak. "And we came through to find the king."

"We couldn't save her," whispered Derek. "We didn't even know where she was."

"It's just as well," said Dad Jayden. "We wouldn't want our students and our guests to put themselves in danger."

"Rajani is *our* friend," I said, referring to Derek and myself. I sent a grateful glance toward Zeke and Trey for putting themselves at risk, too.

"Which is why you'll just put yourselves in greater danger," said Dad Jayden on the field. "Bryony, you're his target. I need you especially to stay out of this one."

I slammed my fists on the desk in front of me. "Rajani is only in danger because of me!"

Mom crossed the room and stood in front of my desk. "All you're demonstrating right now is that you're not in the right headspace to go rescue her."

Glaring at Mom, I leaned back into my chair with a huff.

"Which is why you, Derek, and our visiting princes"— Mom looked to those she named in turn—"are all going to join your brother at your aunt's house on Earth."

"*What*?" I snapped. "Mom, you all said it yourselves—

Aunt Alanna's a target. And around her, we'll be sitting ducks—"

Mom held up a hand. "Alanna is participating in this mission to catch Xerxes once and for all," she said, her voice clipped.

"But then you'll—"

"Bryony, you don't need to know the details. You just need to be safe. I know you're all adults, but you're young yet —inexperienced." She shot Trey an especially harsh look at that. "This is *our* fight."

I bit back a comment about how I doubted she'd ever agreed to step aside when her loved ones had been in danger at my age. Mom had joined Veras at eighteen, before there had been an Academy. They'd just been a small group of Natches trying to make the world a better place for our kind and Typicals alike.

Mom leaned down and put a hand on my shoulder. "Please, Bryony. Just promise me you'll stay safe."

That much I could promise. So long as she didn't know all of the details of how I planned to do so.

AUNT ALANNA AND HER HUSBANDS LIVED IN A COZY, FOUR-bedroom house outside of town, with plenty of acreage to both keep the outside world away and to keep Alanna well out of the range of any passing Natches who hadn't signed up for a training session without their abilities.

Not that my aunt stayed a hermit entirely. She had to get out and stretch her wings on occasion, confused Natches and strange looks turned her way be damned.

I wished she were here right now, even if I knew how foolish that was. With her gone, all the Natches around me still had their powers, and they'd need them if things went according to plan.

Because I'd spent the night at my aunt's, curled up on a spare bed next to Derek, and my parents had yet to give me an update. We'd changed into Alanna's and my uncles' workout clothes, each of us managing to find something that fit, and we were tired of just sitting here, twiddling our thumbs.

I'd tried it their way. Now it was morning, and we were trying it *my* way.

"You want to be bait?" asked Zeke, his Kiwi accent making it especially clear he thought the idea ridiculous.

"Shh!" I said, looking over my shoulder to see if my two remaining uncles who'd stayed behind had heard me. Caspian was outside the front door, talking to one of the prince's bodyguards. Without Alanna around, his skin was rock-hard, his ability always "on," so to speak, though his handsome features were distinguishable through any element he hardened his skin into. Bo was down the hall, in his sister's room, tending to her. With Alanna gone, her abilities were back, which meant she had to literally hold herself together and experience pain all the while.

She'd gotten more used to it since she'd been afflicted with her ability all her life. But it still involved resting often. Renegade contacts had been called in to help guard the students left behind at the Academy, taking over where Lacey might have been tasked to help. Sage had insisted his fiancée stay with him.

Here. In this quiet house. Where everyone inside was of help to no one.

"No," said Rio in his clipped tone. "We are not putting you in danger like that."

Derek frowned. "What if it was someone you cared about who'd been taken? What if Bryony herself was already taken by that criminal?"

"We'd do whatever it took to find her," said Trey. He sighed and leaned back on the couch. "All right. What do you have in mind?"

"*Trey*," said Rio.

"She's a fighter," said Trey, taking a deep breath and then slowly smiling at me. "Not a damsel. And that's why we love her."

"Agreed," said Zeke.

I couldn't believe that it was just two days ago that the princes had all proposed to me and I'd felt too awkward around them to even face them again.

Now I only felt like I could do this because I had all four of them here. I took Derek's hand and Trey's in mine, giving them both a squeeze. "Rio?"

Sighing, he kicked off from the wall he was leaning against and sat down on the couch beside Trey. "I will not let you do this without me."

"We can't get to Nelia without a portal," I said, relieved to have them all on board and without a moment to waste. "So we have to make the news."

"*What*?" asked Zeke, clearly disbelieving. "Make the news and have your parents and our bodyguards on our asses long before some mad elf criminal shows up? Blimey."

"And speaking of," added Rio. "How are we to get anywhere without our guards knowing? They will never agree to such a plan. They serve our parents first before us—protecting us comes before following our orders."

Drat. There really were few options at this point, weren't there?

"Trey? Can you command them to stand down?"

"I could, but as soon as I left, they'd be themselves again." He swallowed, his eyes going a bit hazy.

"You know about when he commanded his brother to fly, don't you?" asked Zeke in a hush beside me.

"Huh?" The sound escaped my mouth, drawing Trey's attention.

"I was four," he said, his leg bouncing. "And he didn't actually *fly*. If it's not possible, I can't command it to happen. I commanded him to give me his brand new toy, and then I walked away from him. As soon as my powers stopped seizing control of him, he came back to himself and ran down the hall after me, screaming at me that I was a no-good Natch thief." His lips pinched. "I told him to fly off the nearby balcony. The door was open. It was just an errant thought."

"He broke his legs," added Rio, his face grim. "He survived. As you say, you were but a child."

"He could have *died*," said Trey, his voice shaking.

"But he didn't." Zeke spoke bluntly.

My heart ached at the look on Trey's face. I hadn't looked into his past at all—hadn't realized his abilities had caused him such heartache.

"In any case, no, Bry, I don't think commanding them to stand down would work." Trey tilted his head, as if thinking. "I could command them to come along and help, but I'd have my hands full making sure none of them cracked and called for backup."

"We'll get around them without your abilities then," I said firmly. I thought a moment more. "Connak?" I ventured. "He was with Rajani when she was taken. He has to feel useless in the infirmary. If he can get a message back to some portal creators to open up a portal here, we can start searching for Xerxes from here."

Zeke drummed his feet against the floor in the armchair he was in. "But I'm sure he's under close watch. So making the news it is. What do you have in mind, princess? Stage another rescue? We just patrol the streets looking for someone in need of help?"

"I think even kissing one of you in public might do," I said, my insides heating. I shoved both hands between my thighs in an effort to stave the throbbing radiating out from my core.

"Why not kissing all of us?" offered Trey, not a hint of amusement on his face. "That would be more likely to get people to do a double-take, get the phones out, the hashtags trending—"

"And however Xerxes is monitoring the news, it'd get

back to him," said Derek. He reached an arm around me and squeezed. "I like it."

He *liked* the idea of me kissing all four of them in the middle of town?

My head became somewhat dizzy.

Rio shook his head. "Not that I am against another chance to kiss you," he said, without a hint of shame about him. I ground my thighs tighter against my clenched fists. "But I fear the plan is too complicated. Ordering the guards to stand down or sneaking out without them noticing—regardless, they would call in the cavalry as soon as they realized what had happened."

"I can't just sit here!" I said, tossing my hands in the air. *"Please."*

"I can provide a distraction," said someone new to the conversation. We all turned to find Sage, his hair ruffled, purple bags under his eyes, leaned up against the wall leading to the bedrooms. "We need this fucker caught. I've spent a lot of time here with Lacey. I think I have an idea." His hand settled on my shoulder. "I'm sorry about Rajani," he said quietly.

"Making the news it is," said Trey, straightening. He looked between Rio and Zeke. "Who has the most experience driving on the right side of the road?"

"You mean the *wrong* side?" countered Zeke.

Rio raised his hand shakily. "I have driven in this country many times, but I have to admit I do tend to turn into the incorrect lane on occasion."

The glint of the sun bounced off a sleek dark limousine in the driveaway, visible through the living room's recessed window.

The keys were hanging on the nearby key rack right inside the front door. "I'll drive," I said, bolting to my feet. "I'd rather make it to town in one piece, thank you."

CHAPTER TWENTY

TREY, ZEKE, RIO, DEREK, AND I HOVERED JUST INSIDE THE FRONT door, the keys in my hand, all fueled up on power bars from a quick rummaging around in my aunt's kitchen and ready to go. Sage pushed aside the very edge of the curtain covering the small window on the back door in the kitchen, peering out. In one hand he clutched a rocket firework he'd found in the basement, in the other a lighter. "It's clear back here," he said in a hushed voice.

"They're still all out front," confirmed Derek.

"Okay," said Sage. "Let's do this."

Slowly opening the back door, he creeped outside and shut it behind him.

With bated breath, the five of us waited in the darkened living room.

Mere moments later, a shriek whistle pierced the sky, followed by what the unexpecting might think was an explosion.

Uncle Caspian cursed in Spanish on the other side of the door, a shuffle of feet indicating he and the guards had started for the back of the house.

"Go, go, go," said Trey, and my hand was on the doorknob before he got the second syllable out.

"Open the limousine doors and get inside!" shrieked Trey as we all bolted outside, his command driving us even more than our own brains. "Bryony, go around to the other side and sit in the driver's seat. And drive!"

This was all part of the plan, none of it unexpected, but I found my muscles moving beyond the capacity I'd attributed to them, my sheer *need* to follow Trey's command pushing me to my limits and beyond. Trey had been right that he could get us to move faster.

That little bit of extra speed was just the edge we needed.

Unable to follow his own commands, Trey lagged just a moment behind, scrambling into the passenger's side seat beside me and clicking his seatbelt into place.

"Seatbelts on, everyone!" he shouted.

We complied.

"What's going on?" shouted Uncle Bo from the front door, but I was already slipping the key inside and pushing the button to start the ignition, the conveniently backed-up limousine ready to go forward without worrying about driving in reverse.

In the rearview mirror, I saw Uncle Bo trailing after us down the driveway and the dirt road, our long vehicle bumping over every little dip and crack in the path. Bo's abilities included super strength but not super speed. His strength wouldn't do him much good.

Uncle Caspian and the bodyguards soon came into view, just little dots in the mirror as we put the house behind us.

Trey chuckled and ran a soft, long finger over my cheek. "I don't think I've ever had so much fun sneaking out."

I laughed despite myself, my hands clutching the steering wheel as I drove down the driveway and made a sharp turn. The back of the limousine skidded off into the grass somewhat. I wasn't used to driving such a long vehicle.

"Bryony, you're in control," said Trey sharply as he clutched the armrest in the door to keep from hitting the window. "Same for everyone. You're in control."

Zeke took that as a signal and flung his hands toward the back of the vehicle. I didn't see what he was doing, but the plan involved camouflaging the back of the limousine with its surroundings so no one headed after us would know where we'd gone.

My muscles relaxed as I realized I'd still been too focused on driving to let up on the gas.

"Your abilities take some getting used to," I said, lifting my foot a bit. But then, thinking of Rajani, I put pedal to the metal of my own free choice. We probably only had a few minutes' lead on any of them, and Zeke's reach only went so far. They could probably make us out ahead of them through the illusion if they hung back just enough.

We just needed to get to town. Make the news. Then hope Xerxes found us before anyone from Veras did.

"I don't think you needed my help after all," said Trey, pointing to the speedometer. "You do know we'll have to slow down when we encounter any traffic."

"Until then, though, there's nothing standing between me and my goal."

"Or between your foot and the floor, I venture."

EVEN WHEN TRAFFIC GOT HEAVIER, I MANAGED TO STAY AHEAD OF any pursuers, parking the limo in a parking lot for an ice cream shop on the outskirts of town. We didn't care if it got towed at this point. We just didn't want to lead any guards or family members to where we were.

Rio had another plan to put more distance between us and them. One by one, he'd carry us to the decorative water fountain in the middle of the city, where I knew there was always a crowd of people meeting up with friends before heading off in different directions to enjoy what downtown had to offer.

Derek agreed, but Trey and Zeke didn't think Rio had the strength to carry them, even one at a time.

By the time he put down Zeke about half a minute later, the last of the bunch, Rio had clearly proven them wrong.

"All right, all right," mumbled Zeke, finger-combing a strand of his hair.

"So," said Derek, looking around. There was indeed a small crowd, most congregated around a food vendor several yards away from the water fountain. Most were minding their own business, but a few turned their heads, probably looking for the source of concentrated, quick wind that had ruffled their hats or in one guy's case, sent his sunglasses flying clear off his face.

"So," I said, throwing my arms over Derek's shoulders. "Let's give them a show."

Derek's lips found mine before I could even blink, his soft lips hungry, his tongue slipping inside and caressing my gums.

"Okay, mate, her kissing just you isn't really a *show*." Zeke tapped Derek's shoulder and my best friend stepped aside as the prince's hands slipped to the small of my back. With a flourish, he dipped me backward, his lips pressing forward to graze my neck, searching for my mouth and claiming it greedily.

Even over the trickle of the water fountain, I could hear a few murmurs.

"If I may?" Rio asked.

Zeke righted me, then gestured toward me, and Rio offered him a slight nod. The Japanese prince cupped my face and kissed my forehead, his lips parking once on the tip of my nose, then on my upper lip, my lower lip, each kiss growing faster, more unyielding.

"My turn," added Trey, the growing whispers turning to the hum of louder conversation and a few clicks of camera apps. Rio stepped aside and I had to take a deep breath as kisser number four made his way to stand in front of me, threading his hands through my hair, tickling the top of one of my pointed ears. "Kiss me, Bryony," he whispered, his voice catching on the words and sending shivers down to my toes.

My mouth was on his, sucking, kissing, never finding it to be enough. My tongue entwined with his, my lips growing swollen as he met my force with his own.

For a moment, there was nothing but him and me, the kisses that would never end and never be enough.

He pulled back. "You're in control, Bryony."

A slight sense of *urgency* leaked out from my pores, but if he thought I was done kissing him, he had another think coming.

It was only after I felt a tap on my shoulder that I pulled away, my hands still clutching tightly to Prince Trey's back.

"We got their attention," said Rio into my ear. Gazing around, I saw that a circle of onlookers had formed, almost all of them with a phone screen held high or projected in front of them.

Prince Trey pulled one hand away from my back and waved as if posing for the pictures.

I supposed we were. I waved as well, and Derek and Rio followed suit. Zeke grunted and folded his arms over his chest.

Slipping his hand into his back pocket, Derek pulled out his own phone, the centimeter-thick bamboo material comprising the screen glinting in the sun overhead. I'd left my own phone at Aunt Alanna's.

"We're trending," he said.

"That was fast," said Zeke. He cocked an eyebrow as he got a look at Derek's screen.

"What?" I asked.

Zeke chuckled.

"'Hashtag Princess Reverse Harem,'" read Rio from the screen slowly, as if questioning each word.

"That makes it sound like princesses are in the harem," added Trey. "Hmm…" He had a far-off look in his eyes.

"Don't you dare even imagine it," I said, play-punching

his arms. "You're all *mine*." The words were out of my mouth before I could even think too hard about them.

They all stared at me, wide-eyed.

Then Zeke laughed. And Rio and Trey. And Derek, too.

I chuckled along with them.

"I was thinking more like if I could clone you," Trey said, grabbing me by the ass and planting another kiss on my head. "All the interesting things we could get up to…"

The last thing I wanted to think about just then was Hazel and her cronies, but the word "clone" set off an image of Sheila and her doppelgänger ability in my mind.

Her doppelgängers that vanish into thin air on command, kind of like Sheila herself did in the library last night.

Unless…

My stomach felt rock hard and my smile slipped.

"What is it?" asked Trey, all concern.

"I just…" I mean, they couldn't have messed with the roller coaster anyway. And they were assholes, but were they *murderous* assholes?

Did Sheila spy on Rajani, Derek, and me, letting her group know once we were separated? Had she been off to tell *someone* asking about me where I was?

Thinking back, there was the Nelian guard I'd thought was Connak stepping outside of a strangely located portal right before the big explosion.

I'd only seen the Nelian from behind. Why had I assumed it was him?

And the bodyguard… The bodyguard's suit jacket had seemed a little short at the wrists, like he was borrowing it or throwing on an old one that hadn't fit him.

He'd been tall, lanky… like *Jerry*.

I turned to Derek, Trey's arms still wrapped around me. He was the only one who could really *understand*.

"I think Hazel and her cohorts might be helping—"

But my sentence was interrupted by a crackle of light in the air as a rip fissured the air beside the water fountain.

Someone had found us as planned. But only the next few seconds would tell if it was someone working with Daddy Alarik or the fugitive who had my friend.

As the crowd let out murmurs and screams and started running away, the five of us turned to the opening, palms out at our sides, knees bent, ready to fight, my men flanking me and slightly to the front so I could project any protection toward them all at once, as planned.

I'd figured, perhaps too confidently, that we could protect any Typicals lingering in the area.

I held up one hand, holding back any attack on my signal in case a friend stepped through that portal.

But then the burgeoning portal before us vanished. There was another crack from behind me, and as I turned around to see the source of it, I came face-to-face with Hazel, the fluctuating glow of an open portal mere feet behind her.

"Good morning, *Princess Whore*," she said, and with a pucker of her lips, she blew. My limbs went stiff, my vision went gray, and I fell to the ground, a solid piece of rock.

DIRT CAKED MY CHEEK, ITS MUSTY SCENT INVADING MY NOSTRILS. The back of my head throbbed and I rubbed it, wincing as the muscles in my arm cracked, like I'd been lifting weights the previous day.

Rolling over, I blinked, hard, trying to remember where I even was. Several yards above me was a lattice of green webbing—vines, I realized—woven in a dome shape.

I bolted upright. "Where the hell am I?!"

It was dim in here, but there was a muted beam of dusky light trickling in from one distant point—the mouth of a cave, I realized, the sun already setting outside.

Around me was dirt and this vine-crafted cage and… Trey, Zeke, Rio, and Derek, crumpled on the floor.

"Wake up!" I said, crawling over to them and shaking

both Zeke and Rio at once. Panicked, I reached over their prone forms to jostle Derek and Trey, needing them—any of them, *all* of them—to wake up and tell me they were all right.

"Oh my god, *please*." I put a finger to Rio's neck, checking for a pulse, found one, then moved on to the others in turn.

They all had pulses. A slight moan escaped my mouth as I realized I'd been fighting back a sob. None of them looked visibly injured—just dirty, disheveled, and out cold.

How? How had this happened? We'd had a plan.

The portal in front of us had been a distraction. There'd been a portal behind us, and *Hazel* had walked out of it.

Motherfucking Hazel.

She'd turned me to stone, putting me into stasis. Had she managed to do the same to the rest of the men? How fast could she work? And then she'd dragged us... *here*?

No. She clearly wasn't working alone.

But she'd surprised us, and that had been enough.

A low groan reverberated beside me and Zeke pushed himself up on shaky limbs. I scrambled to slide my arms around his back, guiding his great bulk to a sitting position.

"Hey," he said, his sexy accent making the word seem so inviting right now. I threw my arms around him and kissed his cheek.

He turned and kissed me back, full-on on the mouth. Then he looked around. "Where are we?"

Turning around, I gestured to our companions. "On Nelia, if I had to guess."

"Guess it does look somewhat familiar. Lots of caves on this planet."

He crawled over to Rio and did the pulse check.

"They're all breathing," I said, and Zeke started slapping Trey's face, a little too hard for my tastes.

"Wait!" I said, but that actually got Trey's eyes to flicker open. He bolted upward.

"It's a trap!" he shouted. "No one move!"

Zeke and I stilled. But something felt wrong when it came to one of his commands. Flexing my hand, I stared at it.

Trey blinked. "Everyone, you're in control," he said, clearing his throat. But there wasn't that *sense* of relaxation that usually came when he said that following an order.

"Would have been nice if you'd managed to say that before that little zebra bitch turned us to stone, eh?" said Zeke, moving on to start slapping Rio.

"Is that what happened?" Trey rubbed his jaw as Rio came to, Zeke yanking him up by the arm.

"She got me first," I said. "What did I miss?"

"Nothing," said Zeke, moving on to Derek. His palm hovered over my best friend's cheek and he looked to me, as if for permission to smack him. Wincing, I nodded. It'd worked for everyone so far.

I brushed aside a lock of hair that had fallen over Rio's eyes as Derek came to with a startling gasp, jumping all the way up to his feet.

"Easy, tiger," said Zeke, but Derek was already pointing his arm ramrod-straight out in front of him, aiming at the wall.

Only nothing happened.

"My abilities aren't working," said Derek, staring at his hand.

My blood ran cold.

Derek got a little wobbly on his feet, swaying, and Rio jumped up to catch him, only he moved as slow as anyone else would, not quite managing to grab a hold of Derek until he was halfway to the ground.

Crawling over to them, I placed the back of my hand to Derek's forehead. It wasn't hot, but sweat dotted his brow.

"What the hell's going on?" growled Zeke. His arms out in front of him, it looked like he was testing his abilities, too.

"My aunt," I said quietly. "She has to be nearby." I scrambled to the edge of the makeshift cage, grabbing handfuls of vines. "Alanna!" I cried out, the name echoing down the depths of the cave.

But there was no reply. No sight of another cage.

If she'd been nearby, I could have asked her to try to fall asleep, let the guys gain their powers back after an hour or so, and then we could bust out of this place.

But she wasn't here. Or she was already asleep and it would just be a matter of time before their powers came back, assuming she didn't wake in the meantime.

Or she was outside of the cave somewhere, fighting Xerxes right now—or a captive of his.

Like I was. Like we all were. Because of *me* and my big ideas.

"Bry?" Derek slipped an arm around my back.

I explained my theories about my aunt to the guys, unable to keep the sense of despair out of my voice.

"Well, if she's out there fighting Xerxes, then she's not alone," pointed out Derek. "And it's just a matter of time before our parents and the rest of Veras storm in here and…" He drifted off when he saw my face. I knew it must have fallen.

"I'm a hostage," I said. "Exactly what that asshole wanted. I played right into his hands!" Turning around, I cried out, "Rajani!" I knew it was hopeless. Surely, she would have responded even to my aunt's name if she'd heard it. The name echoed off into the darkness.

Letting out a choked sob, I leaned onto Derek's shoulder as Rio slipped in behind me and started gently rubbing my back.

"It's not your fault, love," said Zeke, his tone even. "We all agreed to this."

"But I *insisted*," I said, looking to each in turn. "And look where I got us! What if my parents aren't even *fighting* because they know he has me? What if they just let him—" I choked back a sob.

Trey squeezed between Derek and Rio and kissed the top

205

of my forehead. "Don't torture yourself," he said. "We can't change anything in here."

As if struck by inspiration, Zeke got to his feet, striding over to the nearest cluster of vines and shaking them. They barely gave under his grip. "So let me get this straight," he said. "To manage all of this, this Xerxes jerkoff is working with other Nelians who can produce vines like the one here that made this cage."

Sitting up straighter, I wiped a sole tear that had escaped down my cheek. "And at least two Nelians who can produce portals."

"Two?" Rio asked.

I bit my lip. "They need two on the Nelia side to open a gateway to Earth," I explained. "Unless they get a boost from my mom. Then they can do it with one."

Trey cocked his head but didn't ask. "But we know *that's* impossible, your mum helping this criminal out."

I nodded. "He attacked her—kidnapped her. She almost killed him once. She'd never, unless forced to..." My breath hitched. I could see some criminal Nelian forcing his lips on hers if she didn't put up a fight, if she was caught and trapped in a cage like I was.

"And your aunt is either fighting the man nearby, a hostage, or helping him," said Zeke, stroking his stubble.

"She wouldn't be *helping* him," I said.

"She was once his lover," said Derek unhelpfully.

I shot him a look. "Over two decades ago. No, Daddy Alarik said Xerxes carries a torch for Alanna, not the other way around. Besides, she didn't even feel the sense for him like she does with her husbands."

"The sense?" asked Rio.

Right. I supposed most Earthlings didn't know. I hugged my knees to my chest. "Nelians believe in loving whomever you want—however many people you want." I couldn't bear to look to see how they reacted to that. "But they also only consider those to whom they feel the Nelian sense calling them their true mate or mates."

"A bond," said Zeke, rapidly blinking.

"Yes," I said, my face reddening. "I don't... I don't know how to explain it."

"Do you feel this Nelian sense, Bryony?" Trey traced a careful finger over the top of my shoulder, pausing at the exposed skin around my neck. I shivered.

"I don't... I don't know. I don't think so," I admitted.

"You do not *think* so?" asked Rio, leaning forward and whispering closer to my ear.

I could have sworn each was trying to *trigger* a reaction, make the sense jump out of me so I could pick my one true love.

To tell the truth, I couldn't pick between the four of them if the fate of the world depended on it. And at this rate, I really hoped that didn't become an actual possibility.

Zeke cleared his throat. "Sounds convenient."

"Yeah," I said. "Alanna knew without a second thought that her husbands were all meant for her."

"But your mom doesn't have that kind of second sense," Derek pointed out. "I know Alarik feels that for her, but she didn't need to have some magical radar tell her she wanted to be with all four of her partners."

The way he looked at me then, like his eyes were pouring truth directly into my soul, made my heart skip a beat.

"You're all right," said Trey, nodding toward Derek, almost like a blessing to let my best friend into their little tightknit group of princely friends.

Derek scratched the back of his neck.

"Have to say I'm a bit jealous, though," added Zeke. "You've known Bryony all her life."

"All mine," said Derek. "She's a few months older than me."

Chuckling, I clutched his thigh.

Trey tapped his index finger to my nose. "Someone's robbing the cradle."

"I am *not*." I playfully shoved him. "He's my rival-slash-best-friend." I patted Derek's leg again. "And maybe something more."

"Rival?" asked Zeke. "I have to hear about that."

"Bryony," said Rio, squeezing my shoulder as he stood. "As much as I feel this conversation must be had between us all, have you tried your ability?"

I hadn't. I knew it would work, though. I alone was immune to Alanna's nullification power. But what use would it be? "I can keep people out—if I see them approaching." I muttered the last part slightly under my breath. "I can keep them safe if I need to, if they're panicking and about to run off into danger."

"Or flying off a roller coaster," added Trey, his blue irises twinkling.

"Or that." I stood, extending my arms and summoning the pink glow. "But I can't *move* something or break it."

The bubble expanded, pushing past Rio and Zeke and over to bars of the vine cage. At first, it expanded right past it, protecting the vines inside it, and then I tried to manipulate it back, sliding it just inside the cage, like a dome of its own as the pink butted up against the vines.

Grounding my feet into the dirt, I concentrated so hard, the back of my head began to ache, as if the action caused strain augmented by my overall soreness.

I didn't know what I hoped for. But they were right. There wasn't anything we could do stuck in this cage. And who knew when our captors would return? I could protect everyone if I saw them coming, but what would we do for food? For water?

We needed to get out.

But the vines didn't so much as quiver.

Gasping, I let my arms fall, tumbling forward. Zeke

managed to catch me under his arm one-handed as if I were a sack of sand.

Rio, Trey, and Derek scrambled to provide me more support, gently guiding me to the ground, laying me on my back. Rio brushed some hair off my forehead.

"Why is it you can use your ability and we cannot?" he asked.

"I don't know," I said hoarsely. My heartbeat was slowing from the exertion, though a tingling sensation permeated my every fiber at the spots where my body was in contact with any of theirs. Trey held my head in his lap, the back of my head flush against his groin. Derek laid a hand on my thigh, and Zeke was down at my ankles. Rio traced his feather-soft touch over my face.

"Your hair," he said, his head tilting.

"What about it?" I started to get up.

"The roots are growing in green," said Derek, his mouth in a thin line.

I laughed. "Well, yeah. I dye it." I reached up to grab a lock. "Though I guess I've been a bit too busy to touch it up —" My mouth clamped shut when I saw half of my long strand of hair was green. And wavy, any straightening conditioner I'd managed to use on it yesterday worked out through all the exertion and the stress.

But that didn't explain the color coming back so rapidly. The hair wasn't even any longer.

"Perhaps the strain of the power called out to your Nelian nature?" Trey proposed.

"Or the planet itself," suggested Rio.

Whatever it meant, it was the least of my problems. But there was something gnawing at the back of my mind that I just couldn't brush off.

CHAPTER TWENTY-ONE

"What if it's our touch?" suggested Derek out of the blue.

All of the heads in the cage turned toward him.

"You might want to elaborate on that one, mate," said Zeke.

"Hear me out." Derek pushed up his glasses one-handed. I had to admit I was a little surprised they'd survived Hazel's petrification, even if I knew her abilities didn't directly do damage to anything she petrified. "It wasn't until we had her lying here that her hair started changing."

I stared at the lock of my hair again. "Well, maybe... Who can say?" I admitted. "I don't know how this might help us, though."

Derek gestured around him. "You're on Nelia most likely. And you're its *heir*. Perhaps it's reacting to you, responding to you feeling loved."

My heartbeat grew wilder at the suggestion, but when I looked to Zeke, Derek, and Rio in turn, I found nothing but openness and honesty in all of their faces. I shifted slightly to observe Trey, who took a deep, savoring breath.

"May we show you we love you, Bryony?" he asked.

I blinked rapidly. "I... I... But how?" I whispered softly.

The men all glanced at one another and nodded, a silent conversation passing between them.

"Your first time should be special," said Rio. "Together, we can make it special."

My voice caught in my throat. My "first time"? Going all the way?

…With all four of them at once?

Zeke ran a hand up my leg, tracing the curve of my calf over the tight workout leggings. "If you're okay with it."

"Just let us know," added Derek, his own finger trailing down to the crack between my knees, teasing up the fabric of my leggings and toward my trembling apex.

"Yes," I whispered hoarsely. "All of you. I want all of you. *Please.*"

Zeke peeled off his tank top in two seconds flat, flicking a lock of his long, fiery hair over his shoulder as Derek stood and removed his own T-shirt, kicking off his sneakers and grabbing for the waistband of his pants.

I leaned back, my thighs and pussy already turning to jelly just watching the strip show going on in front of me.

Rio and Trey stood, removing their own clothes piece by tantalizing piece until I was there on the ground of this awful, filthy cage, not minding as much as I ought to have because I was surrounded by love.

And supreme examples of the male physique. Rio was the leanest, followed by Trey, and then Derek, but each had finely sculpted abs that begged for my touch. Zeke was the hairiest, that scorching-hot hair clashing against the smooth tan of his skin all the way down to his thick, elongated member.

Each had a cock far larger than I'd ever imagined I'd encounter—too large to fit inside me, I worried. Grinding one thigh against the other, I squirmed as I took a look, lingering just a tad longer at Trey's plump member, the only one I'd never had a peek of yet. His faint blond hair continued over his pecs, leading a trail across his navel and down around his awaiting stalk and sack.

"Well?" asked Trey, the corner of his mouth twitching upward. "Are you going to be the only clothed one in the room?"

"I don't know," I teased, kicking a leg up. "Why don't you all give me a hand?"

Derek grabbed the leg and pulled my sneaker off, then bent to grab the other to do the same, this time keeping the leg up in the air, stretching it, sending a slight tease of pain down my leg and to my groin, but in a good, burning way. Zeke bent to take hold of my waistband, reaching in and grabbing the pants along with my panties all at once. Practically *yanking* it off, he helped me shimmy my ass into the air so they could fold the leggings down each leg and off entirely.

Derek kissed my ankle as Zeke's hand slid down my crotch and to my folds. My mouth opened to gasp and both Trey and Rio were on either side of me, each taking a side of my workout shirt, peeling it up, slipping their fingers beneath my sports bra to take it all off in one go. I raised my arms and let out a moan as Zeke's hand went to work on my clit, Derek still massaging my calf, my ankle, peppering it with kisses. I hardly noticed as Rio and Trey gently guided my head and shoulders up off the ground so they could fling the rest of my clothing aside.

The whimper crawling out of my throat was unlike any sound I'd made before as Zeke's fingers slid down my folds, dipping into my juicing pussy, bringing out the moisture and slicking it all over my labia.

At the same time, Trey's lips were on my breast, taking careful nibbles of my nipple, making it tighten before I finished taking a breath. Rio's mouth was on mine between my gasps, his breaths coming heavy across my face, Derek's hands and lips still working their way up my leg.

I let out a moan.

"Who do you wish to be first?" asked Trey, coming up for air.

There it was. Decisions again. Choosing one.

Zeke chuckled, his hand never stopping, playing with my clit and sending my breathing into jagged, hitching wretches. "Let's just surprise her, eh? I think we could all claim to be her first." One of his fingers dove right up inside me.

Yelping, I arched my back, but what little pain there'd been was over, overwhelmed by the sensation of Zeke adding another finger, widening my pussy, prying it open in smooth, massaging movements.

"What about condoms?" asked Rio.

"I'm on birth control," I said through heaving breaths. "For medical reasons," I added. As if I needed to justify myself.

Zeke seemed amused. "Perfect."

"I don't exactly sleep around," said Derek, letting one finger dance across my calf. I shuddered at that, at all the touching all over my body, at Zeke's fingers being where I wanted—*needed*—to feel a thick, throbbing cock just then.

"Don't worry about it, mate," said Zeke. "Desperate times and everything."

Without saying a word, Zeke pulled his fingers out and straddled me, Derek lowering my leg to the ground and taking a seat at my feet, his hands massaging the soles.

Trey took a turn kissing my face as Rio moved to my breast, working with his fingers before landing a kiss atop each one.

My groin pushed up against Zeke's, pulsating with need, burning up with sheer heat.

He reached down to his cock, which already dug harshly into my thigh, thick and juicy and waiting.

Slipping it inside, he readjusted himself, the tip poking in as he clutched either side of my waist. "All right, love?" he asked.

Gasping, I nodded, Trey's lips under my chin as I threw my head back.

Zeke thrust in farther, harder, with such great force, I

trembled beneath him. He pushed and pushed until he could go no more and then, his body grinding against mine for a moment more, he pulled back, slow at first, and then faster.

A scream tore from my burning throat, and Zeke pushed back in, harder, faster, with more urgency. In, then out. In and out and in again, faster and faster, my skin alighting with a tingling sensation everywhere one of these men touched me, my vision growing darker. Then his cock twitched inside me, spilling forth, massaging me from the inside out.

A low gasping grunt escaped from Zeke's lips as he pulled out once more, the final movement sticking sort of like a suction before he lifted one thigh and then another to shift to the side of me.

I was still breathing harshly, still moaning, as Derek and Zeke switched places, Derek's palm grazing up against my inner thigh. He didn't hesitate, moving forward to kiss my mons, his tongue lashing out to my labia, to the clit in particular.

"*Oh…*" I groaned.

Sucking and sucking for a while, Derek went to work. Trey and Rio were still taking turns massaging my breasts, kissing my swollen lips, Zeke sending shivers up my legs by tickling my feet.

Derek sat up straighter, straddling my legs, and with a quick sleight-of-hand, his cock pressed deeply inside me, sliding in with no resistance as if on a slick slide.

He thrust in, leaning forward, his hands splayed against my abdomen applying just the right amount of pressure before he was pressed up and up as far as he would go. He took his turn pulling out, pounding in, steady, savoring every minute, his teeth biting his bottom lip as the momentum built and built. I shuddered, feeling like I was on a ride, my arms flailing up above me until both Trey and Rio took hold of one, giving Derek more room to play.

His hands slid up to cup my breasts, my legs and arms

barely able to move beneath the princes' firm grip and then Derek's cock throbbed inside me, releasing his load.

Breathing hard, he slowly slipped out, stopping only to kiss my right breast before sliding out and off me entirely.

My head was swimming. I didn't know how much more stamina I had, but I wouldn't dare stop to question this moment, to think about what troubles awaited us out there. I was here with my men. In the now.

"Let's change it up a bit, shall we?" suggested Trey.

The princes let go of my limbs and between peppering me with kisses, guided me to flip over onto my stomach. I hardly had the energy to protest, even if I'd wanted to. The cool dirt felt like an ice pack on my feverish-hot cheek and I welcomed it, panting, sweltering, sticky, and wet, but not wishing it were any different for the world.

Behind me, someone took hold of either side of my ass, yanking it upward, another set of hands adjusting my knees until I felt like I was doing nude yoga.

A smack against my bare ass cheek. I recognized that touch immediately.

"Trey?" I croaked.

"It's me, darling," he said, his British accent so sexy with those few special words. He smacked my ass again—hard, the stinging slowly melting into a throb of tingling pleasure radiating back to my pussy.

His cock pressed hard against my exposed vagina, his fingers reaching down to adjust himself and line his thick member perfectly inside me. Sleek and quick, it got all the way up without resistance, my muscles relaxed and ready.

He inched out again, smacking my ass as he moved.

I groaned, rubbing my cheek harder into the dirt. He thrust back in. Then out. He smacked my ass with each go, the sound echoing out into the darkness of the cave around us.

My legs trembled, my knees threatening to slide out from under me, but two sets of hands steadied each thigh. As I looked out, I saw Rio standing beside me, stroking his cock in time with Trey's relentless, insatiable thrusts.

Crying out, my head swam as he shivered inside my pussy, releasing until he was spent.

Breathing deeply, we stayed there a moment more, and then he pulled out, giving my ass cheek one last soothing slap as he stepped back.

I collapsed to the ground, my mons back flush against the dirt.

"Sorry, sport, looks like she might be spent," said Trey to Rio, and Rio stood there, his erection calling out, *demanding* my pussy.

Shaking my head, I rolled over. "Rio," I said quietly, reaching toward him.

Rio gestured to the other men. My muscles limp, I let them do whatever it was they had planned, draping my back over Trey's and Zeke's legs joined together, knee to knee, Derek taking care to cradle my head.

Rio took hold of each of my thighs and tugged upward. The other men stood slowly, carefully, keeping hold of me all the while.

I was being held aloft in the air by all four of them, Rio directing my legs around his torso to embrace his back. The last little bit of my strength locked my ankles around him just as his erect cock pushed into my tunnel in one simple movement.

None of us moved for a moment, a lock of my hair tumbling down between Derek and Trey, my body tingling all over with a sense of weightlessness.

Then Rio pulled out slightly and pushed back in, the three men holding the rest of me stumbling slightly but quickly shifting my body to push me back against Rio's thrust.

We moved faster and faster, Rio's cock like a magic wand calling forth some life I hadn't known I had left in me, the friction making me sizzle and seep.

At last he spurted out inside me and I screamed in ecstasy, the sounds reverberating out against the cavern walls.

It took some maneuvering, but Rio pulled out, leaving my pussy spent as all four men helped me to my feet. I collapsed back against the nearest broad chest, my hand reaching for the nearest arm to steady me.

Between the gasps of breaths, there was the slightest shift in the wind, the slightest sound of dirt squelching against footsteps.

The voice that spoke was icy and familiar. "You *are* a whore."

CHAPTER TWENTY-TWO

DEREK WAS THE FIRST TO MOVE, SCRAMBLING TO PICK UP MY clothes, which he handed to me before grabbing his own. Prince Trey and Zeke stood naked between me and the edge of the vine cage where Hazel and her cohorts had appeared as I dressed, and I didn't fail to notice the bemused arch of Hazel's brow as she watched us, her arms crossed tightly in front of her.

The workout clothes stuck to me like a second skin, rolling up obnoxiously as I quickly slipped into them. Rio gathered his and the other princes' clothes and passed them out, but Trey and Zeke simply took them from him, their eyes narrowed on the Veras Academy students out there on the other side of the cage.

"You *are* fine specimens," said Hazel, and Pepper licked her lips suggestively.

"What the hell are you doing here?" I asked, stepping in front of Trey. "How did you manage this?" I gestured to the vine cage.

Sheila tittered, an obnoxiously high-pitched laugh. "The heir to Nelia doesn't even have all her people in line, does she?"

"Quiet, Sheila," snapped Hazel.

She needn't have bothered. I knew they couldn't have gotten us here or created a vine cage without Nelian help.

Which meant that Xerxes still had some followers on his home planet, however few they might have been over two decades ago.

"You're working with the fugitive," I said, gripping the lattice of vines keeping me from smacking the smiles right off those faces. "How? Since when?"

"I noticed you didn't bother to ask *why*." Hazel threw her head back.

"I could ask that, too," I said. "But I'm sure whatever reason you give me would be some complete bullshit. My family's actions to save the planet led to your family being millionaires instead of billionaires. Or you thought *you* had a shot with a prince." The bumps on the vines dug into my skin. "You don't deserve to be Veras Academy graduates."

"Oh, heavens me, whatever will we do without our diplomas from your slutty parents?" mocked Pepper. Everyone laughed, except Hazel, whose eyes narrowed.

"You think you just get everything handed to you, don't you?" she said. "The Thornes *worked for* their money—"

"Inheriting the position of CEO of a pollutive company. Yes, *such* hard work," I snapped. "Thorne Plastics' employees likely worked five thousand times harder than any of your family, and they got only a tiny fraction of the profits to show for it."

Hazel's face got redder and redder. "What about you? You inherit a kingdom, get a husband handed to you on a platter —and you can't even bring yourself to share!"

Someone snorted from behind me—Zeke, it seemed like. "We didn't come here to find just any spouse." His deep voice rumbled. "So stop acting like you ever had a chance."

"Shut up, hairy," snapped Hazel. Pepper's face fell a little. "I wasn't *interested* in you." She tossed her hair over her shoulder.

Glancing at my own, I saw it was completely green—the guys' plan to *relax* me had worked.

Only I wondered if it would mean anything, this connection to the planet of my ancestors?

Almost as if on cue, a strange feeling filled my gut. There was tingling to be sure, a brief sense of euphoria, but something else, too. Like someone was tapping my shoulder without anyone actually touching me.

I turned. And though it wasn't actually visible, in a sense, I felt as if I could reach out and touch it. There was this compulsion, this *need* driving me back into the cage, right toward...

All four of the men in here with me.

Whatever I'd felt before, it hadn't been this.

It hadn't been the Nelian *sense*. Which was real. Which I could feel, even with my half-human parentage.

My face must have lit up or somehow given it away because my four human men would never know exactly what I felt—but they softened then, all four of them, just looking at me.

"Hello?" said Jerry in an unkind tone. "We're still here."

I rounded back on these bullies turned complete assholes. "So you've hated me since the first day you transferred, what's new about that? Do you honestly hate me enough to throw your lives away like this?"

Sheila stiffened. "We're not in danger."

Laughing, I checked off the items on my fingers. "You kidnapped four royals—that's an international, *interplanetary* incident. You sided with a fugitive whose idea of saving the planet was basically *killing all of humanity on it*."

"Not Natches," said Pepper, interrupting me. "At least not the ones willing to fight for him."

Glaring at her, I continued. "And you're putting yourself up against Veras, the Renegades, *and* the majority of the Nelian population." I shrugged. "Seems like putting your lives at risk to me."

"Hazel, you didn't—" started Sheila.

But Hazel shushed her. "We can take them. Xerxes has a plan."

"You don't even like Nelians," I said. "And now you're working with one?"

Hazel gazed at her manicure coolly. "We don't have to *like* someone to work with them. We did projects with your lot all the time at school, didn't we?"

"Besides, Xerxes promised a new order," said Sheila, piping up in her squeaky voice. "Where Natches who help him wind up on top—"

"Shh," snapped Hazel, cutting her off.

"How did you even meet up with a fugitive?" asked Rio, stepping closer.

Jerry answered. "He's been snooping around the Academy for days. Pretty much since he got out. The other him was a decoy, paid for by the senator. When the Nelians heard what had happened, those loyal to him came to get him."

"And you've been in on this since the start?" asked Derek.

Hazel jutted her chin toward him. "Hey, handsome. Does your *princess* know those lips touched mine first?"

"*Yes*," I said, taking Derek's hand in solidarity. "Now answer the question."

Hazel examined her nails in the low light from the cave entrance. "We didn't help stage a prison break, idiot. But we have brains. Sheila spotted the Nelians creeping around campus." She nudged her.

Sheila rubbed a hand down her arm. "I sometimes send my doppelgänger to class and walk around out of sight of the windows to let off steam."

Pepper snorted. "She makes her doppelgänger do *all* her studying. Dumb as a rock, this one."

"Shut up." Sheila clenched her hands into fists at her sides.

"Forgot I'm talking to *the dumb one*," snapped Pepper. "Feeling lost without your body double to rely on, are you?"

Without meaning to, perhaps, Pepper had confirmed that standing here, they were without their abilities as well.

Hazel was a little more alert. Her lip curled. "Quiet, both of you."

Jerry spoke up. "Rotten elf asked how Sheila *liked* Veras Academy. When it was clear she didn't, she got us and he filled us in. He asked about the king and his children, his weaknesses."

So it wasn't just me making the news that had gotten Xerxes the information he'd sought. He'd had firsthand witnesses.

They'd already been scoping out an opportunity to try something, had already been talking to the rebel elves when they'd followed me to the amusement park.

Jerry could restore broken things back to their original condition. What if he could restore a roller coaster's manufactured cart back to its original pieces, encourage the safety bar to turn back into a chunk of metal not fastened by a bolt?

"Yeah, it was me at the Jollity Land," he said, maybe reading how my face had gone pale. "You didn't even notice me blending in with the crowd getting off the coaster before you when you were boarding. Unfortunately, you moved. I got the wrong seat."

"You could have killed them!" I shouted. "You were trying to *kill me*?"

"Oh, grow up," snapped Hazel. "We knew you'd protect your way out of it. Probably." Her voice went quieter. "Just thought your date could do with a little disaster."

Trey stepped forward and put a hand on my back. "I'd say that idea backfired."

Hazel's nose upturned. "Perhaps. But the Nelian rebels got more antsy after that. Insisted we help them nab a hostage that would get Veras to stop breathing down their necks. And I wasn't about to let that handsome slice-of-fresh-air Sage get kidnapped, even if he never had a clue about the lush right in front of him." Hazel's stance grew wide. "Hooking up with that granny instead."

"You shut your mouth," I said. "Lacey is a million times the woman you are."

Pepper giggled. "You mean a million times more the pile of stretchy, gooey mud?"

"I don't like hitting a lady, but you are asking for it," said Zeke, his fist trembling at his side.

Pepper looked cowed for a moment.

I got us back on track. "So you offered me—or my best friend."

"Whatever it took to get you to lower your guard like the complete tosser you are," said Hazel. "And don't give me this crap about you being valedictorian. There's a difference between book smarts and street smarts, and you don't have the one that really matters."

"And I suppose you do?" offered Trey. He sneered. "I've seen your type a hundred times at court. Spoiled rich Daddy's girl thinks she's something special because she was born into wealth or with a title. I have to capitulate to them all the time at home. Enough. Fuck off, twat."

Hazel stumbled a little.

Since she didn't have a comeback, I turned to Jerry. "You dressed up as a bodyguard."

He shrugged. "They've been crawling all over the Academy the past few days. I have a suit and sunglasses. Fairly no-brainer disguise for wandering around the yard."

So the *how* all made sense now. But the why... "What was in it for you?" I asked. "Besides seeing me fall? How could *that* be worth throwing away your lives like this? I mean, we're about to graduate. We wouldn't have to see each other ever again. I didn't think you were capable of this level of—"

"We'd see *you*," said Hazel stiffly. "Every time I'd turn on the TV, I'd see you, canoodling with your princes, dictating to the Earth's people. No. Xerxes promised absolute freedom to any Natch who helped him."

I'd had about enough of her skewed view of things. "Where's Rajani?" I said, shaking the vines. "And Alanna?"

"Your friend is right here."

Everyone turned to the sound of the voice, a baritone, thundering timbre behind each of the man's words.

From the fading outside light marched in Xerxes, the fugitive, his cropped hair unmistakable, though now he was dressed in green-and-brown leathery Nelian attire. Behind him strode two Nelian women I didn't recognize, one holding a flaming torch aloft to add more light. And behind them were two Nelian men, each holding one arm of my best friend, her wrists bound with vines in front of her, her mouth covered in a thin vine that wrapped all the way around her head.

"She's been quite the interesting conversationalist," said Xerxes, and I couldn't help but notice Sheila and Pepper shrink back as he neared. "She had a lot of *truth* to reveal about you, princess."

He reached through the gaps between the vines and stroked a finger over my cheek. "You look a bit like your aunt…"

Revolted, I pulled back, and Zeke's hand shot out to snatch his finger, bending it before any of us could blink.

Xerxes' screech bounced off the cavernous walls.

CHAPTER TWENTY-THREE

Xᴇʀxᴇs ᴄᴏɴᴛɪɴᴜᴇᴅ ᴛᴏ ʜᴏᴡʟ, ᴘᴜʟʟɪɴɢ ʜɪs ʜᴀɴᴅ ᴀᴡᴀʏ ᴀɴᴅ shaking it. "You Earth scum. You're *dead*."

The guys all gathered closer around me, two on each side, following my lead as I backed up just out of reach of anyone on the other side of those walls.

"Let her go!" I said. Rajani's eyes went wide and she shook her head. She didn't want them to let her go…?

Xerxes pulled out a dagger from his belt and held it up to Rajani's throat. "I don't need her anymore," he said, his finger swollen but not stopping him from clutching the hilt of the dagger even harder.

"Wait!" I screamed.

He sneered.

"What do you want?" I asked. "Where's my aunt?"

"Alanna is outside this cave in much the same shape as your little friend here," said Xerxes. "I personally incapacitated two of those human scum she called husbands before I nabbed her. She was the one who thought to look for me on Nelia even when those foolish Earthlings of yours were chasing after my double."

Sheila whispered something from the other side of the cage and Hazel hushed her. The diminutive natural redhead

225

trembled, like she might collapse at any time, but Hazel stood, braver than she had been in front of the boar.

In my opinion, she needed to feel a little of that fear again.

I prayed for my uncles' safety, but there was nothing I could do from in here. A flicker of the Nelian's torch danced off the shiny stone of the blade, and I flung my arms out, projecting my bubble of protection, aiming it at the fugitive. The shimmering, pink dome put Rajani and the four Nelians I didn't know on the one side, and the rest of us on the other, the line separating precisely between the tip of the blade and my friend's neck.

Xerxes chuckled, looking at the pink dome above him. "She told me Alanna's negation doesn't work on you. I wonder why." He clonked his dagger against the pink, but it bounced helplessly, though Rajani still slumped over. Her head lolled back as she was held upright by the two Nelians.

At first I thought he'd struck her somehow, but then I realized perhaps she'd fainted at the sight of the blade headed for her throat.

"Well?" asked Xerxes, stepping toward the vine cage. "Are you going to keep me in this bubble with you? Or wrap you and your little Earth scum lovers up in it, leaving all your friends here vulnerable to my attack?" He gestured back to Rajani and to Hazel and her companions, too, as if that threat would have the same impact on me.

Hazel stiffened. "We're on your side."

Xerxes stormed over to her, his blade brandished threateningly. "You're Earth scum and you'll do as you're told, even if that means bleeding at my feet."

Hazel stumbled backward. "No. You promised—"

Xerxes spun and clobbered his elbow straight to her eye socket, knocking her to the floor out cold.

Sheila and Pepper screamed.

Xerxes pointed his dagger toward them. "Anyone else have anything to say?"

They shook their heads, clutching each other's hands.

Jerry just stared at Xerxes, his eyes widening, and then he turned and vomited right next to Hazel's head.

While Xerxes was distracted, I tried my theory, recalling the bubble of protection to the inside of the vine cage, lining it up just right behind its surface.

Xerxes chuckled darkly. "So you'd surrender all your friends to me, leave their fates in my hands? No matter. I have you right where I need you to get your coward of a father to show up. You can't keep that little bubble of yours up forever."

Trey put a hand on my shoulder, and Derek on the other. Rio slipped his hand beside Derek's and Zeke his beside Trey's. That beautiful sensation flew through me, spreading all the way down to my toes.

Mother Nelia herself seemed to be soaring through me.

Focusing all my concentration, I told that protection bubble extending from my hands that I needed it to shred those vines to pieces. To protect me, to protect everyone I loved—and even those I didn't—those vines had to *go*.

With a mighty roar that ripped free from my lips, the bubble pushed out between the holes in the lattice cage and squeezed through like one of those banned things called balloons being jammed into a tiny space. Xerxes turned on his heel at the sound of the vines ripping, straining, but it was too late. With a pop, the vines shattered, raining down on the ground like streamers.

"What have you—" started Xerxes, but I compressed my bubble and turned it toward him, slamming him clear across the cave and into a wall.

There was a scream from the other side of the cave and the two Nelian women charged toward us, the one tossing her torch to the ground as she drew a stone dagger from her belt. The men dropped my friend like a sack of potatoes and joined them in charging against us.

"Get behind me!" I snapped in Pepper, Sheila, and Jerry's direction.

"What about Hazel?" asked Pepper.

"*Now!*" I screamed.

They actually moved.

Sending out a projection bubble around the eight of us was easy enough, but there was Hazel's prone body off to the side—assuming she was all right—and more importantly, Rajani out there *behind* the advancing row of rebel Nelians. I'd just have to keep drawing their attention.

Zeke growled and raised his fists, everyone but Sheila and Pepper taking a fighting stance around me, but I wouldn't let anyone inside this bubble.

Spreading its range farther, the first Nelian woman came in contact with it and her dagger bounced off with a clatter as if stabbing into a rock. She tried again and this time I focused on the area of the bubble where her dagger would hit, molding it, making it almost gelatinous. Her blade slid in, and though her brow furrowed as she tugged and yanked, it wouldn't pull back out.

She screamed in frustration and two of the other Nelian rebels who'd been slashing with their own stone daggers uselessly pulled back.

I looked around. Where was the fourth Nelian? Near Hazel, helping Xerxes to his feet.

Xerxes struggled, then shoved the other Nelian man in order to stand on his own, a trickle of blood running down Xerxes' temple and across his cheek.

He didn't say anything, his breath coming out so raggedly that I could hear him clearly even some yards away.

Then, before I could blink, he bolted across the cave—straight for Rajani.

"No!" I screamed.

But as I moved to reshape the bubble of protection, the Nelian woman's dagger falling to the floor with a thud, a force of energy shot through it from the inside, an icy ball roaring with power that popped through the bubble and landed with precision on the ground right behind Xerxes. It exploded, sending shards everywhere, some of which bounced off the outside of my bubble. Several shards lodged like knives into the back of Xerxes' calf.

I stared at Derek and blinked. His powers were back. Which meant my aunt was either asleep or—

A gust of wind rose up from beside me and Rio was gone. I blinked again, taking note of how the Nelian rebels' hair all flew up in one motion, my arms falling in the gust and the protection bubble blinking out. Then Rio was behind me, gently placing an unconscious Rajani on the ground beside Sheila.

I was at her side in a second, searching for signs of life. Her chest rose and fell, and her head lolled, clearly groggy.

She was okay.

Unbidden tears welled up behind my eyelids.

Around me, grunts and growls told me the battle wasn't over. Even Pepper got into the fray, shooting light out against the Nelian rebels she'd just been helping.

But it only went on half a minute—ice pinning a Nelian rebel to the ground by his foot, a Nelian man running from the sudden appearance of an illusion boar, a Nelian woman spinning like a cartoon character as Rio ran in a circle around her—until Trey's voice rang out, echoing across the cave. "Everyone, stop!"

Everyone went still, the slight crack of Derek's breaking ice the last remaining sound in the cavernous space.

Trey took a deep breath and looked to me. "Bryony, you're in control."

The tension in my muscles relaxed, and I stood, getting a better lay of the situation, looking for Xerxes. He was crouched, frozen while headed toward Hazel on the ground, his face scrunched in pain.

"Zeke, Rio, Derek," continued Trey, "you're in control." My other men sprang to life again, gathering back round me.

Sheila, Jerry, and Pepper stood obnoxiously still behind us, their limbs bent out in weird positions, as if playing Red Light, Green Light and giving it their all.

With the precision touch of a surgeon, I projected my protection bubble again, manipulating it across the room to the five Nelians, shaping it to cocoon each one like budding leaves on a tree. Stretching and straining the bubble, I gathered the rebels all together, shoving their still forms against one another one by one.

Trey looked back at Hazel's cohorts and nodded, not releasing them from their spell.

"How long do people have to follow your orders?" asked Derek.

"As long as I want them to," said Trey. "Or as long as I'm near them, I suppose."

A crack of light broke through the darkness, right behind Trey and Zeke.

I only had time to look over my shoulder a second, to make out what I thought was—Mom? Normak? Had she boosted his portal-creating powers so he could act alone, and from the Earth side of things?—when Trey stumbled from the force of the portal opening and fell backward into it.

I *felt* the slam of force against my bubble before I saw it, whipping back around to focus back on my powers, but it was too late. Xerxes had seen his chance and taken it, diving to grab hold of Hazel's prone body as my protection bubble shattered to pieces.

"Bryony!" shouted Mom through the portal, reaching a hand out, almost touching Rio, who'd stood nearest to Trey before he'd fallen through.

Xerxes shouted at his companions and one Nelian man and one Nelian woman held their hands out toward each other, creating a portal of their own.

Hazel under his arm, limping from his leg wound, Xerxes was halfway through the portal.

And before I could confer with any of my men, I recreated the protection bubble around me and slammed myself forward toward Xerxes, pushing up against his back and sending the three of us alone tumbling through it.

There'd be no more of this. We were ending it today.

With a crack, the portal snapped out of existence behind us as we continued to tumble, Hazel's golden-white hair flying as she went rolling into the grass and clonked against a swing set.

A swing set.

I blinked, pushing myself up, looking around. Veras Academy's back yard.

We were home.

And he was fucked.

He seemed to understand this as he raised himself up on one forearm, his leather Nelian vest torn in several places.

A wry chortle escaped his lips. "You followed me? Why? Tell me."

I'd had no intention of telling that asshole anything, but I found my lips moving before I could stop them.

I'd forgotten about his truth-pulling ability.

"You took Hazel."

He glanced at her prone form, arching an eyebrow. "She told me you were her enemy."

Settling on my knees, I brought my bubble of protection out and wrapped it around him before he could get any ideas. He could ask me whatever he liked, so long as he wasn't going anywhere.

"Do you show pity to your enemies?" His voice shook slightly as he spoke. "Tell me."

"I do," I answered, the truth surprising even me. All the rage burning inside me at my plan gone disastrously wrong, at Hazel's idiocy and cruelty, and that was the answer that was my truth.

"How fortunate for me," said Xerxes. He groaned as he attempted to sit up straighter.

"Tell me, did Alarik's plan work?" he asked. "Is your world saved from destruction?"

"It is," I said, drawing on everything I'd learned about this planet's history, how close it had come to permanent detrimental change to its climate and life forms. "You'd understand that if you bothered to pay attention during your decades on Earth."

"I've been in a prison," he said darkly. "A place I never even knew could exist before I encountered this putrid species."

I let the comment slide. The door to the Academy flung open and out burst Trey—he'd simply fallen through to the school, thank Mother Nelia—followed by Mom and all four of my dads. So many of my professors, along with a cluster of Nelian guards and bodyguards, funneled through the door like a massive wave and spread out in the yard, headed toward us.

"You had help," I said, my bubble not wavering. "And not just the idiots here." I jutted my chin toward Hazel. I didn't even know if she was alive. Her face was swollen, her chin dyed with red.

"Not every Nelian embraces King Alarik's methods of letting humanity's hubris and stupidity go unpunished," said Xerxes. His mouth turned up in a cruel smile. "Saving this Earth of yours was only half the job Mother Nelia tasked us with."

"You're wrong," I said.

"Oh?"

"Not everyone here deserves your hatred."

"Well, princess," said Xerxes, his gaze turning toward the mass now just a few yards away, his voice almost hard to hear beneath the shouting. "When you're queen, I hope you'll remember that not all of your people feel that way."

I would.

I'd stop thinking of my destiny as some kind of dull fate.

"Then I'll show them what humanity has to offer," I said, offering him my truth unbidden.

EPILOGUE

"Mom, I'm fine. I remembered the sunblock." I shook the bottle in front of my phone so Mom could see the proof.

"But remember you have to reapply it," she said. "And watch out for sharks in the water—"

"Okay, darlin', I think that's enough smothering," said Papa Zander, directing the hovering phone screen away from her. In my head, even across these hundreds of miles, he was able to speak. *"Sorry, pumpkin. It's just that you've never been out on your own like this. And so soon after last week. She can't help but worry too much."*

I'm not alone, I told him in my head back, taking in the beach all around me.

This was nothing like the beach surrounding the lake back home. The sand was warm beneath my toes, the water bluer, the sun brighter overhead. Beside me on the towel beneath the beach umbrella sat Rajani, as fit as a fiddle, sipping on a piña colada.

"Nothing's going to take me by surprise again," she said, flexing her arm and letting her metal scales grow. "Not even a fucking shark, Professor Aurora." She spoke loudly so my phone could pick her up and I readjusted the screen to get her in the video.

233

"See?" I said. "I'm fine."

Papa Zander smiled. "I know you girls are. Probably don't even need the—what was it? Five men you brought along?"

"If Bry was going to bring her four dates, I figured what was one more?" She turned and looked toward Connak, who was dipping a toe carefully in the lapping water, his chest still covered in a bandage from the wound Xerxes' rebels had dealt him last week. He jumped and Rajani laughed, taking another sip of her drink. "I like them buff and dorky," she said under her breath.

Pop Nash got on the phone. "Rou and Darien asked me to remind Derek not to lose track of his passport." Yeah, the "spring break road trip" had become more of an all-expenses-paid tropical vacation to the Caribbean. I *was* dating three princes, after all. And Natch engineers had figured out how to make air travel less pollutive in the past couple of decades.

Derek lounged next to me on a beach chair, his Hawaiian-style shirt open and exposing his broad, chiseled chest, his flower-patterned swim trunks nothing out of the ordinary but really setting off those calves like no one's business. His nose was in an old-fashioned book, but almost like he felt me looking at him, he looked up and beamed.

I grinned. "Derek can take care of himself, too."

"Yeah, but you know how he is. Head in a book. I'm surprised the kid takes so well to a workout," Pop Nash added.

"He does indeed." I peeled my sunglasses off and bit the ear piece as I watched him.

"Okay, okay," said Pop Nash, reddening. "You be careful, kid."

Dad Jayden took over the phone and got right to business, giving me an update on the situation back home. "Xerxes is now in Nelian custody. There's no one to blackmail on his home planet. They're building him a special jail cell outside of the heart of Nelia."

Daddy Alarik appeared in the camera beside Dad Jayden's

shoulder. "It's a cabin," he explained. "With guards posted—guards I can trust." He ran a hand through the top of his thick, green hair and muttered under his breath. "The others are getting their own cabins. Separate from him."

Since there was no prison on Nelia—there'd been no need for it before the schism between Daddy Alarik and his former best friend—this was something, even if it might have seemed rather cush, considering what they'd threatened to do. But Daddy and I had discussed it. It was time for Nelia to serve out punishment—but in *our* way. A gentler way. A way more likely to change hearts than letting a man rot in a cell for several decades.

"What about Uncle Rhett and Monroe?" I asked.

"Fine," said Dad Jayden. "Wade discharged them last night. They just need time to recuperate and they should be back on their feet in no time."

"Alanna is taking good care of them," Daddy Alarik added.

"But what about her head?" I asked. Despite being bound outside of the cave we'd been imprisoned in, Alanna had managed to knock herself unconscious by striking her head against a rock in order to let everyone's powers return and give us all a fighting chance.

"Nelians heal quickly," said Daddy Alarik. "She's doing better than her husbands are."

That was a relief. She *had* looked fine when I'd seen her last. Then there was the question I was dreading. "And Hazel?"

"She's almost well enough to go home," said Dad Jayden matter-of-factly. "Though she'll need plastic surgery if she wants to fix her nose."

I grumbled under my breath. I hoped her nose never settled quite right again. It would be the least punishment she deserved.

"The royal family of Britain is working on how to handle her once she's arrived. Since we had her deported," said

Daddy Alarik, his nose in the air. "I wish I could banish the rest of her traitors away from you."

"It's fine, Daddy. They were all expelled—just two months before graduation. I think that'll give them plenty of cause to regret their actions."

"Well, we'll let you get back to it," said Papa Zander, taking over the phone. *"Don't have too much fun,"* he added in my head.

I sent him an image of me sticking my tongue out in my head, but I was all smiles on the phone.

He clamped his lips together, his eyes sparkling in amusement.

"Bye, honey!" called Mom. I said *goodbye* to each of them, blowing a kiss before ending the call.

After slipping the phone back into my beach bag, I put my sunglasses back on and stared out at the beach around me. We were missing a few of our group. They'd only gone inside for something in the hotel room; it shouldn't have been taking them this long, especially not with the fastest man on Earth among them.

Maybe it was just the events of the last week, but the back of my neck prickled as panic started brewing in my gut.

"Did your brother get in trouble?" asked Rajani.

"Huh?" I turned toward her.

"Sage. For the firework distraction you told me about," she said.

"Oh, no. Least of my parents' worries, I guess," I said. "He and Lacey are having a staycation over the break. She seems to be doing better. Must have been nerves about sharing the news about the engagement on top of everything else."

"That's good," said Rajani, though her thoughts seemed to be elsewhere. I followed her gaze to find Connak jumping from one foot to the other as if trying to avoid a snapping crab. "I'm going to go see what he's up to," she said, tracing her fingers gently over her neck.

Placing her cocktail glass on the beach towel, she put on

her sunhat and headed to the shoreline. I sat in silence beside Derek, watching as Rajani threaded her arms up Connak's chest and then exchanged a kiss with him, his skittishness around the water quickly quelled, the waves moving in and out around their calves.

"Professor Kouta said you left the test unfinished," said Derek out of nowhere, slapping his book closed.

"What?" I asked, drawn back into the moment.

"The political science test you made up last week. When Rajani got—"

"I know. He offered to let me take it again, but I told him to just leave it."

"But you know that means I got a higher score on it."

Shuffling over to him on my knees, I placed my cheek against his swim trunks. "You deserve it," I said. "You work hard for valedictorian. I'll do just fine with salutatorian."

"But it's not the same as winning it fair and square."

I rolled onto my back and looked up at him.

He swallowed and ran a hand through my hair—green and wavy and shoulder-length now, no effort made to hide my pointed ears.

"Are we really going to do this?" I asked.

"No," he said quietly. "I just want you to know… You're the smartest person I've ever met."

"Just because I'm good at taking tests and regurgitating facts doesn't mean I can't also appreciate *your* kind of intelligence," I said. "You work hard for your good scores. You deserve this." My hand reached up and caressed his cheek.

"Don't take what Hazel said to heart," he said, cupping my hand in his. "You'll make an incredible queen."

"And thanks to you and the others, I'll be seeing as much of the Earth as I can before I take on that responsibility."

After the events of last week and the full force of feeling the Nelian sense for each of the four men in my life, I knew there was no way I could ever choose between them. We'd all agreed to take it slow, to see what marriage or lack thereof could mean for the royal families interested in a political alliance. Nelian tradition allowed for more than one spouse if they'd agree to it. But for now, for this first year after graduation, we were taking a page out of Derek's book and exploring the world. Together. The princes had plenty of political work they could do, and Derek and I didn't plan on parting from them.

We were a group now. All five of us. I wouldn't be queen if I were missing even one of them.

"We're gone for all of five minutes and Derek takes advantage of it for some special Bryony time?" said a deep voice with a familiar London lilt.

Grinning, I let my hand fall, not moving my head from atop Derek's crotch at all. "It was more than five minutes," I said, realizing that my own special "Derek time" just now had helped quell my fears about what had taken the princes so long. Bodyguards with or not, I knew for a fact they could give them the slip when inclined.

Zeke was beyond gorgeous in a tight pair of navy swim trunks, which seemed perfectly at home with his tanned, sculpted hirsute chest. Rio, paler and more svelte, nonetheless looked like a swimming champion in long, black swim pants like a pro might wear. The leggings-like material left nothing —not even his bulging crotch—to the imagination. Trey wore green speedos, his thick thighs bare and muscular, not a blemish to be found across his broad chest. Their hair was still damp even after they'd left the ocean behind for a bit, and the effect was like it'd been professionally styled and slicked back to be fresh-from-the-shower gorgeous.

"We wanted to bring you something special," explained Rio.

I sat up and watched, mystified, as Zeke handed Derek a small jewelry box. Derek took it as if he'd made some request of Zeke, somewhere between page 50 and page 89 of the book he'd had his nose in since we'd come out to the beach for the day.

All four held matching jewelry boxes and as one, they got down on their knees and extended the boxes toward me.

"Guys," I said. "We talked about this."

"It's not quite what you think," said Zeke.

"No running off without a word this time," added Rio, bouncing slightly in that way I knew meant he could quickly move to grab me if I did.

I laughed.

"All right." I crossed my arms. "You may proceed."

"Why, thank you, love," said Trey, his eyes twinkling. They each opened their boxes and revealed a different-colored ring.

Trey's was pearlescent, an almost reddish color.

Zeke's was black and just as shiny.

Rio's was a deep gold, more metallic color.

And Derek's was blue, as effervescent as the ocean.

"This looks almost *exactly* like what I was expecting," I pointed out. Sure, there were no gems, but...

"They're promise rings," explained Trey.

Rio reached into the pocket of his swim pants and pulled out a gold chain. "If you accept them, you can wear them all around your neck with this chain."

"*If* I accept them?" I asked, my heart nearly fluttering out of my throat.

"You haven't heard what we promise with them yet," Zeke said, his voice colored with mirth.

"All right." I curled my legs beneath me.

Rio took out his ring. "I promise to be devoted only to you. I promise to show you the world, to grow old with you, to be at your side. Will you accept that promise?"

"Yes," I said, shaking as he placed the chain in the palm of my hand and added his ring on top of it. I grabbed him by the back of the neck and kissed him, his lips soft and sweet.

"I promise to be your partner," said Zeke. "In life, in love —in everything. You are the only woman I'll ever love." With a flourish of his hand, he made a miniature globe appear over the ring. "I'd give you the world if I could. Both worlds. Will you accept my promise?"

"Yes!" I said again, and Zeke leaned forward to add his ring to my palm, nibbling at my ear as he neared. I sighed contentedly.

"I promise that I shall take no other lover, put no other person's needs before yours," said Trey. "I'll support you in any way you wish. Do you agree to this promise?"

"Of course." I accepted Trey's ring added atop the others. He caressed my cheek and kissed the top of my head.

"And I promise that no matter what life throws at us—no matter how many men your Nelian sense shows you you can love, I won't make you feel like I'm jealous ever again," said Derek. "I promise to love only you, to go where you need me, be it on Earth or on Nelia." His eyes sparkled. "Will you accept my promise, Bry?"

"I will!"

Derek added his ring atop the others and kissed me on the nose.

My heart pounding, my skin tingling, I worked to quickly slip all four beautiful rings on my chain and moved to clasp it around my neck.

Rio slid in behind me, taking hold of one end of the chain as Derek took the other. Zeke reached forward to smooth my hair out of the way as Trey looked on.

The necklace affixed and in place, I felt the cool, smooth surface of each ring under the hand I pressed to my breast.

"And I promise to love you equally," I told them. "To be there for you, for your people when they're in need of Nelia. I love you all."

There was no way to describe the Nelian sense that floated in the air between us, the bond they could never truly feel; but the way they all looked at me, it felt like somehow they did feel it. That they knew.

"I don't have rings to give any of you," I added.

"Looks like we'll have to settle for a gift of another nature," said Zeke, wriggling his eyebrows.

"Later. In the hotel," added Rio, as if that needed to be explained.

Laughing, I nodded.

"But first," said Trey. "You fly all this way to visit this beautiful beach and you're just sitting here, dry as a desert?"

He stood and the other men followed suit, each grabbing hold of a part of me until I was up atop Trey's shoulders, my legs wrapping around his neck, my groin flush up against the back of his head. The top of my head clipped the umbrella above us.

Giggling, I held on tightly as Trey rushed forward toward the water, the other three men each holding on to a leg or my back to steady me as we rushed ahead.

Straight past the dozen bodyguards out of place on the beach in their dark suits, past other vacationers, past Connak and Rajani making a sand castle at the water's edge.

Straight into the ocean and into our life ahead. Together.

THE SUCCUBUS SIRENS SERIES

Read more sexy reverse harem stories set in the Succubus Sirens world of superpowered heroes, villains, and elves:

Succubus Lips – Succubus Heart – Mutiny's Rebellion – Succubus Soul: Veras Academy

These standalone, interconnected novels can be picked up in any order, but if you want to avoid spoilers, start with Book 1!

Praise for *Succubus Lips*:

"This is probably one of the most bizarre yet satisfyingly creative books I've ever read... If you're into kickass heroines and book boyfriends that make you swoon, this one is for you!" -The Lovely Books

"*Succubus Lips* is well-written and subversively funny, willing to toy with the reader's expectations and do the opposite... sexy without being tedious." -The Romance Reviews

Praise for *Succubus Heart*:

"This book kept my interest from the very beginning, and I enjoyed every scene. Absolutely recommended." ~The Romance Reviews

ABOUT THE AUTHOR

Lina Jubilee loves reading, writing, drinking tea, and rooting for her favorite fictional romances. When not lost in a book, she cooks dinner at lunchtime, plans errands in fewer trips, and does everything she can to get back to romping through fictional worlds ASAP.

Ravenous readers, if you liked this book, please consider joining my Facebook street team! Connect with me:

https://authorlinajubilee.wixsite.com/books/

amazon.com/author/linajubilee
bookbub.com/profile/lina-jubilee
instagram.com/linajubilee
facebook.com/authorlinajubilee

Nothing can keep Rose away from Romance Book Club at the library—not even the snowstorm of the century. Catching a ride home through the storm with Lance, the stunningly attractive librarian who happens to be her neighbor, and Vaughn, his chiseled, alluring housemate, Rose takes them up on their invitation to drop by sometime and join them for their own book club. Rose gets more than she bargained for when she's introduced to Rafael, their magnetically charming third roommate, and the surprising genre of books they love to read and discuss. As the blizzard rages, Rose joins the Racy Reverse Harem Book Club, whose members are open to trying just about everything together to get warm.

A standalone novelette by Lina Jubilee, author of the reverse harem urban fantasy series Succubus Sirens.

REVERE ME: FLEEING FROM
THE FAE KING
STANDALONE FANTASY ROMANCE

Brecc

I've waited an eon to find you. You, my bride, the other half
to my soul. But I noticed you too late, the annual fete that was
supposed to bring us together not your time to shine. My
need for you threatens us all… Nonetheless, I will have you.

The world is meaningless without you. Love me. Bow to me. Revere me.

Edony

I was supposed to be safe. My years as an eligible maiden were behind me, so no fae should have sought my hand at the Fae King's Fete. Yet you caught me breaking the rules, and my fate rested in your hands. Instead of banishing me to the labyrinth of madness surrounding your castle, you vowed to let the world crumble to have me at your side. But I won't let you sacrifice everyone I care for—everyone in your kingdom —for me. To escape you, I'll go willingly into the maze. I'll keep running so you never find me. You will never break me. I will never yield to your desires.

Even though I crave you. Even though when I close my eyes, all I see is your face.

Revere Me is a steamy fantasy romance recommended for ages 17+ for mature themes and scorching romantic tension. First serialized on Kindle Vella, this episodic novel reads as a dark fairy tale in the vein of *Beauty and the Beast*.

MY MINI LIBRARY ROMANCE
STANDALONE CONTEMPORARY
ROMANCE

Wallflower bookworm Quinn curates her neighborhood's Mini Donation Libraries, paying special attention to the Ooh-La-La Box filled with romance reads. When a series of steamy donated books wrecks her life for a few days, she's left wondering if the author is local. Before she can get her sleuth on for long, a friend introduces her to Allen, a man with deep pockets who wants Quinn to set up a Mini Library on his street—and can take her wildest fantasies from the page to under his sheets.

First serialized on Kindle Vella, *My Mini Library Romance* is a contemporary romance with plenty of sizzle and a dash of humor. Perfect for every booklover who's ever dreamed of becoming a romance novel heroine.

READ MORE HOT ROMANCES
FROM CRIMSON FOX
PUBLISHING

Crimson Fox
PUBLISHING

A love story written in the stars.

Hunted for being a witch, Madelyne longs for somewhere to belong and performs a full moon spell to find her true love.

Across the galaxy, Kalas completes the aeons-old celestial ritual to show him the location of his fated mate.

Enchanted by Madelyne's beauty, Kalas flies to Earth to find her. And, with nothing left for her on Earth, Madelyne agrees to accompany Kalas to his home planet.

But as Madelyne adjusts to her new life, old doubts linger, and she just cannot understand why someone like her would be worthy of the crown prince.

Madelyne has spent her entire life being told she doesn't belong, and now Kalas must convince her it's more than just 'fate' that makes him want to claim her as his own.

THE HEART OF DOCTOR STEELE

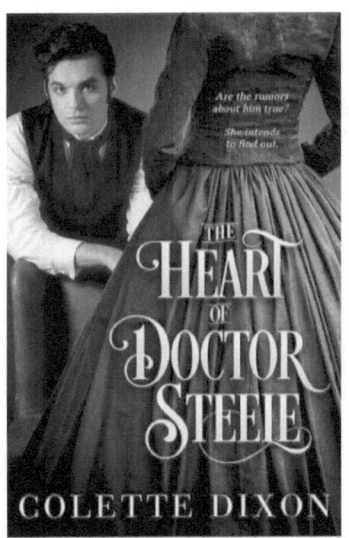

Are the rumors about him true? She intends to find out.

The mysterious Dr. Steele has taken up residence next door, and scandalous rumors about him are spreading through Margaret Landeau's small Massachusetts town. Rumors of women he's ill-used and exploited for his experimental surgeries. Never one to believe gossip, Margaret arms herself with a basket of baked goods and ventures to discover the truth from the man himself.

John Steele has lost everything. His parents, his aunt, too many women he intended to save, and his good name. All he has left is his aunt's home in a far-flung village and a library he's stocked with whiskey. He has nothing to offer anyone. Especially not the bold woman next door whose passion for healing reminds him of the man he once was.

But when a dangerously ill girl arrives on his doorstep, pleading for help, Margaret is thrust into his world. She will learn who the real Dr. John Steele truly is, and soon, not even his dark past can stop her from fighting for the brilliant doctor she now loves. But he must deny his crushing desire for her—loving a man like him can only cast a shadow over her own bright future.

www.ingramcontent.com/pod-product-compliance
Lightning Source LLC
Chambersburg PA
CBHW031940240626
47153CB00003B/810